Praise for *Sisyphus Wins*

Sisyphus Wins is a profoundly honest and personal novel about what it was like to grow up gay in a staunch Catholic family in the '50s, '60s, and beyond. Jonathan navigates his way through the treacherous course of self-discovery and eventual self-affirmation through childhood, adolescence, and adulthood in the context of unyielding religious and traditional values that were often best at inflicting dehumanizing shame and guilt. No matter your creed or philosophy, this is an important book to be reflected upon and discussed.

—Rev. Joseph Holub, retired pastor,
Evangelical Lutheran Church in America

Jonathan's coming-of-age as a gay boy raised in a Roman Catholic family in 1950s Pennsylvania is both disturbing and brave. Creating moods matching the high elevation of the Colorado Rockies and the low elevation of Pennsylvania, Fabyanic alternates between the life of the self-actualized adult Jonathan and the broken boy Jonathan. Every detail is thoughtfully placed to offer the reader a heart-wrenching and intellectual experience through Fabyanic's use of Christian imagery and a modern twist on Joseph Campbell's mono-myth. This read is a journey worth taking.

—Nanci Hubbard Morse, MA,
International Baccalaureate English Teacher/Coordinator
Summit High School, Frisco, CO

A sobering story of one man's struggle with himself, his family, and his church. Jerry Fabyanic's *Sisyphus Wins* is a real page-turner even when the reader is afraid of what the next page will reveal. Jerry masterfully dances back and forth between distressing life events, deep philosophical ponderings, and lighthearted experiences. The reader is ultimately left wondering where the line is between truth and fiction.

—Jason C. Steinle, author of *Upload Experience*

Walking back through the '50s,' 60s, and '70s with Jonathan is both nostalgic and painful. Like many Catholic children, he grows up in a parochial environment that offers comfort and structure to those who adhere to its rigidity. His emergence as an adult who is different than his siblings leads to self-doubt, fear, anger and loneliness. The journey to Colorado and up many mountains leads us all to a self-examination of who we truly are.

—Sen. Joan Fitzgerald,
former President of the Colorado Senate

Mr. Fabyanic tells one story of those who have grown up scapegoated and hemmed in by bigotry and conservative religion. Like no other I have read, this book demonstrates the pain of being forced to choose between a life of cowardice or one of shame and self-destruction. Through Fabyanic's masterful storytelling, the reader travels with Jonathan Slovanco on his heroic journey to wholeness.

—Sean Guard, Dept. Chair and Teacher Leader
for English Language Development
at Aurora Central High School

Sisyphus Wins is the honestly told story of Jonathan Slovanco, who must ultimately discover who he is and how he fits into the world as a gay man. Feeling separate from others does not work for him, yet tradition and all he knows comes into question when he ultimately decides that the truth will set him free. This truthful book shines a light on the obstacles faced by modern gay men. Family, religion, and universal knowledge all must be reckoned with. This is a remarkable read.

—Dr. Marilyn Buehler, Retired IB English Teacher, and Advocate for Multiculturalism with Through Each Other's Eyes Intnl. Center for Cultural Education

SISYPHUS WINS

a novel

JERRY FABYANIC

Georgetown, CO

Sisyphus Wins
By Jerry Fabyanic
Copyright © 2016 by Jerry Fabyanic
All rights reserved.

This is a work of fiction. All names, characters, places, and events
portrayed in this book are the product of the author's imagination or are
used fictitiously, and any resemblance to actual persons, living or dead,
business establishments, events, or locales is entirely coincidental.

Published by Western Exposure
Georgetown, CO 80444
www.JerryFabyanic.com

ISBN 978-0-9969636-0-2 (soft cover)
ISBN 978-0-9969636-1-9 (hard cover)
ISBN 978-0-9969636-2-6 (ebook)
Library of Congress Control Number: 2015917675

References:
The Holy Bible, Douay Rheims Version, TAN Books & Publishers, 2000
Holy Bible, King James Version, Thomas Nelson Publishers, 1976
Saint Joseph Daily Missal, Confraternity Edition,
Catholic Book Publishing, 1959

Cover and interior design by Nick Zelinger, www.NZGraphics.com
Edited by Melanie Mulhall, www.DragonheartWritingandEditing.com

First Edition

Printed in the United States of America

"But I say to you, that whosoever is angry with his brother, shall be in danger of the judgment. And whosoever shall say to his brother, Raca, shall be in danger of the council. And whosoever shall say, 'Thou fool,' shall be in danger of hell fire. If therefore thou offer thy gift at the altar, and there remember that thy brother hath anything against thee; leave there thy offering before the altar and go first to be reconciled to thy brother, and then come and offer thy gift."

Matt: 5:22–24.

1

July 10, 2015

JONATHAN SLOVANCO SIZES UP the day through his bedroom window even though it will be nearly two more hours before dawn breaks. The huge ponderosa outside his window sways gently, helping to fill his room with sweet pine scent. The forecast promises a warm, sunny day, but in the Colorado Rockies, anything can happen. Still, it seems that the KMGH weather forecaster, Mike Nelson, will be right. For the past two weeks, from the end of June through the July 4th holiday, a stable atmosphere has dominated the Centennial State, much to everyone's relief. It had been a hellacious winter, great for skiing and other backcountry winter adventure, but brutal for traveling and underground waterlines. The current warm stretch has been accelerating the snowmelt, thus quickening the pace from mud season to summer.

Stretching, Jonathan notes the tiredness that has overtaken him of late. His mind and will say get up and go, but his body fiercely protests, craving one more rollover. After a moment, Jonathan rolls to his left and slowly sits upright. He stretches and reaches for the hiking garb he set on his dresser the night before: shorts, long-sleeved merino wool hiking shirt, tech shirt, and wool socks.

After dressing and performing his morning ablutions, he makes his way to the kitchen where he swallows his daily regimen of supplements, brews a cup of green tea, and prepares a bowl of granola.

As he slowly munches his cereal, he once again kicks around which mountain to summit. Elbert seems fitting given it is Colorado's highest and can be reached an hour sooner than Mount of the Holy Cross. It would also be an easier ascent because it is just a steady climb up a steep hill with no serious bouldering.

Mount of the Holy Cross, on the other hand, would be far more arduous. While crunching the granola, he opens his well-worn copy of Gerry Roach's classic fourteener guide to the description of Holy Cross, which had earned its name because of the cross-shaped snowfield on its northeast face and had been ascribed religious significance by some for the same reason. The fact that Thomas Moran painted it and Henry Wadsworth Longfellow wrote about it just added to its mystique. Jonathan knows the hike is considered to be a difficult one and, in fact, he has had personal experience with its dangers.

He thinks fondly about the day when he, two friends, and his chocolate lab, Augie, made an attempt of it. It had rained steadily from the time they left and remained unrelenting during the ascent. At thirteen thousand feet, the rain turned into sleet and then snow, making the final push dubious at best and quite dangerous for Augie, who looked more like a polar bear than a dog and who glued himself to Jonathan in fear. At that point, he and Augie turned back, leaving his friends to finish it off. Ironically, just as they got down near the tree line, the sun broke through, drying and warming them. He promised Augie they would come back and try it again as they snacked on their provisions. Augie never would come back, but the memory of that day helps make up his mind. Today he will reattempt the ascent of Mount of the Holy Cross, tired legs and out of shape lungs notwithstanding.

After rinsing his bowl and placing it and the teacup in the dishwasher, Jonathan lifts his day pack, noticing its heft due to the rock he placed in it the night before. He puts it back down and checks the compartment where he stores his rain-wear, compass, sunscreen, and bug repellant. Then he stuffs into the pack two cinnamon-raisin bagel sandwiches filled with almond butter and blueberry preserves, a tube of cheddar cheese Pringles, and a large plastic baggie containing several handfuls of trail mix. In addition, he stuffs a smaller bag of trail mix into his shorts pocket to nibble on while walking.

Just as he begins zipping the pack shut, he remembers the orange, which has become sacred and requisite since the time climbing Mt. Elbert with two friends some years past. They foolishly had brought no supplies other than flasks of water, with the exception of an orange Jonathan stuffed into his fanny pack at the last minute. They learned a tough lesson, parched but determined at thirteen thousand feet where they shared the orange. When he recalls the incident, it reminds him of the loaves and fishes parable. For some inexplicable reason, two oranges seem warranted this time. Trusting his intuition, something he has learned over the years, he tosses two into the pack. Lastly, he wraps a long-sleeved shirt around the food to help insulate it, zips up the compartment, and leans it against a chair.

After checking the water bladder he filled the night before to be sure he filled it to the max, Jonathan snags four plastic bottles of cranberry juice, stuffing them inside the mesh sleeves on the pack's sides. He steps back and smiles as he looks at the ensemble, thinking about how far he has come over the past three decades in terms of being prepared for mountain climbing. He lifts the pack, groans as he hoists it over his right shoulder, and makes his way down to the mudroom.

After lacing up his running shoes, he pulls on his windbreaker and grabs his hiking boots before stepping out into the chilly predawn air. He inhales deeply and scans the abundant stars in the still-dark sky. "Sweet."

Jonathan stashes his gear in the Explorer, careful to shut the tailgate softly to avoid waking his still-sleeping partner and neighbors. Inside, he rummages through the collection of CDs he keeps in the console, decides on Enya, and slips her *Memory of Trees* CD into the slot.

Ninety minutes later and with dawn appearing, Jonathan pulls off the highway and makes his way through paved county roads to Tigiwon Road, which leads to the Holy Cross trailhead. The road is only suitable for four-wheel-drive vehicles and is single-lane in places. Fortunately, he is early enough that he does not have to negotiate with vehicles making their way down. Nevertheless, the road is rugged with rivulets and washes from the spring runoff still flowing across it and protruding rocks that would have been daunting to less-intrepid drivers.

It takes him just over an hour to make his way to the trailhead parking lot where he discovers nearly two dozen other vehicles, near which campers and hikers stand in various stages of waking and getting ready, their shoulders hunched over mugs of coffee to stave off the morning chill. After finding an open spot to park, he steps out to the morning chill and the smell of coffee and frying bacon wafting through the atmosphere, mixing with the smell of pine trees.

Sitting on a large, flat boulder, he laces up his boots, double-knotting them, and hoists his pack onto his shoulders. He shakes his torso to see how snug the pack sits and satisfied it is properly secured, moves toward the trailhead. He waves to one small group in the process of donning their gear and to one younger guy sipping something hot while standing next to a Subaru with a California plate. *Kinda cute*, he thinks. *Sure hope he dresses warmer than that if he's doing the climb.*

A check of his watch tells him it is 6:32 a.m. At the registration stand, he completes the form: date, name, address, vehicle type and color, and license plate number. He indicates he will be hiking only for the day, not camping overnight. As he slips the white copy into the box, he thinks about how the day might be toasty but a good one to hike. Cumulus clouds float lazily in an otherwise clear sky and there is a slight breeze that hints of the overnight shower. He walks back to the Explorer, places the yellow copy on the dashboard, and folds the pink copy and stuffs it inside his shorts pocket.

Approaching the trailhead, Jonathan takes note of the damp rocks strewn over the trail and reminds himself to watch his footing while stepping across several larger rocks. His left boot slips a bit as he places it on a large root that forms a natural stairway up the first rise and comes down lightly onto his right knee, but he saves himself by bracing himself with his hands.

After righting himself and situating his pack securely, he begins making his way up the switch-backing trail, this time being more intentional about foot placement. As he does so, he notes more closely the contour and aspects of the trail itself. The seemingly chaotic bedlam of rocks and roots has taken on a certain orderliness about them, as if each was deliberately assigned to its particular location and role. Collectively, they exist in the realm of nature, of Mother Earth, not dissimilar to how each human, animal, and tree exists independently, yet together form tribes, herds, and forests as an interconnected organism.

Turning his gaze and attention to the pines, spruce, and occasional shrub, Jonathan takes in the infinitely varied characteristics of each and recalls his class discussions when his students were reading the transcendentalists. He had taught that nature does not duplicate. "Each of her creations is unique and in continual process of change. Yet, men feel compelled to alter and mold her into uniform shapes and sizes and have the chutzpah to believe there is permanence to their actions. Further, nature abhors rigidity in form. A smooth-hewed ninety-degree angle is a human notion, not hers, and that's what society works to do to the human spirit: conform it by reshaping, shaving, and honing it to be like everyone else. I doubt we'll ever understand that in the end, nature always has the final say."

Surveying the well-worn trail, he recalls as well the symbolism of the path for the transcendentalists: Henry David Thoreau comparing the deeply rutted path outside his cabin at Walden to tradition and Nathaniel Hawthorne depicting it in *The Scarlet Letter* as something for his lovers Hester Prynne and Arthur Dimmesdale to slip onto to escape the oppressive Puritan community.

Stepping beyond the canopy of trees and into an open area populated with paintbrush and columbine, Jonathan breathes deeply, and for a moment, the tiredness that has pervaded his body and spirit dissipates. Taking the hose from the water bladder between his lips, he draws a few long sips while gazing towards the rising sun above the craggy rock faces that are aspects of this particular range, which in turn are part of the larger Sawatch Range, which in turn are part of the Rocky Mountains.

Once again he moves towards Half Moon Pass at 11,640 feet, about 1.7 miles from the trailhead. The trail has smoothed as it graces its way through the blossoming meadow. As he looks off to his right to take in the vista that is part of Holy Cross, his toe catches the edge of rock protruding from the otherwise dirt path. For the second time he stumbles. He manages to catch himself, but the weighted day pack pulls him to his right throwing him momentarily off balance. After he regains his footing, he notes how snuggly he has secured the pack as if making the man and his burden one entity. He chastises himself for getting sloppy with his foot placement. He is fatigued, but that is no excuse.

Crossing Half Moon Pass, he begins the 970-foot descent into the valley to East Cross Creek. The trail becomes quite steep and once again rugged, far more than the initial part since it serves as drainage for melting snow and torrential rains. This time, larger rocks, some boulder size, populate the course requiring Jonathan to scale them despite going down-hill. Larger roots network vein-like across the trail. Looking down the trail, Jonathan can see how cascading water has eroded it, carving depressions and providing obstacles that require full concentration.

Be careful, he reminds himself, noting again the tiredness that pervades his body. Runoff has eroded the ground under-neath a large root, forming a six-inch gap nearly a foot wide, and just as he takes note of it, he begins to fall, face first. At first he cannot believe it is happening. His left boot toe catches in the chasm under the root and he twists to the right. Seeing a huge granite rock quickly rising to meet his head, Jonathan braces himself with his right forearm and misses the rock by inches. Thanks to that split-second maneuver, he manages to land on his forearm, but as he slides headfirst downhill, he feels rocks and grit abrade and grind into his forehead.

Lying facedown, stunned, his face buried in the sleeve of the shirt that protected his arm and cushioned the impact of his head, Jonathan finds himself incredulous that the fall actually happened but quickly realizes that he might be in serious trouble. Though there were dozens of potential hikers at the parking area, he doubts any will be coming soon. For now, he is on his own.

Jonathan wiggles his fingers and then his toes, and with all twenty digits moving at his command, he senses he might have avoided traumatic injury, though he does feel pain in both legs. His right knee hurts more than his left, but at least there is sensation in both, which means the nerves are working.

He lies still for a few moments trying to calm himself and regain his wits. Compounding the dilemma of lying facedown with his head pointed downhill is the snuggly secured day pack atop his body. It has not shifted, despite doing its part in aiding and abetting the fall. Its bulk prevents him from rolling onto his side. Debris digs into his skin as he attempts to work his left hand free to force it between his chest and the ground to unhook the straps, but there is not space enough for him to manipulate the buckles.

His left leg has more mobility, so he flexes his left ankle and mentally gives a sigh of relief, realizing it has suffered no apparent trauma. Slowly, he begins inching his leg to the right and his torso begins to move as well. A few moments later, after using his otherwise pinned arms to raise his torso enough to allow him to pivot, Jonathan manages to get his entire body crosswise to the trail. With that, the pack becomes an asset. He pushes up with his left hand and arm and rolls to the downhill side, allowing the weight of the pack to aid the maneuver. Now atop the pack, it is only a matter of working his legs downhill. After having done that, Jonathan is able to maneuver himself up into a seated position.

Jonathan draws his knees up towards his chest and checks out the abrasions on his shins, then feels his forehead and notes abrasions there, too, but at least there is no blood flowing. A few tentative stretches and prods tell him he does not seem to have broken bones or pulled muscles. After extricating himself from the day pack, he pulls out a package of antiseptic wipes and begins cleaning the abrasions. Satisfied his wounds are as sanitized as he can get them, he stuffs the wipes into the empty plastic bread bag he has brought for trash and zips both packages into the pack.

Once he is upright, he completes an inventory of body parts to insure their functionality and determines that everything is fine. He feels confident that he has not only avoided breaking any bones, he has avoided a concussion.

What he is not confident about, though, is continuing the climb. He has survived the ordeal, but it has added to his fatigue, draining energy he cannot afford to waste. The summit will certainly take several hours to reach. Not only are there several hundred more feet of descent and then over three thousand feet of climb to the summit, with a large part of the trail requiring bouldering, there is also the return, which will require him to ascend this same portion of the trail. It makes him recall the tale of Scylla and Charybdis in *The Odyssey* and concludes that it would be like passing through the clashing rocks twice.

Jonathan turns and looks back up the trail toward the switchback that would return him to Half Moon Pass and his vehicle and surmises that it is about two miles. If he chooses that option, he can be home for lunch. Then he turns back to take in the plethora of rocks and roots awaiting him. He shakes his head, reaches down for his pack, and hoisting it back onto his shoulders, secures it snugly, again becoming one with it. After a long sip of water, he again turns and looks back up the trail from whence he has come, then turns to the path ahead, steps up onto a large rock, balances himself, and jumps down.

"You start a journey, you finish it," he mumbles as he picks his way down the trail towards East Cross Creek, taking the time and effort to be intentional about every foot placement. When he has reached the bottom, he sees that East Cross Creek is still swollen from runoff. There is a makeshift foot-bridge, but there are also stretches of logs barely above the waterline and other places with just the snouts of protruding boulders. It is an obstacle course. Crossing will require concentration, careful footing, and complete presence.

Jonathan reaches into his shorts pocket and extracts the small bag of trail mix. Tossing a handful into his mouth, he chews deliberately, savoring the intermingling of sweet and sour, the slight bitterness of the almonds, and the concentration of flavor imparted by the dried fruits. He takes one more handful and after swallowing the last morsel, pulls the water bladder hose to his mouth, then hesitates.

Eschewing the water he has carried and what he knows about the danger of giardia, he kneels in the mud beside the creek, settling his scratched and still-throbbing knees into the muck, and immediately feels the pain dissipate, thanks to the icy water. He cups his hands, dips them into the stream, and pulls up a handful of melted snow to his mouth. He sloshes it in his mouth, swallows, and repeats the action twice more before splashing the water onto his face. Its coolness is both invigorating and comforting, especially on the gashes on his forehead. The fatigue and exhaustion leave his body as if his spiritual gas tank is being refilled.

Absorbing the energies emanating from and within nature's heaven, he inhales deep breaths, and then slowly exhaling, he allows himself to feel the restoring energy purveying and pulsating throughout his body. While doing another body scan, he notices the mud caking and forming a natural poultice on his knees. He then stoops, swathes his right hand through the mud, and smears the paste onto his forehead wounds.

Feeling restored in body, mind, and spirit, he stands, bows, puts his hands together in prayer fashion, and whispers, "Namaste. Gratitude for all blessings bestowed and to come."

As he scans the world in which he stands, replete with pines, firs, flowing water, rocks, flora in abundance, and unseen creatures, Jonathan recalls what led him, inexorably, to this ritualistic climb of Holy Cross, laden with a weighted burden. He begins crossing to the other side, confidently but carefully stepping across rocks and nearly submerged fallen trees that serve as a bridge from this land of time to the land of timelessness that holds his memories of that day of death, of the archbishop, and of the father he never knew.

2

November 2, 1995

THE STUDEBAKER CARRIAGE SLOWLY made its way down the deserted street. It was November 2, the Feast of All Souls, that Day of the Dead. The sky's darkening clouds hinted at the advent of winter. From the north, a cutting gale swept the landscape, blowing withering leaves of maple, elm, and oak across the street, lawn, and sidewalk. Four geldings, strong with heads bowing low, bore the hearse into the wind, heightening the darkened dignity of the occasion. In the lead, one white and one black were teamed, and behind them, a roan and a green-eyed palomino.

The church the carriage was making its way to was a century old, its cornerstone placed the same year in which Pope Leo XIII issued his encyclical *Rerum Novarum*. The immigrant bricklayers that made up the church's first congregation, along with fellow old-country coalminers, steelworkers, craftsmen, and artisans, had carefully and reverently laid its reddish-brown bricks, striking the lines of mortar with precision.

The building was nearly as wide as high, giving its expanse a broad appearance as if its purpose was not so much to reach to heaven as to serve as the foundation for the community. As such, it dominated its surroundings. Two steeples rose above the entrances to the left and right sides with elongated spires, though the steeple on the right, which doubled as the belfry, towered thirty feet above its counterpart. Each was adorned with a simple cross. For one hundred years, the bells called the devout to Mass on Sunday mornings at 6:00, 7:30, 9:00, 10:30, which was the high mass, and 12:00. On weekdays the bells reminded the faithful of the Angelus. But on this occasion, only one tolled every twenty seconds.

The carriage rolled across a bridge, crossed railroad tracks, turned left onto Locust Street, and came to a halt in front of the church. Pure white snow—not the ash-soiled snow once caused by Pittsburgh's steel mills—covered the courtyard. It was now being tracked with pallbearer footprints and the imprint of the bier.

At the heavy oak doors stood the archbishop, attired in the customary black vestments of a funeral Mass. On the archbishop's head rested the miter, symbolizing the two-part story of God's history with mankind, the Old and New Testaments, and pointing to heaven in a flattened double helix. In his right hand, the archbishop gripped his crosier, the staff that symbolized his authority and doubled as a walking stick. Two black silk ribbons descending from the miter rounded onto the soft curvature of his back just below his nearly negligible neck.

His visage was pallid white accentuated by the liver spots that speckled his skin. The jet-black mane that had once given him an austere but distinguished look was now gray, wispy, and sparse. His wrinkled brow was punctuated by coal-black, preternaturally wide-spaced eyes, which, it was said, gave him unusual peripheral vision. These, along with his wire-rimmed glasses, aquiline nose, and a crooked jawline, gave him a fierce but dignified look. This was offset a bit by the pronounced limp evident when he walked. The archbishop stood over six feet in height, quite tall in his family, and his legs, hampered by the debilitated one, struggled to carry his disproportionate weight.

Despite his physical limitations, he seemed to Jonathan to be as tempered as steel, brooking no error, falsehood, or deviation from the path. But there was a bitterness to him, as if his responsibility for holding back Satan was a burden more rightfully belonging to those in the archangel realm.

The four pallbearers hoisted the casket from the wagon, holding it aloft on their shoulders as the four pillars held the earth, and solemnly placed it atop the bier. Strands from the choir singing Mozart's *Requiem* hovered in the air throughout the darkened church that struggled to get light from innumerable candles and ancient light fixtures hanging by chains from the ceiling.

Jonathan took his place in the sixth pew and turned to watch the archbishop standing before the great doors, which had been opened wide. Inside, awaiting the procession, were immediate family members along with a scattering of relatives, friends, and neighbors. In the balcony, the black-robed men of the choir, now having ceased their initial dirges, awaited their cue from the archbishop.

Jonathan had chosen to sit in that sixth pew, for it had been, in a deep personal way, as much a home in his childhood as any. He had sat there in the company of his mother countless minutes, hours, and days, and on occasion, they were joined by a couple of his siblings. He gazed upon the scene recalling a past that seemed never to have happened. How long ago had he sat there, knelt there, and stood there feeling he was as much a part of the whole church as every statue, candle, pew, and altar? It was impossible to grasp, so he did not try. But as if he could look outside himself and make an assessment, he thought of that child as a good boy who deserved better but was fine now.

Listening to the mournful pealing of the lone bell, Jonathan wondered how many times and for how many souls it had tolled over the past century. Conjointly, he directed a part of his attention to another sound, a dirge emanating from the pipes of the great organ in the loft, and closed his eyes to absorb every note from both bell and organ, allowing them to resonate in his soul. He breathed deeply, inhaling the wafting sweet incense and the subtle scent of the beeswax candles. Beneath him was the firmness of the cool wooden pew contoured to the small of his back and in his hands, the warmth of the two pieces onto which he held firmly: his old Latin rite missal and his journal.

He opened his eyes and flipped through the pages of his journal to find the place where he had copied, in near-perfect Palmer penmanship, two pieces composed by the great seventeenth century English poet and cleric John Donne that had resonated with him from the time he had first read them in college. Over the years they became sources of comfort and inspiration to which he could turn to help him make sense of it all.

The first, the tenth of Donne's *Holy Sonnets* and commonly known as "Death Be Not Proud," he read through slowly, attempting to listen to its message with his heart, not his brain.

Death, be not proud, though some have called thee
Mighty and dreadful, for thou art not so;
For those whom thou think'est thou dost overthrow
Die not, poor Death, nor yet canst thou kill me.
From rest and sleep, which but thy pictures be,
Much pleasure; then from thee much must flow,
And soonest our best men with thee do go,
Rest of their bones, and soul's delivery.
Thou art slave to fate, chance, kings, and desperate men,
And dost with poison, war, and sickness dwell,
And poppy or charms can make us sleep as well
And better than thy stroke; why swell'st thou then?
One short sleep past, we wake eternally
And death shall be nor more; Death, thou shall die.

No, he thought, *I no longer fear death. It cannot kill me. It will merely be a prelude to my resurrection and rebirth.*

Next he read the lines from Donne's "Meditation XVII" that he had highlighted.

"Now this bell tolling softly for another, says to me, Thou must die. Perchance he for whom this bell tolls may be so ill as that he knows not it tolls for him. And perchance I may think myself so much better than I am, as that they who are about me, and see my state, may have caused it to toll for me, and I know not that."

Jonathan looked up, gazed at the sanctuary light, and reflected. Looking back down to the highlighted text, he read more. "No man is an island, entire of itself; every man is a piece of the continent, a part of the main; if a clod be washed away by the sea, Europe is the less, as well as if a promontory were, as well as if a manor of thy friend's or of thine own were; any man's death diminishes me, because I am involved in mankind, and therefore never send to know for whom the bell tolls; it tolls for thee."

The organ ceased its dirge, and from the rear of the church, the archbishop called upon the saints and angels to come to the assistance of the deceased's soul. The choir rejoined, asking that Christ lead the soul to Abraham's bosom. And with that, the archbishop proceeded into the nave that had served as a womb for Jonathan and leaning heavily on his staff, led the procession slowly towards the sanctuary. He was followed by the bier, carrying the black-shrouded coffin and wheeled by the four pallbearers, then the servers and acolytes. With the aid of his scepter, the archbishop stepped haltingly, limping with dignity towards the sanctuary.

After guiding the bier to its proper place, the pallbearers took their places in the first pew to their right, the Saint Joseph side, so called by the faithful due to the smaller altar on that side of the sanctuary upon which stood a statue of Saint Joseph. Across from them, their sisters sat on the Blessed Mother side.

Through the gate of the communion rail stepped the archbishop, moving solemnly to the foot of the altar, where he stood, allowing for the movement behind him to cease. The acolytes followed the archbishop into the sanctuary and parted, three to one side and three to the other, where chairs and kneelers had been placed.

All was fit and proper, everything necessary present, and the family in their places. The gathered would participate in the bloodless Sacrifice of Calvary, with the archbishop in the role of Jesus Christ, offering himself as a most acceptable victim to the Eternal Father for their salvation, and the congregants as witnesses to the act.

Jonathan sat back in the pew and tugged at the five frayed ribbons of his weathered missal. He felt the outline of the raised cross on the black textured cover, tracing it with his index finger, as well as the indented dedication to Saint Joseph, the patron of the universal Church. Next he ran his finger along the edges of the pages, originally cardinal red but faded and bled inward over the years, and noted that the spine was soft and a tad broken, even though the book was otherwise in relatively good shape.

When had he last used the missal? After a moment of hesitation, he opened it to the first page and read in his fifth grade handwriting that the missal did indeed belong to him. He had written in the address of their home as well as the date: May 9, 1961. He recalled that day and the days preceding his confirmation, even the conversation his mother had with Sister Lucinda about whether he was old enough to have an adult-level missal. His mother had put her arm around him and told the nun not to worry, that he had begun reading his sister's books about the saints in the third grade. He had swelled with pride by the demonstration of his mother's confidence in him, and the memory of it had accompanied him into adulthood.

Out of curiosity, he pulled at the first ribbon, the red one, and the missal opened to the proper for Ash Wednesday. He smiled at the irony as he read the antiphon from the prophet Joel that pleaded with the Lord to spare his people. Jonathan turned his gaze to the front center pews where his brothers and sisters knelt, except for Christopher, who sat resolutely and stoically with his head upright and gaze focused forward. James, Juliana, and Mary Agnes read from their missals following the liturgy of the traditional Latin Mass, while Ruth fingered her rosary beads, and Elizabeth, Paul, and Andy knelt in rapt attention. He listened to the heavy bell that had begun tolling once again, which added to the strains of Mozart's *Requiem* the organist was playing. One lone bell.

As the archbishop and the two servers made their final movements and preparations to begin the Mass, Jonathan read over Psalm 42, ordinarily recited during the Prayers at the Foot of the Altar but omitted in requiem Masses, words that once made sense but did no longer. He raised his eyes and looked straight ahead to the statue of Saint Joseph standing on his altar holding the babe, his son, the Son of God. As a boy standing or kneeling next to his mother, he would stare at the image in wonderment. There was a time, he thought, when he was an innocent babe and his father held him like that. Of that, he mused, he had no doubt.

Using his left index finger as a bookmark, Jonathan closed his missal and continued to take in the image of Joseph holding Jesus. He let his mind wander back to his boyhood, a time that seemed both past and immanent. The archbishop's resolute voice brought Jonathan back from his reverie as he began the Mass. "*In nomine Patris, et Filii, et Spiritus Sancti. Amen.*"

Jonathan turned the page of his missal to the Confiteor, the Confession. He watched the archbishop bend forward and listened to his voice, now barely audible in the otherwise still church. "*Confiteor Deo omnipotenti, beatae Mariae semper Virgini . . .*"

He read along. "I confess to Almighty God, to Blessed Virgin Mary." Then he looked over at the confessional booth to his right, where as a boy, he had shared a trove of offenses. The Church, he had learned, categorizes all sins, no matter how trivial or heinous, succinctly into two categories: venial and mortal. Mortal sins from missing Mass to genocide, if not forgiven before death by a priest, provided the individual a one-way ticket to hell. But if they were forgiven by a priest before death, one got to walk right through the pearly gates. Unforgiven venial sins required time in purgatory, but eventually, once they were burned away, heaven was achieved.

He recalled the first time he stepped into that booth, all of seven years of age, and recalled his youthful apprehension in anticipation of the ordeal. He was in second grade, and it was his first confession. Scared and nervous, Jonathan felt his heart racing, beating hard. He had done what Sister Immaculata called his examination of conscience and had memorized the list. Four times he had been disrespectful to his mother by being sassy. Several times—he could not recall the exact number—he had gotten lazy and did not finish his chores as good as he should have and did not do his best on his homework. As far as he could remember, he had gotten angry with his sisters and brothers at least six times, and once he had nearly gotten into a fight with his friend Billy when playing with their little army men.

Jonathan had been unsure about which ones the priest would consider venial and which ones mortal, so he figured it would be best to get them all off his chest. Breathing shallowly with his throat constricting, he stepped into the booth for the first time in his life and began a ritual he would follow into his adult years. It opened with Jonathan making the sign of the cross and saying to the priest, and therefore to Jesus, "Bless me, Father, for I have sinned."

1957

JONATHAN SNUGGLES CLOSER TO his mother, her cloth coat providing the soft warmth he craves. He loves coming to church with her. At age seven, it is nothing he can comprehend, but the scent of incense and the flickering candles fill him with a sense of comfort, and he knows he is safe.

The church is grand to his little boy mind and body, and each time he goes, he is filled with awe. Romanesque in structure, the domed ceiling is a scene of the eternal with a heavenly, star-filled background of God in his majesty sitting on his throne with Jesus and Mary to either side. Jonathan gazes for stretches at the scene, absorbing every detail with wonderment, trying to figure out where his place will be when he gets to heaven. God is father, Jesus's father. To Jonathan he looks mighty powerful and even scary with his long white beard and stern eyes. Jesus, though, looks kind and loving. Jonathan begins thinking that it would be okay for God to be Jesus's father, but if he has his choice, he prefers Jesus to be his dad. The idea of a strict father who scares and smacks his kids around like old Mr. Isaacson makes Jonathan uncomfortable. To him, a father should never be scary or mean.

Mary is kindly looking too, like Jesus, but Jonathan has his own mother, so he has no need for another. He figures his mother must be blessed as well because she prays a lot in church and even at home. And she is usually patient with him. She makes the best goulash and, when they can afford it, breaded pork chops. She is not good at baking cookies though, but the pies she bakes from the fruits and berries he picks with his big brother Paul and his little sister, Mary Agnes, are the best. He does not think Mary would be as good a mother as his, so he hopes that when he gets to heaven, he can keep his own. He does not think Jesus would mind.

There are four paintings of evangelists on the ceiling, one in the center of each of the four isosceles triangles that sweep down to the rounded Roman columns that support the roof. He does not really grasp what an evangelist is, but he knows they are the men who wrote the stories of Jesus's life he loves to hear when the priest reads them in Mass. In Sister Bernadette's class, he learned that they were "authors." The gospel has become his favorite part of the Mass. The only bad part about listening to the priest read the gospel is having to stand, which tires him. And when the priest gives his sermon, the warmth and closeness of the packed congregation makes him feel drowsy. Then he finds his mother's ample arm in her soft cloth coat a perfect pillow to lean on and nap.

As for the writers of Jesus's story, he always wonders why in the paintings three of the men have animals with them. The one exception is Matthew, who has wings like an angel. This confuses him. Is he an angel or a man? Sister Bernadette taught him and his classmates that men are closer to God than angels, but that does not make sense to Jonathan since the angels are already in heaven with God and can fly. We would have to be dead like his dad to be with God, and that is another scary thought.

The one called Mark intrigues Jonathan because he is with a lion. Jonathan loves animals, especially wild ones in the jungle. He likes going over to his friend Billy's house to watch the Tarzan movies on their family's television set. When he sees the tigers and lions and other wild beasts, he imagines how much fun it would be to be Boy, Tarzan's son. Then he would be able to swing on the vines with his dad. It would not be as good as being able to fly like an eagle, the bird that sits on John's shoulder, but swinging on a vine would be okay. It would be like swinging on the bull rope over the creek, which he and Billy already do. And with his big chest and his strong arms and legs, Tarzan also seems like a good father to have.

Jonathan does not care too much for the one called Luke, although he likes his gospel best. He loves hearing Luke's story of the birth of Jesus, with the angels singing, the shepherds visiting, and the cattle and sheep in the stable kneeling in adoration. He figures that animals must be like people because the story shows they understand that baby Jesus is also God. Still, Jonathan does not care for the ox pictured with Luke. It makes him think of the bull on Uncle Henry's farm. He is not mean, just stubborn, and he does not like kids around him. So Jonathan always keeps his distance when Uncle Henry asks him to spray the bull with powder to kill the flies that swarm around and pester him.

Jonathan's favorite evangelist is John. He looks young, like Jesus, and has no beard. He thinks John and Jesus must have been very close because in the picture he has seen of the Last Supper, John has his head on Jesus's arm, much like Jonathan rests his head on his mother's arm in church. But that is somehow different because Jesus and John are both men. Still, it seems okay that they are very close. Jonathan thinks that maybe someday he will have a close friend like John.

It is the eagle, though, that captures Jonathan's imagination, even more than Mark's lion. He loves looking at the pictures of big birds. Sister Bernadette calls them raptors. They are big and strong and could maybe even fly up to heaven. He imagines himself being one, soaring above the earth to the highest point in the sky, and then diving faster and faster. It would be like being in a plane, only better because you would be the plane.

The red lamp with the candle hanging in front of the sanctuary catches his eye. He whispers to his mother, "Why is that red lamp hanging in front of the altar?"

"It means Jesus is here."

"But I don't see him!"

"He's in the tabernacle on the altar."

"But I thought he's everywhere. If he is, then he can't just be in that box."

Jonathan loves to argue, not to be disagreeable, but because he wants to know why things do not make sense.

His mother hushes him as she continues praying her rosary. It is Friday, so Jonathan knows she is reciting the Sorrowful Mysteries. He is not quite sure what that means, but knows enough to understand they are about the time of Jesus's suffering and death. Since Jesus was nailed to the cross on a Friday, the priest wears black vestments when saying Mass, but not for the Benediction.

Death is scary. You only hope that when you die, you would not die with sin on your soul. He thinks about the talk he and his friends had in class about their families with Sister

Bernadette earlier that day. She asked him to tell the class about his family.

"It's me, my mother, my five brothers, and my four sisters. Mother cooks our meals and does our laundry and works in the garden in the summer. She grows lots of vegetables. My brother Theodore is the oldest, and he's in the navy. Elizabeth is next. She's married and just had a baby. Then there's James, who works and goes to night school. After him comes Ruth, who just graduated. Then comes Christopher, who's in the eleventh grade, and Juliana, in the ninth grade. Paul is my next older brother and he's in the seventh grade, and Mary Agnes is my little sister. She's five. And Andy is my little brother. He's three."

"What about your father? Tell us about him."

"I can't, Sister. He's dead."

One of Jonathan's classmates waved his hand. "What does that mean?"

"It means he's in the ground," Jonathan replied.

"I'm sorry to hear that, Jonathan. How did he die?" Sister Bernadette asked.

"I don't know, Sister. He's just dead."

Another hand waved excitedly. "Sister, what happens when somebody dies?"

"Well, he goes to heaven if he's been good. Then he will be with Jesus."

Almost everyone seemed to have questions at that point.

"Where's heaven? Is it up in the stars? That's what my mother says."

"Yes."

"Could we go there? What if we got a very fast spaceship like the one the Russians have? Could it take us to heaven?"

"No, you have to die first, and then your soul goes to heaven, not your body."

"But if heaven is a place, then we should be able to go there."

"It's not a place like this. It's a place for souls, so there are no bodies like ours there. Your body stays on earth, under the ground."

"Isn't Jesus's body in heaven? Father Keegan told us Jesus and the Blessed Mother both went to heaven, body and soul."

"That's true, but all the rest of us have to wait for the Final Judgment before our souls are joined back with our bodies. Then we will be with God too, body and soul."

"So, Jonathan's dad's body is under the ground but his soul is in heaven?"

"Yes, that's right."

"But what if he was bad? Would he still be with Jesus?"

"No, he would go to where the devil lives. If a priest forgave his sins before he died, then he might go to heaven. But he might be spending time in another place called purgatory if God decided he needs to suffer a bit before he is allowed into heaven."

"What are sins, Sister?"

"Sins are bad things you do like being disrespectful to your parents or missing Mass on Sundays. When you're seven, like some of you, you are at the age of reason. That means you know right from wrong. So if you do something really bad, God won't let you into heaven, and you will have to spend eternity with the devil. So it's very important to be good at all times."

"What does eternity mean, Sister?"

"It means forever. It never ends."

"So, if I don't go to Mass and the priest doesn't forgive me, I will be with the devil forever?"

"That's right."

"My dad never goes to church. He tells my mother she's wasting her time when she goes, and they end up fighting. Will my dad go to the devil, Sister?"

A look of exasperation came across the nun's face. "I don't know," she said. "That will be for God to decide."

"But that's not fair! My dad always helps me with my homework, and we have fun together. He's teaching me how to build model airplanes, and he works all the time around the house after he gets home from work."

"It's not a matter of being fair. It's a matter of being good."

"But my dad is good. He just doesn't like going to church. Why is that bad?"

"It's not up to us to decide. The Church tells us what we must do and we cannot do. If we disobey the Church, then we cannot go to heaven."

"Jonathan, did your dad go to church?"

"I don't know. I think he did, but my brother Christopher says he didn't."

"Do you think he's in heaven?"

"I don't know. All I know is that he's dead and in the cemetery."

"Does that scare you?"

"No," he lied.

"I'd be afraid to go there. My big brother says ghosts haunt cemeteries and come out at night."

"He's just trying to frighten you," said Sister Bernadette.

"Are ghosts real, Sister?

"I don't know. Maybe souls that have been bad stay here because they're afraid to see God."

"Yeah, like in Mrs. Anderson's old, creepy house. I get scared every time I walk by it. But I like being scared."

A number of the children began to shout, "Me too!" and the class descended into cacophony. Jonathan, though, sat quietly amid the chatter as Sister Bernadette worked to restore order. Uncomfortable thoughts came to him. *I'm afraid, but I guess I'm not supposed to be.*

Jonathan is seven, so he has reached the age of reason. All he can understand is that he is supposed to know the difference between good and bad—like telling the truth and not lying or not going to church on Sundays and holy days instead of staying home. Eating meat on Friday is bad too although he is not sure why since fish seem to be meat, just meat from animals that live in water. He does not mind the fish his mother cooks, except the kind that has the needlelike bones in it. Maybe being stabbed in the roof of the mouth by one of those bones is some sort of punishment, so he always offers it up to God.

Jonathan is at an awkward height, too tall to be standing on the padded kneeler like he did when he first started coming to church but too short to see clearly above the heads of the people in the pews in front of him if he stands on the floor. And when he kneels, his forehead rests against the top of the pew in front of him. So he alternates between kneeling and standing, sometimes on the floor and sometimes on the kneeler. It seems a good compromise to him.

Jonathan tries to remember the day his dad died almost four years ago but has only a vague memory of it—the quiet commotion, his brothers standing in mute silence, except for Paul, who kept crying when the police officers came to tell his mother what had happened. Neither his mother nor his brothers and sisters ever talk about it. When he asks about it, all they say is that it was an accident. Although, one night he woke up and heard his mother and Christopher arguing about having a hunting rifle in the house. She told Christopher he could not have one because that was how his dad died.

But one scene, one that comes when he is about to fall asleep, repeats itself.

Jonathan is standing behind his dad's old recliner. It has dark brown fabric and heavy black buttons all along the arms where the material meets the curved wood finish. Beside it is a yellow pole lamp with ridges, an ornate pedestal, and an off-white shade. Inside it are six lights shaped like Christmas tree bulbs that make them look like candles.

He is almost four years old and wearing a white shirt, brown corduroy overalls, and high-top brown shoes. He is wearing glasses that have a patch over the right lens to force his left eye to do the work because he has what they call a lazy left eye that drifts when he stares. There are patches on the knees of his trousers, too.

There were women in the house, neighbor ladies, he thinks, preparing food. Every once in a while, one comes to talk to him or tries to pull him from behind the chair, but he refuses to come out of his hiding place and stands quiet and scared, clutching his threadbare teddy bear. He is not sure where his mother and big brothers and older sisters are, but they're not at home.

None of it makes sense, but when it passes through his mind like a bad dream, he becomes really scared all over again. He always feels better, though, when he goes to church with his mother.

He loves the big church. It has nice smells: the wood pews, the incense and candles, the soft sweet scents of perfume on the ladies, and the pipe and cigar tobacco smell on the men. Jonathan looks around with reverent curiosity. He is particularly awed by the size of the pipes in the choir loft from which the organ music flows. He loves listening to the choir and thinks about how he wants to sing in the choir when he grows up, like his brother Paul, who is in the boys' choir. Christopher teases Paul when his voice cracks. Mother says the reason it cracks is because he is growing and becoming a man like Theodore and James. James always sticks up for Paul. One time, he broke Christopher's nose in a fight, and there seemed to be blood everywhere.

High Mass is best to go to even though it can be long, especially when Father Stanislaus celebrates it.

Jonathan hears his mother whisper softly, "Hail Holy Queen," which means she is nearing the end of the rosary. Soon the priest will come out to start the Benediction. He likes to come to Benediction but has to admit that all the "Pray for us," especially in the Litany of the Saints, starts to get boring after a while. He does, though, like the Litany of the Blessed Virgin Mary. In it, Mary is called all kinds of fun and strange names, like Mystical Rose, House of Gold, and Morning Star. They have mysterious meanings, none of which he can comprehend.

A few moments later, the altar boy rings the bells next to the sacristy door signaling the time for Benediction. The people, mostly old women, stand, as Father Keegan, his favorite priest, and the two altar boys enter. They all kneel and the priest repeats the ritual of the rosary Jonathan's mother has just finished, leading the first part of the prayer and allowing the congregants to respond.

Father Keegan leads one Our Father and three Hail Marys, and concludes the introductory aspect of the rosary by praying the Glory Be. Then he proclaims, "For a true contrition, the first Sorrowful Mystery, the Agony in the Garden."

The participants recite one Our Father, ten Hail Marys, one Glory Be, and move on to the second Sorrowful Mystery, the Scourging at the Pillar. After concluding the five mysteries, in unison they pray the *Salve Regina*.

Jonathan's eyes focus on Father Keegan as the altar boy wraps the vestment around his shoulders. Father ascends the altar steps and unlocks the tabernacle from where he retrieves the cup that holds the Host, the body of Christ. He swings open the little glass window in the center of the monstrance and places one Host inside. He closes it, and with his hands wrapped in the shawl, raises the monstrance and turns toward the people. Slowly, he makes the sign of the cross with the monstrance three times, once to his left, then to the center, and finally to his right. He sets the monstrance on the altar, descends the steps, kneels, and announces, "The Litany of the Blessed Virgin Mary."

The congregants join with the priest in recitation, with Jonathan alternating between joy at the proclamation by Father Keegan of the titles for Mary and boredom with the incessant, monotone "Pray for us" by the people after each. When concluded, the priest once again ascends the steps, removes the Host from the monstrance, and places it back into the tabernacle. He descends for the last time and in his deep baritone voice, he intones the first line of "*Tantum Ergo.*" The music, its cadence uplifting and comforting, fills Jonathan with a sense of peace and belonging. This is his place, the place where he feels safe, protected, and loved.

∽o∾

1959

JONATHAN FINISHES PUSHING INTO the garage the dirt, dust, lint, and other grit that has found its way into the basement. One of his chores every other Saturday morning is to move the ironing board, the boot barrel, a metal tub three feet in diameter and two feet high that holds the family's collection of winter overshoes, and the assorted pairs of shoes sitting along the wall that separates the room from the garage. After sweeping the basement floor from corner to corner, he returns each item to its assigned spot. He needs to get it done before his mother does the laundry, a daily ritual, so she can hang the sheets, Saturday's target, on the rope line strung from the overhead joists. It is raining, so hanging them outside is not an option. Also, she refuses to use their recently purchased dryer except for emergencies. It saves on the utility bill. The chore is not as hard as it used to be before his mother replaced the old coal-burning furnace, which had left coal dust and soot everywhere, with a natural gas one.

Next, Jonathan tugs the dented and dinged metal garbage can from its corner in the garage and sweeps the debris from there. Using the coal shovel as a dustpan, he pushes the pile into the shovel and deposits the debris into the can. The rest of the garage will have to wait until James pulls the family car, a 1952 Ford, out to wash and wax later in the day, that is if the rain stops. Otherwise, James will complete the job with buckets of soap and rinse water in the garage. Rain or shine, that task, like all others, gets done.

After restoring everything to its original spot, Jonathan pulls a frayed jacket from the basement rack where all the family's outerwear hangs. He inherited the jacket from Paul, who had in turn gotten it from Christopher. Jonathan assumes he is the fifth wearer, and little Andy will finally wear it out and put it to rest. He struggles with the zipper because its teeth are bent and gone partially missing over the years.

After manipulating it up, he takes the only yellow slicker available and slips it over the coat. The slicker's hood has long been missing, and he considers a wool hat he wears when it is snowing, but thinks better of it.

Next, he pulls on and ties up his high-top Keds and pulls his knee-patched overalls over them. There is no sense pulling the rubber overshoes from the barrel because they are no longer waterproof, thanks to the holes in them. Besides, they would only delay the inevitable and slow him down. And squishy toes can be fun, that is, when they are not cold.

It is April, and the spring rain already feels warm to his skin, so getting chilled is not a problem. Keeping his newspapers dry is another matter, so he uses a worn carrying sack to drape over the one with the cache of *Sun-Telegraph* newspapers.

Jonathan's mother comes down the steps with a load of laundry as he heads toward the door. "When it stops raining, don't forget to burn the trash," she says.

"I won't, Mom," he replies.

Jonathan trudges down the driveway with the eighteen newspapers he is to deliver. The misty rain feels good and the air smells sweet. Jonathan inhales deeply and notices his hair is already soaked. Rivulets begin to flow into his eyes. He blinks to clear them, but it is a hopeless cause. He decides that there is nothing he can do about it, so he might as well enjoy it.

It is Paul's paper route, but two months earlier, Mr. Rudovich hired Paul part-time at his grocery store to stock shelves. Until he is able to find another boy to take it over, Paul has given Jonathan the smaller part of the route, the neighbors down their road, while he continues to deliver to the forty-two other households that cover a much larger territory.

Most days, the newspapers weigh down Jonathan's nine-year-old body to the point that he struggles with the sack draped over his left shoulder and hanging on his right side. Waterlogged today, it sags almost to the ground and constantly brushes against his lower right leg. Because the lower parts of his trousers are saturated, the friction caused by the rubbing burns his leg, but not in a warming sense.

Jonathan loves his new job. He earns a penny and a half for delivering each daily paper and five cents for the Sunday edition. He has done the math, now that he can multiply with decimals, and calculates that he is earning twenty-seven cents a day Monday through Saturday and ninety cents on Sunday, which adds up to $2.52 a week. Since he is careful to put the newspapers inside the screen door or in another place where they will not get wet or blow away, as Paul trained him to do, most of his customers tip him five or ten cents weekly. Occasionally, he gets more, especially if Mr. Morey answers the door instead of Mrs. Morey. Mr. Morey jingles the change in his pocket and offers to pay Jonathan however much it is instead of the weekly bill if Jonathan agrees to take the chance. At first, Jonathan is suspicious, but decides to take a chance. He never loses because Mr. Morey always has well over a dollar in loose change, which is way more than enough.

Because of his willingness not only to do the job, but also to take care of his customers, he usually makes between four and five dollars a week. With his mother's help, he has opened a savings account at the bank at which she cashes her Social Security check, and because he already has $17.50 in it, he figures he is getting pretty rich. The lady at the bank has told him that he has enough to buy a savings bond if he likes.

It used to take Jonathan over thirty minutes to deliver all his papers, but over the past two weeks, he has managed to get it down to nearly twenty minutes by finding shortcuts through yards and by getting stronger. Unless the rain slows him down, as it is doing on this day, he can almost fly while delivering the Saturday papers because they are very thin. But the Sunday paper more than makes up for it. Before delivering them, Jonathan has to stuff the Sunday papers with three additional sections, including the funnies, before heading out. Further, he has to get up way early to get it all done. The tradeoff is that he is allowed to go to the 6:00 a.m. Mass with James, Juliana, and Paul. He likes that but misses going to the 11:00 a.m. High Mass. There is something about the choir singing everything in Latin that he loves, but he figures he is growing up, so it is fine if he does not accompany his mother, Mary Agnes, and little Andy.

Jonathan feels closest to Paul, who is his next older brother. More than his other three older brothers, Paul looks out for him since their dad's death. Quiet by nature, almost to the point of being shy, Paul says little but does much. Unlike Christopher, who is four years older, Paul does not get into trouble, at least of his own doing. Paul can be quite sensitive to events and the emotions of others, although he masks it well. Despite his young age, Jonathan is beginning to understand the idea of intuition. He has an awareness about those around him that transcends observation and analysis, and he is learning to trust his intuitive power to guide him. He is also learning to appreciate the choices others make instead of judging them.

Paul's insight, though, is different from Jonathan's. While Jonathan has an uncanny knack for reading those around him, Paul seems to know when something is going to happen before it does, such as his sensing their father's unexpected, tragic death before it occurred. That particular premonition has already become family lore.

Jonathan recalls the time the police came to the house to take Paul in for questioning. Apparently, the local school had been vandalized, and the other kids pointed a finger at Paul. Paul was there when it happened but had not participated. Still, he was an accessory and a witness, which meant he was held accountable for the vandalism, along with the others. It was through that experience Jonathan learned the difference between commission and omission when it came to wrong-doing. It was hard to understand, but someone could get into trouble not only with the law but also with the Church for *not* doing something.

Although Jonathan is perceptive and shares a full-sized bed with Paul, Jonathan struggles to understand what is going on inside his favorite brother's head at times. It is as if Paul is in turmoil about whom and where he is and is itching to be somewhere else. Jonathan notes how Paul talks about seeing the world and traveling to faraway countries. He also notes that Paul never seems sure of himself, constantly doubting his abilities. Jonathan wonders why Paul is so hard on himself, as if he has something to prove.

On the other hand, Christopher is very confident in himself. Jonathan likes staring at the autographed picture of the late actor James Dean his sister Juliana has framed and set up on the mantel. Christopher has his hair styled like James Dean and even has a black leather jacket like the one James Dean is wearing in the picture. From his nine-year-old perspective, Jonathan calculates that Chris seems destined for trouble. It has become almost a weekly ritual for their mother to take a strap to him, something totally out of character for her, because he drinks, smokes, and comes in after curfew. On occasion, she slaps Jonathan on his shirtless back for wrongs he unsuccessfully protests he is innocent of, but it is nothing compared to what his older brother receives. The amazing part is that Christopher merely laughs at her attempts to discipline him.

Ever since he can remember, Christopher has fought with their mother about going to church. He was the only one who refused to go to the Catholic high school, finding his place, instead, in the newly opened public high school, where he could have and should have been first in his class. Of all his siblings, Jonathan views the sullen and introspective Christopher as the most intelligent. As far as Jonathan is concerned, this is evident from his choice in books and music. On the living room end table, Christopher keeps books written by authors whose names Jonathan finds difficulty pronouncing—Nietzsche, Asimov, and Schopenhauer among them—and even though Jonathan is one of the top readers in his class, he does not understand any of the writing.

And with eyes softly closed, Christopher oftentimes sits quietly on their mother's reupholstered rocker absorbing the strains of Tchaikovsky or Beethoven emanating from the hi-fi set James has recently purchased along with a matching TV set. The music is heavy and powerful, like Christopher, despite his small frame and fine, sandy, curly hair. While Paul's journeys need to be literal, Christopher's are metaphoric, traveling to heights Jonathan suspects are unimaginable to the rest of his siblings and peers.

Unlike Christopher's small ears, which subtly rest amid the shroud of his greased-up, slicked-back hair, Jonathan's ears are pronounced and have become a source of embarrassment. With an evil laugh, Christopher often tells Jonathan that he looks like a car coming down the road with its doors open. Cutting and painful to the point of humiliation, Christopher's taunting perplexes Jonathan, who sees that his brother's intellect and physical beauty belie the meanness that can spew forth without warning. There is irony to the seeming contradiction of how brilliant and beautiful people can have within them the capacity to be the cruelest of people towards their fellow humans. Even as he wonders if being good-looking is a blessing or a burden, Jonathan feels empathy for his handsome brother with the giant intellect because he has been drafted. This has upset Jonathan, who thinks that Christopher should be going to college to study instead.

In the third grade, thoughts of college lie beyond Jonathan's capacity to dream. Being second-generation Americans, no one in the family has gone to college to earn a degree. It is simply beyond their means and culture. Survival was the first order of business for both sets of Jonathan's immigrant grandparents. Their children, Jonathan's parents and aunts and uncles, had been trying to experience the American Dream, but the reality was work first, dream later.

Education beyond high school for the boys and beyond eighth grade for the girls was a dream, not reality. The idea that education is the key to success, happiness, and financial stability is only recently beginning to register with some of the Slovancos. The eldest brother, Theodore, whom Jonathan idolizes, left home after the tragedy and joined the navy, where he is taking college-level classes. When he has completed them, he will be the first to earn a degree. But the idea of attending a college and earning a degree separate from military obligations is as foreign to the family as was the language Jonathan's grandparents struggled with three-quarters of a century earlier.

Juliana hollers as she strides into the room. "Hey, ears, you better not make dog ears on the pages of that book!"

Jonathan seethes. "Don't worry, I'm not."

He has been lying on his stomach on the living room floor, under the lamp, reading a story about Saint Isaac Jogues, a French missionary who had the fingers of his right hand cut off by Indians so he could not hold the Host to consecrate it into the body of Christ and give Communion. The pope gave Isaac Jogues a dispensation that allowed him to use his left hand instead.

Juliana orders the books on the saints from a Catholic book club, and though they are for older kids, Jonathan has little problem reading them, except for an occasional vocabulary word. Then he lugs the huge dictionary with tissue-like pages from the hall closet and looks it up. His mother recently purchased a set of encyclopedias from a traveling salesman. They really could not afford it, but she told James, who was not keen about the expenditure, that it was necessary because education is the best way to become more successful in life.

Oftentimes, Jonathan chooses a letter of the alphabet and picks the encyclopedia with that letter on its spine. Then, after saying his nightly prayers and climbing into bed, he opens the book randomly and simply reads on whatever the topic might be, from a famous person to a country. Because of that, he has memorized every state capital, including Juneau, the capital of the newest state Alaska, and can name every president in order up to President Eisenhower.

His mother calls to him, "It's 9:00. Time to hit the hay."

It is Saturday, so he is allowed to stay up an extra hour. However, since he has to get up at 4:00 a.m., he does not argue. "Okay, Mum."

Lying in the bed, Jonathan considers, with fear, how his family is coming apart, despite outward bravado. Their mother is doing everything possible to hold them together since their father's death, despite the pressure from the parish priest to put a couple of them, including Jonathan, in an orphanage. Her strength of will has refused to bend. He pictures her, with his younger brother Andy still inside her, standing resolutely in the rain at the funeral, strong and unshakable.

Remembering he has forgotten to say his prayers, Jonathan climbs back out of bed, kneels beside it, and makes his examination of conscience, numerating the offenses he committed over the day. Satisfied he has accounted for all he can recall, he makes a silent act of contrition.

Reaching across the bed and underneath his pillow, Jonathan pulls the rosary beads his mother bought him for his first Communion two years earlier and clutches them tightly in his right hand. Silently, he recites the Memorare imploring the Virgin Mary to help him and his family, confident that the Mother of God will hear and answer his prayer. When he finishes, he adds a personal plea to his heavenly mother. "Help us, Mother Mary. Everyone's hurting so much, especially James, Christopher, and Paul. They miss our dad more than the rest of us. And please help Christopher and Paul stay out of trouble, and help me be good."

Jonathan crosses himself, climbs back into bed, and curls up pulling the blanket over his head. After a few minutes, he is satisfied he is warm enough, so he rolls onto his left side to face the wall and pokes his face out from the blanket to breathe the cool, moist air. The sound of running water in the bathroom, which is on the other side of the wall, catches his attention. He hopes it is Paul in there though he is pretty sure Paul has not come home yet.

Spelling bee Monday, he remembers. He is the best speller in his class, but the competition will be strong. Michael, John, Nancy, and Susan are no mental slouches—s, l, o, u, c, h, e, s—but he feels pretty good about the list. Margaret, his cousin in the eighth grade, has grilled him over and over, not only on his words but also on some from her vocabulary lists. If he wins, he will get a trophy from the men in the Holy Name Society at their meeting the following Sunday after the 7:45 Mass.

The running water catches his attention anew and he allows it to overtake his mind, which soon puts him into a deep sleep.

4

November 2, 1995

CLOSING HIS EYES AND clenching his teeth, Jonathan surveyed the countless times he had bared himself in that confessional booth by divulging his inner life, his private world, to a another man not of his choosing. *It is about power,* he said to himself. *I gave them my power for no purpose.* Mild anger rose within him for allowing himself to be subjugated and debased, his dignity shredded, but when he realized what was happening, he recognized it, honored it, and let it subside. He thought of the running water that had lulled him to sleep countless times as a boy.

Responding to the servers who had finished their professions of the *Confiteor*, the archbishop in a raised voice said, "*Misereatur vestri omnipotens Deus, et dimissis peccatis vestris, perducat vos ad vitam aeternam.*"

Jonathan read along in his missal. "May Almighty God have mercy on you, forgive you your sins, and bring you to everlasting life."

As the archbishop and the servers continued in Latin, Jonathan followed the remainder of the preparatory prayers in English. He stifled a yawn and remembered how, as a boy, he would yawn at this point of the Mass, almost without fail. Though early in the Mass, there was a monotonous drudgery to it, but the tempo would pick up quickly with the choir singing the *Kyrie*. Jonathan sat back onto his pew, closed his eyes, and waited.

He opened his eyes as the archbishop ascended the three steps to the altar, bowed, kissed it, and stepped to the right side of it to read the Introit. Jonathan pulled at the blue ribbon in his missal, turned to the page titled "Mass on the Day of the Death or Burial," and read the biblical verses that implored God to grant eternal rest to the deceased and let his perpetual light shine upon them.

The archbishop stepped back to the center of the altar, turned to the congregation, and intoned in his most majestic and baritone voice *Kyrie, eleison,* the one prayer in Greek in the Latin Mass: "Lord, have mercy."

In response, the organist pumped the ancient organ peddles and pressed down on the keys. Its pipes came alive, and the choir filled the church with Mozart's *Kyrie*. The archbishop turned back towards the altar and stood silently with head slightly bowed, seemingly absorbing every chord and note into every sinew of his body and mind. One by one, Jonathan's siblings sat back in the pews, a few staring ahead, the others with eyes closed and heads bowed.

The choir sang *Kyrie, eleison* three times, *Christe, eleison* three times, and *Kyrie, eleison* three more times, their repetitive blends echoing and resounding from the domed ceiling, walls, stained glass windows, columns, pews, altars and statues.

"Lord, have mercy, Christ, have mercy, Lord, have mercy."

༺༠༻

1961

A LIGHT COMES ON in Jonathan's head as he and his little brother Andy play in their camp. "Jude. That's it!" he says.

Choosing a confirmation name has proved to be more of a challenge than he thought, and with the date getting close, the pressure is on. While the other boys joke they will pick names like Hercules or Mickey (after the Yankees centerfielder or Mickey Mouse) to be silly, Jonathan has taken a serious attitude towards the task. Besides, he knows they all have to pick a saint's name, and there is no Saint Hercules or Saint Mickey. He did his research in the *Book of the Saints*.

Picking a name for yourself is a bit strange, Jonathan thinks, given your parents already gave you one when you were born. But at the same time, it is very exciting. He cannot quite put his finger on it, but he senses the name will be symbolic of him for his entire life and thus, meaningful. Jude, the patron of hopeless causes, was one of the more outgoing apostles of Jesus and a favorite of everyone, especially Jesus, because he cared about everyone else and was always there to help those in desperate need. That is the reason Danny Thomas is naming the new hospital he is building after him.

"So, whaddya you think, Andy?"

"Sounds goofy to me. Sounds like a girl's name."

Jonathan becomes a little miffed at the suggestion. "Jude's a man's name. A girl would be Judy or Judith. Besides, Pat can be a boy's or a girl's name."

Andy shrugs his shoulders. "It doesn't matter to me, so if you like it and Mum says okay, then okay."

At seven years of age, Andrew is already showing signs of sophistication. On points over which Jonathan gets all agitated, Andrew simply shrugs his shoulders. It is not as if he does not care. He really does. It is just that most things do not rise to being worthy of an emotional response. Even at seven, his life philosophy seems to come down to one simple construct: into every life comes pain. Suffering, on the other hand, is a matter of choice. And when either comes, do not avoid it, deal with it.

In the fifth grade, the idea of becoming a soldier of Christ through Confirmation has deeper meaning for Jonathan than for his classmates. It means he is to become an active fighter, an actual soldier for God and for the Catholic Church, God's kingdom on Earth. Only twenty percent of the world is Catholic, so there is a lot of work to be done.

To prepare for battle, Jonathan trains like every soldier. He is becoming disciplined in mind and spirit, arming and girding himself with the truth of Christ and of his Church. Lenten fasts, in particular, have a hardening effect. It is not good enough to simply give up candy and other sweets. Daily Mass is obligatory, followed by the rosary in which he recites the Sorrowful Mysteries—the Agony in the Garden, Scourging at the Pillar, Crowning with Thorns, Carrying the Cross when Jesus falls three times; and the Crucifixion—all begun on Ash Wednesday. It is then the priest smudges ashes on his forehead, reminding him that from dust he came and to dust he is destined to return.

On Fridays, he walks two miles to the church for evening Benediction with his mother along the winding, tree-lined road that has a narrow dirt shoulder on which they step to avoid passing cars. On Sundays, he again attends High Mass, since he no longer delivers newspapers because Paul has found someone else to take the route. That means he fasts from Saturday evening supper so he can receive Communion.

The life of Saint Isaac Jogues still fascinates him, and he is now prepared to suffer or even die for his faith like the French saint. When he was nine years old, he really did not grasp the reason why the priest holding the Host with his right or left hand mattered, but at age eleven, he understands that it does matter. That is the way it is done, so that is that.

It is not just the story of Saint Jogues that stirs his emotions, so does the setting. There is something he loves and craves in that primordial environment. The thought of living in nature excites his imagination. From the time he was a little kid, he has loved to play in the woods up on the hill behind his family's home. Though only a few square miles in size, the forest seems to stretch without end. Each summer, he and his pals play cowboys and Indians quite often, tracing old trails and creating new ones, wondering what it was like when the Indians lived there hundreds of years before them.

Jonathan likes playing Cochise, which is Michael Ansara's role on *Broken Arrow*. Jonathan's other favorite role is Bronco Lane, played by Ty Harden. In the forest, Jonathan strips to his sneakers and walks naked through the lush greenery and fallen logs. There is something about this that makes him feel alive and primal. And despite the lessons he has learned in catechism class, it does not seem to be impure. Far from unchaste, walking naked in the woods seems to be a true and natural way to connect with the sacred, as profound and holy a ritual as the sacrament of confirmation.

Nonetheless, here in the woods he can pretend to be an Indian, but in real life he is a Catholic white boy. Here he can be Cochise, but there he will be a soldier of Christ, so he needs to adopt a name fitting for that role. He thinks of the banter with his friends in the school cafeteria about the upcoming ceremony in which the bishop slaps the cheek of the one being confirmed and calls him by his new name.

His friend Archie was having none of it and guffawed. "When he slaps me, I'll slap him right back."

"Like heck, you will," Jonathan chided. "He's the bishop, so he can slap you. Besides, he's not really going to whack you like Sister Francis did when she heard you cussing."

"Like hell! No one slaps me and gets away with it."

"Sister Francis did."

"It's a matter of time before she gets hers."

"What are you going to do? Hit her? You wouldn't hit a lady, especially a nun!"

"Like hell I won't. It's bad enough when my dad smacks me around, but when my mom does it, it really hurts."

Jonathan wonders what will become of Archie. He is a crazy kid, always in trouble. But he is the funniest kid too, doing things Jonathan never dreams or dares to and getting away with pretty much everything. He is an anomaly, a complete contradiction: incredible pain masked by a cheerful, invulnerable exterior. Try as he will, Jonathan finds he is not able to mask his pain like Archie. Putting on such an act requires an intensity and mental focus he is incapable of. At age eleven, he is beginning to sense an inkling of deep personal pain, but the source of it remains unintelligible.

One day Archie attempted to explain his crazy behavior to the gang. "I do it so I don't hafta make stuff up when I go to confession. Besides, it's all bullshit, all this stuff about going to heaven or hell when you die. When you die, you're just dead. That's all. No sense worrying about it. So you might as well have fun living before you croak."

Jonathan wanted to argue, but did not because he knew that Archie would just start tormenting him in front of all the other guys, and that was never a good idea. He thought of Lawrence, his cousin in the seminary who is getting ready to be ordained. With his ordination, Lawrence will become a commander in the Army of Christ while he will only become a foot soldier with his Confirmation.

The idea of becoming a real soldier when he grows up excites Jonathan. He remembers Teddy coming home on leave, wearing his uniform. Jonathan was six or seven years old and completely spellbound, hardly able to take his eyes off him. Teddy would leave his cap with the shiny brim on the mantelpiece, and in the morning when everyone else except their mother was asleep, Jonathan would take it down and put it on his head. Even though it was much too large, it made him feel different somehow.

Jonathan made sure he sat as close as possible to Teddy at the dinner table during that visit, simultaneously trying to be as unobtrusive as possible. During a rare and special dinner of pork roast, sauerkraut, creamed corn, mashed potatoes, and cranberry sauce, Teddy told stories of his overseas tours that mesmerized them all. And later that evening, with all their brothers and sisters present except for Christopher, he showed slides with pictures of faraway, exotic places like Spain and Japan. During the showing, Jonathan stole a peak at Paul and noticed him focusing intently as well.

That was the first time Jonathan heard of the Naval Academy, and he quickly decided he wanted to go there to college. Then he would become a fighter pilot, taking off from an aircraft carrier. Of course, there would be the problem of his lazy left eye and his inability to swim. The latter he could learn, but the former was definitely a problem. The attempts to correct the lazy eye when he was three or four had not worked. Now he has glasses that make him look like a genius, he thinks, but he knows, from conversations he had with Teddy when he first thought about going to the Naval Academy that his eyesight will likely disqualify him. He has decided he will just have to work harder, whether learning to swim or finding a way to become a fighter pilot.

When the boys tire of playing in their camp, Andy asks Jonathan if he would like to play some catch.

Jonathan is halfhearted in his willingness. "Yeah, sure."

He is embarrassed about his inability to throw a ball. He cannot seem to coordinate his hand and eye. Four years younger, Andy already throws a ball harder and far more accurately than he. Jonathan really likes Andy, which is good because he and James are the only brothers still at home. James is home because he is the main source of income for the family, which gave him a deferment from the draft. His other three brothers are gone from home, Chris drafted into the army and Paul in the Marines, doing his basic training at Parris Island. In the meantime, having Andy helps make life complete.

For their game of catch, the boys use the road in front of the house, and Jonathan takes the downhill end. He is a pretty fast runner, so if the ball should get by him, he is able to catch up to it before it gets to the steep hill that rolls down to the creek. And with his wild throws, if Andy misses, the ball will not roll too far going uphill.

Looking up the road, Jonathan sees James driving down on his way home from work. He hollers to Andy, "Here comes James."

After Andrew runs to the side, James pulls their Ford into the driveway.

"Good day at work?" Jonathan asks James as he gets out of the car.

"Yep. I'm leaving the car in the driveway because I got class tonight, so you better not hit it."

"We're on the road," Jonathan says defensively.

"Yeah, but I've seen how you throw," James replies. "And keep your glove in front of your face. Those glasses aren't cheap."

Jonathan sheepishly pushes his glasses up off his nose. "I'm working on it."

Turning his attention back to the game of catch, he tells Andy to go long and hurls a high lofting throw with everything he has. The throw magically goes directly in Andy's direction. Andy turns and runs up the road, stretches, and makes the catch over his shoulder.

"Wow!" Jonathan shouts. "That's a great catch, Andy!"

Andy grins ear to ear and nonchalantly tosses the ball back.

The thought that he makes a better big brother than a little one crosses Jonathan's mind. Maybe, he figures, it is because Andy and he are closer in age. "Okay, my turn. Throw me a high one."

Andy lets it fly, and Jonathan sees it is going to go over his head, so takes off running down the road. At the last second, he stretches out his glove and the ball drops right into the basket. But as it does, Jonathan falls onto the gravel and tumbles, and as he does, his glasses fly off and break in two.

"You okay?" Andy hollers as he runs down to him.

When he sits up, Jonathan lifts both arms to reveal raspberry burns. His left knee has a gash with stones embedded in it. As he picks up the two halves of his glasses, he feels his throat tighten and begins to sob.

"I'll get James," says Andy.

"No! He's going to kill me when he sees these."

Andy tries to comfort him. "They're only glasses. You can get new ones."

"No we can't. These cost thirty dollars, and we don't have that kind of money."

Andy gets down on one knee next to him. "But you're okay at least."

"Yeah, I guess I am," says Jonathan looking down at his bruises and the caking blood on his knee. "I'll just be dead."

Later that evening, Jonathan awakes to hear his mother's and James's raised voices. They are arguing about him.

"He needs the suit for Lawrence's first Mass," his mother says. "He can't be dressed in dungarees while singing in the choir."

"If he doesn't ruin it, like he broke his glasses, he'll just outgrow it in a year," James replies. "We don't have that kind of money. Borrow a suit! I'll have to work an extra shift just to pay for his new glasses. Stupid kid!"

"He's not stupid, and don't ever say that again. He's smart, and one day he'll prove it when he graduates from college. Besides, at least you and the other boys had your father around when you were growing up. He and Andy just have you to guide them."

James's voice lowers as he acknowledges his defeat before his mother's will and determination. "Don't remind me."

In the quiet that befalls the house, Jonathan listens to Andy's soft breathing in the bed he used to share with Paul. He rolls onto his left side and sidles up to him. The pain from the bruise and stinging from the brush burns remind him of his spill earlier that evening. He reaches his right arm gingerly around Andy and snuggles closer. In a moment, he hears James come into the bedroom, undress, and slip into his bed.

Jonathan whispers to the sleeping Andy, "I'm scared. I just don't know how we are going to get through all this. It's not fair to any of us."

The thought of singing in Lawrence's first Mass comes to mind. He wonders whether he can go to him for confession when he becomes Father Lawrence, but somehow the thought of confessing his sins to a cousin makes him uneasy. He tries to figure it out in his head. There is something weird about it, but it is more than that. He does not think he could trust Lawrence to keep his confession confidential.

Jonathan buries his face deeper in the pillow he shares with Andy, and with his forehead lightly touching the back of his little brother's head, he breathes deeply, smelling the sweet scent of Andy's hair. He holds the breath for a few counts and exhales, then repeats the rhythm and soon falls into a deep sleep.

5

November 2, 1995

AS THE CHOIR FINISHED singing the *Kyrie*, Jonathan opened his missal and noted that the Gloria, which follows the *Kyrie* is omitted in requiem Masses. He briefly pondered that practice, trying to remember the reason for the omission. Recalling the truth he came to understand in the fifth grade, he decided it must be because that is the way it is done. That was all a Catholic needed to know.

He looked up to see the archbishop standing in the center of the altar facing the congregation. The archbishop raised and spread his arms and said, "*Dominus vobiscum.*"

"*Et cum spiritu tuo,*" the servers replied.

"*Oremus,*" intoned the archbishop, who then stepped to the right side of the altar to recite the prayer.

As the archbishop began to read the prayer in Latin, Jonathan again tugged at the blue ribbon in his missal and flipped a few pages to the proper of the Daily Mass for the Dead instead of the Mass on the Day of a Burial. There were other prayers for the dead, more specific ones—including those for a deceased pope, priest, relatives, and benefactors—and he was unsure which the archbishop was reading. He chose one and began reading it, then paused when he read the line about Mary, ever virgin, interceding on behalf of the dead.

"So you never 'knew' your husband?" he asked, cocking his eye at the statue of the Blessed Mother. "However did he take care of his manly needs?"

∽o∾

1963

AS USUAL, JONATHAN WAKES with an erection. At least the embarrassing wet dream phase has passed. When they began a year or so ago, he was not sure what was happening. He had already gotten accustomed to his penis becoming hard, especially when looking at pictures of some of his baseball heroes like Dick Stuart and imagining what it would be like to be with them.

At first, he did not understand it, but when the other boys began to talk about getting hard-ons and sticking them into a girl's private area, he began to piece it together. When their conversation went in that direction, which was becoming more often, he would go along with them and agree that he would like to screw one of them too. Charlene McAndrews, a high school girl three years older with big breasts, was the most-named object of their desires.

Reaching into his briefs, he feels the soft patch of hair sprouting around his penis and begins stroking his erection. Within a minute he is ready to ejaculate, so he reaches under his pillow and grabs the ball of tissue he stuffs there each night. The sensation is overwhelming, and he sighs with pleasure while the cream spurts into the tissue. He hears both James and Andy softly snoring, satisfying him that he has not awakened either.

Jonathan stuffs the sticky gob into his underwear, slides out of bed, pulls on his jeans, and goes to the bathroom, where he flushes the tissue after he pees. He turns on the hot water and allows it to run until it becomes really hot and washes his face. Then he looks in the mirror and studies the darkening patch of hair under his nose, imagining what he will look like with a mustache. Both Jeff, who is two years older, and Alan, who is the same age as Jonathan, already sport hairy lips. Alan's is not very thick, but fuller than Jonathan's. Jeff's looks like a man's, even though he is only fifteen. In fact, Jeff is already growing sideburns, which Jonathan finds very attractive. That is the reason he likes to wrestle with him more than his other friends. In the rough and tumble, he can rub his facial hair and sometimes grab his crotch and pretend it was accidental.

Knowing he has another hour to sleep before having to get ready for school, he returns to bed and tries to crawl in, but Andy has rolled onto his side and has his legs spread so wide they take up most of the room. Jonathan goes to the bottom of the bed and climbs in from there, on Andy's side, against the wall. Just as he begins to doze off, James's alarm clock begins ringing, reawaking him as well as Andy, who rolls back over onto his left side, draping his right leg across Jonathan's legs. Andy falls immediately back to sleep, and James gets up and goes into the bathroom to get ready for work.

Through the wall, Jonathan can hear the buzz of James's electric shaver and after a few minutes, the shower. Just as he begins to drop off again, James comes back into the bedroom and turns on the ceiling light, which rouses him once again.

Andy, however, continues to sleep, blissfully unaware of the activity around him.

From under the fold of his blanket, Jonathan watches James apply his Old Spice underarm deodorant and sucks in its sweet fragrance. He likes watching James dress. He is always perfectly attired in a shirt and tie when going to work, and Jonathan is amazed that James is always able to tie the perfect knot without the benefit of a mirror. When he finishes dressing, James slips his wallet and a folded handkerchief in his pockets and goes out, flipping off the light and closing the door. Shortly thereafter, the aroma of percolating coffee wafts into their room. He vaguely listens to James and their mother talking before falling back to sleep.

He is jolted out of sleep by his mother. "Come on! Let's go! It's 7:00."

"I'm up," he replies groggily. Then he tells Andy to rise and shine.

Andy sits up immediately and looks around wide-awake. "Hey, how did you get on my side of the bed?"

Jonathan kicks him gently. "Because you took my side when I got up to pee."

Andy pounces on him. "Watch it, four eyes!"

Jonathan is stronger than Andy and knows he can take him, but he pretends to be pinned to the mattress. Andy takes advantage of that and kneels on Jonathan's shoulders.

"Say uncle," says Andy.

"Aunt!"

"Quit horsing around or I'm coming in with the cold water," their mother yells from the kitchen.

Andy leaps off the bed. "Huh! She saved you again."

"Yeah, right. She's always coming to *your* rescue."

The boys make their way to the dining room where Jonathan begins making toast and filling Andy's and Mary Agnes's cereal bowls with Cheerios. Andy notices Jonathan is only sipping tea and asks him why he is not eating.

"It's First Friday, so I can't eat until after Communion, which reminds me . . ." He hollers to his mother, who is stripping the sheets from their beds, "I need a quarter for my donuts and milk."

"A quarter? I thought they're only five cents each."

"They are, but I ordered a glazed and two chocolate-covered donuts and two chocolate milks. Last month I was starving after eating only two donuts and a milk."

"How many First Fridays does this make?"

Jonathan winks at Andy. "Seven, so I'll only have November and December to make nine. Then I go straight to heaven."

"Yeah, right," Andy says, rolling his eyes. "I think you'll end up in the other place no matter what. Better make sure you take a lot of Kool-Aid when you die."

Their mother walks through the dining room with their sheets. "Did you get to Confession last Saturday?"

A twinge of guilt arises as he thinks of the personal act he performed earlier. "Father Keegan is hearing confessions before Mass," he says.

"Come down with me. I want to talk to you."

Jonathan follows his mother down the wooden steps to the basement, noticing how worn the rubber of the treads has become. Several pairs of shoes sit to the side of the four lower steps. Jonathan sits on the third step next to the wooden rail, long worn of the paint that once covered it.

His mother loads the sheets into her old Maytag wringer washer. "In case you've forgotten, this is the tenth anniversary of your father's death. So when you go to Communion, offer it up for his soul."

"What about my First Fridays? I have to make nine in a row so I can go straight to heaven when I die."

"You can go to ten in a row. I'm sure it would be okay because you'll still be making a good Communion even though you are offering it up for another. You barely knew your father, but that's not your fault."

"I kinda remember throwing his beer bottle down these steps."

"You were always breaking your own bottles, and I couldn't stop him from drinking beer, so I had to do with what I had. It worked because the nipple fit very snugly over the top."

"I don't think I'll ever drink beer. I hate the smell of it. It's got to taste sour."

"I hope you don't, but that's something you'll have to decide when you're faced with the pressure from your friends. Temptation can be a powerful force, so it's an ongoing battle to remain pure in thought and mind."

"I guess it is," he replies, then changes the subject. "Do you miss him?"

Her attention is focused on the laundry, a chore she does six days a week. After a moment, she responds. "I'm too busy."

"I do, I think. But the only way I know how he looked is through the pictures in the album. I guess I don't look much like him. But maybe I will when I grow up."

His mother looks up at him for a moment and then averts her eyes back to her chore. She says nothing.

Jonathan's voice becomes subdued. "I miss my brothers, too." He sits quietly for a moment but then raises his voice so much that it startles his mother. "It's not fair. How come they all have to go to war? It's so stupid. We learned about Vietnam with Mrs. Lafferty in geography class. It's just a little country and so far away. I don't get why President Kennedy is sending guys to fight for something that has nothing to do with us. The Russians are our enemies and we have more missiles than they have."

"President Kennedy says the Russians and the Chinese are supporting the Vietnamese communists."

"So what! North Vietnam is already communist. So what if all of it becomes communist. Lots of countries are."

"He says that's the problem, that if we don't stop them there, they'll soon take over the world."

"I don't believe that. I just think if enough people want to be free, then they'll fight to become free. Isn't that what we did in the American Revolution? If the people in Vietnam don't like being ruled by communists, then they should start a revolution."

When his mother doesn't reply, Jonathan sits for a moment and then blurts out, "I think it's stupid. That's all."

For a few moments he sits quietly while his mother continues with the laundry. Finally, he pulls himself out of his reverie and stands. He looks back to his mother raising her face from the wash to look at him. "We have to get going or we'll miss the bus."

"Be a good boy today."

"I will, and I'll offer my Holy Communion for daddy. Besides, he might need it more than I do."

Jonathan takes two steps at a time and begins to prompt Mary Agnes and Andy to hurry, which neither is inclined to do.

Mary Agnes taunts him when Jonathan's urgings become more forceful. "You're not my boss!"

"Oh yeah I am until you're both big enough to be responsible for yourself."

"Ooo, mister bigshot."

The three of them run down the stairs, pull on the well-worn shoes and coats, and step into the fog that has descended on the neighborhood. Silently, Jonathan drinks in the mist and smells of the rotting leaves still covering the ground. They kick through the heaps of maple, oak, and willow leaves that cover the road that soon turns into a steep decline down towards the creek.

Mary Agnes notices Jonathan is not wearing his patrol belt and points it out.

He has the patrol belt with him, but he is not about to tell Mary Agnes. "Too busy worrying about getting you ready."

Mary Agnes puts on a smug look. "Well, if you're the boss, I guess you should remember to do everything."

Jonathan glances back at Andy standing behind Mary Agnes's left shoulder. Andy begins to twirl his index finger around his ear and mouths cuckoo.

"I know," says Jonathan.

"You know what?" Mary Agnes demands.

"Nothing. Just hurry up."

As they reach the little bridge that connects their street with the main road, Jonathan sets his books on the concrete abutment and begins to strap on his patrol belt, first over his right shoulder and then around his waist where he clicks it closed. He watches Andy chase a few of their neighborhood friends who also go to Our Lady of Perpetual Help Grade School.

Soon, Jonathan hears the big, dark brown, ancient machine noisily chugging up the hill, its gears grinding as the driver shifts. "Here comes the bus," he yells. "Line up!"

The children haphazardly form a queue, elbowing and jostling to get on first, but Jonathan steps to the front of the line. He smiles at the driver as he hops up the steps. "Good morning, George."

The driver smiles warmly in return. "Good morning, Jonny."

"Two to a seat!" Jonathan shouts as the children scramble to claim their own.

With some effort and a few tugs, Jonathan manages to get the children seated in the arrangement he likes before the next stop, where nearly a dozen more scamper on and he begins the process anew. After several more stops, the bus is filled to capacity. Jonathan walks up and down the aisle to be sure order is maintained, and settles into the front seat by the door once he is satisfied they are all being compliant.

He watches George shift gears and use both arms to turn the huge steering wheel. George's dark brown hair has thinned, but he looks as if he needs to shave at least twice a day to keep a smooth face. He smells lightly of tobacco, but it is a sweet aroma. *He must smoke a pipe*, Jonathan surmises, and begins to imagine what George looks like with a pipe clenched in his teeth as he reads the paper with soft smoke twirling upward.

He closes his eyes, recalling the photo of his father standing on a porch and smoking a cigar. In the photo, he is a young man, maybe around George's age, and he is wearing a light colored pullover shirt with the sleeves rolled up to his biceps. It is likely summer, given the leafy bush that hangs over the porch.

His expression is hard to read, not as if he is trying to hide something but as if he is self-confident and self-assured. It tells Jonathan his dad was a happy man, relaxed and comfortable with himself. His dark trousers are pulled high up on his waist, held snug by a wide leather belt, and droop over his two-tone shoes.

At home, Jonathan sometimes stares at the photograph nestled in the family album, wondering what it would be like if his father were still alive, wondering if he would be as close to him as he is to his mother, wondering if they would even get along. From what Jonathan has learned, his dad was a hunter and played golf, neither of which is of interest to him. He prefers to read, cook, and bake.

He is learning to play baseball—actually softball since the baseball is so small he has a hard time judging it when pitched—but he has found he likes playing not so much for the game, but because he gets to be around other boys. They tease him sometimes about his poor skills, but they also try to teach him. One thing he can do better than all of them is run. Not one of his friends is faster than him. Jonathan dreams that if he could become a major league baseball player, he could steal bases as good as Maury Wills because it takes smarts as well as speed to be a base stealer. The problem is all the other stuff, like hitting, catching, and worst yet, throwing. He concludes that he should, perhaps, become a schoolteacher.

The other problem is Theodore. Jonathan's other brothers do not seem to mind the fact that he is not athletic and would rather be baking than swinging a bat or working on a car. But Theodore minds, greatly. In fact, when he is coming home for a visit, their mother mentions it with a tone in her voice and a look on her face that seems to be cautioning him. He remembers all too vividly how Theodore taunted him the last time he came home by calling him a sissy for baking the cookies and made him sit through a lecture about what real men are supposed to be like and to do.

His voice was stern. "God intends it to be that way, Jonny. You're too young yet to know about such stuff, but God meant for men to be with women and for men to do men's work and women to do women's work. God hates it when men do women's work like cooking, cleaning, and sewing. In fact, he hates it so much, he made it a sin. So is touching yourself."

Jonathan winced, thinking about how his penis would get hard and how good it felt to rub it, making him all tingly. "Then how come you're not married yet?" he asked, jutting out his chin. "James is dating Sally, and I know Chris and Paul have girlfriends. You're almost thirty-one, and I never have heard Mum talk about you with one."

"I am what is called celibate. God has other plans for me after I leave the service. Further, it's not your place to question me. Since our father has died and gone to heaven, I'm your father and head of this family!"

"No you're not!" Jonathan shot back. "Mum is!"

The light chatter and occasional outburst of laughter from

the children bring him back from his reverie but then fade into a distant sound as Jonathan's eyes begin to close. He feels another erection coming on, so he is glad he has worn his heavier and longer jacket to cover the bulge, which he is sure will still be there when they get to the school in another ten minutes. He coyly slips his hands into his jacket pocket, and when he feels it is safe, he begins to massage his penis. He begins to think about Mr. Sherman, his first male teacher, who was a classmate of his older sister Ruth. He likes Mr. Sherman a lot. In fact, he fantasizes about being with him despite the paddling he got from him the year before when Mr. Sherman substituted during the second semester. When Jonathan learned his name was Philip James, he began calling him PJ in the schoolyard when playing at lunchtime.

Mr. Sherman had heard him and threatened to use Big Sam on Jonathan if he referred to him that way again. Big Sam was the name of his wooden paddle, which was a foot long, three inches wide, and had little holes drilled into it to allow air to pass through as he swung it.

"Okay, PJ," Jonathan had yelled as he ran off, not considering that he would be in the room with Mr. Sherman and Big Sam again after lunch.

After they returned to the classroom, Mr. Sherman ordered Jonathan to go to the cloakroom, and Jonathan sensed the pain he would feel from the paddling would be nothing compared to the embarrassment he would feel when he faced his classmates afterwards. But Jonathan knew he was wrong and understood why he was being disciplined. The next day, he brought an apple from home with a note apologizing for being disrespectful and set it on Mr. Sherman's desk before class began. Later, he looked up to see Mr. Sherman reading it while the class was reading silently. He looked over to Jonathan and without smiling, nodded his head. When the day was over, Jonathan tried to slip out and get to the bus, but he felt a strong arm wrap around his shoulder and looked up. Neither said anything, but this time, Mr. Sherman smiled when he nodded, and Jonathan knew all was forgiven.

Jonathan is the first off the bus, and after watching to be sure the rest of the children get off safely and do not push from behind while stepping down, Jonathan heads directly to the church. He sees a short line has formed near Father Keegan's confessional booth. Mostly they are boys from his eighth-grade class, and Jonathan wonders if they are going to tell Father the same things he is about to tell him.

He looks around the church, which is beginning to come to life. His friend Mark is lighting the long candles atop the altar, and Jonathan breathes deeply, detecting the sweet fragrance of incense permeating the air. In the back pews are a number of old people, mostly women wearing babushkas on their heads and fingering their rosary beads while moving their lips in silent prayer.

A few men that just got off their all-night shifts at the factory, including his uncle Leo, also kneel and pray silently. Jonathan likes Uncle Leo a lot and has felt sad for him since learning that because Leo married a divorced woman, he was excommunicated. That has not stopped him from attending Mass, although receiving Holy Communion is out of the question.

Up in the choir loft, he hears the boys beginning to assemble, their light laughter seeping down to those gathered. He hears one shush the others and all grows quiet. When the line moves again, he realizes there is only one ahead of him, so he begins his examination of conscience. He knows the one act he will need to report and tries to count the number of times since his last confession nearly two weeks ago but runs out of fingers.

One of the doors opens and out steps one of the eighth-grade boys who winks at Jonathan as if he knows exactly what he is going to tell the priest. Jonathan steps into the dark confessional booth, kneels, and waits for the panel that separates him from the priest to be slid aside. In the quiet hush, he hears the unintelligible whisperings taking place between the priest and his classmate. In a minute, the priest slides the panel aside. Jonathan looks through the screen, which partially obscures the view between the priest and the confessor, to the tired and bored countenance of the priest.

"Go ahead," the priest sighs, and Jonathan begins.

"Bless me father, for I have sinned. It has been nearly two weeks since my last confession. Since that time I have . . ."

November 2, 1995

JONATHAN LOOKED UP FROM his missal to see the archbishop standing on the right side of the altar with his hands folded in prayer. Jonathan figured he had likely concluded saying the Epistle in Latin and was saying the Gradual. He turned his missal back to the proper for the Mass on the Day of a Burial to find the Gradual. The second line, Psalm 111:7, caught his eye. "The just man shall be in everlasting remembrance; an evil report he shall not fear."

Jonathan looked to the altar and watched the Archbishop step to the center, where he bowed and said in a low voice, "*Munda cor meum*." Jonathan began to read the prayer in English: "Cleanse my heart."

With his arms raised and in a louder voice, the Archbishop pronounced, "*Dominus vobiscum*."

The congregants stood in unison as the servers rejoined with, "*Et cum spiritu tuo*."

The archbishop took three halting steps to the left side of the altar to where a server had moved the funeral Mass missal and read the gospel in Latin. Jonathan found the selection for the occasion. It was John 11: 21–27, in which Jesus tells Martha that her brother, Lazarus, will rise—which, of course, he does.

The archbishop bowed and kissed the book. Then he returned to the center, bowed again, kissing the altar, turned back toward the congregation, and descended the stairs. One server reached out to assist and balance him, but he brusquely pushed the helping hand away. After negotiating the final third step, he turned to his left and, flanked by the servers, limped more than walked to the bench seat. With what seemed to Jonathan like great effort, he lowered his awkward frame onto the center bench. The two servers bowed to him and sat beside him. The three sat erect in posture with hands resting on their laps as perfect stillness covered the church.

Jonathan and his siblings each sat in similar fashion in their pews. The quietude that descended was broken only by a stifled cough, an occasional throat clearing, and the almost imperceptible sound of rosary beads. Jonathan looked up from his brothers and sisters and focused his attention for a moment on the sanctuary light, recalling his mother's reminder about Jesus's presence. He gazed on the altar for a few more moments and then closed his eyes.

∽o∽

1965

JEFF RACKS THE BALLS. The boys are in the basement of Jeff's house, which also serves as Jeff's bedroom. The pool table nearly fills the front area where one steps in from the garage. The floor is unevenly tiled because the tile was glued directly onto the rough concrete. Because of that, the boys periodically need to re-shim the table legs to keep it level, an ongoing process given the number of times someone bumps it when passing through. The worn green felt has more than one tear, which adds another challenge when lining up a shot. The cue sticks show their age and usage, with re-glued tips and curvatures from shooters leaning on them while waiting their turns.

The walls are paneled with wood knotty pine and stained amber. Mounted on the wall abutting the garage is a cue rack, where stand another dozen cues, ranging in weight and length, some in need of re-tipping. On either side are paint-by-number felt portraits of Spanish conquistadors and bullfighters. The boys often brag about how one day they would do the running of the bulls in Pamplona staying one step ahead of a potential goring by the horn of the charging bulls.

A broken-down couch has been pushed against the wall that separates the front area of the basement from the back where the furnace, hot water heater, and Mrs. Jackson's newly purchased automatic washer and electric dryer are located. Above the couch hangs a poster of Forbes Field, the home of the Pirates.

Just past the pool table and facing the entry from the garage sits a makeshift shelving unit that divides the front from Jeff's bedroom area. His full-sized bed, upon which the boys lie when not shooting or playing, dominates the back area. Balled-up, off-white cotton socks, along with T-shirts and briefs are strewn across the carpet remnant that helps soften the yellowing tiled floor and keeps it warm to the touch of bare feet in the colder months. The musty scent of teenage sweat hangs in the air.

A Johnny Mathis album spins on the turntable of Jeff's hi-fi player, which sits on a stand next to the couch. Mathis is one of Jeff's favorite singers, and Jeff is singing along to "Chances Are" while holding his cue, anticipating Alan's break.

Jonathan lies across Jeff's bed slowly leafing through the Pirates' black-and-white annual album, taking time to completely absorb not only each player's statistics, but also his profile. Dick Stuart is the player he has secretly admired, but his real hero is Roberto Clemente. Jonathan always tries to mimic Clemente's stance at the plate and basket-catch style when fielding a fly ball. He has gotten both of those down fairly decently but knows it is hopeless to copy Clemente's "needle arm." No other outfielder, including Willie Mays and Henry Aaron, has a more pinpoint throw than Clemente's. Like a rope, Jonathan has heard others describe it. A crash of balls explodes throughout the room. Alan and Jeff watch as several roll toward pockets. The purple 4 ball falls into a corner one.

"Solids," says Alan, taking aim at the orange 5 ball.

Alan and Jonathan are wearing cutoff jeans for shorts. The fringe that appears after a washing gives them the standard necessary cool look that allows for display of the recently sprouted hair on their legs, which in turn gives them a distinct masculine look. Both are wearing sleeveless T-shirts that likewise have been properly tailored to accent their burgeoning biceps and underarm hair.

Jeff, in his own style, is wearing his customary off-white jeans. He is tall and lanky and self-conscious about his pencil-thin legs. He is several inches taller, just over six feet, and two years older than the other boys. In the fall he will be eighteen and a senior. The great thing about Jeff, in addition to his cool room and hi-fi set, is that he can drive. He is the group leader. With thick black hair and dark brown eyes that shine through black-framed glasses, Jonathan cannot help but feel excited when he is near him. Lying on Jeff's bed and reading the magazine, Jonathan savors his friend's distinct scent emanating from the sheets and pillow.

Without looking up from the game, Alan calls over to him, "You coming to the game?"

"Wouldn't miss it," Jonathan replies, keeping his eyes glued to the Pirates' album.

Alan plays American Legion-level ball. Jonathan has become the equipment manager for the team, a subservient role he relishes. He makes sure the team's equipment is properly inventoried and loaded before and after every game. Jonathan also serves as the team's official scorekeeper and statistician, calculating batting averages, fielding percentages, and earned run averages. Though math is not his strong suit, he is meticulous when it comes to records. Because of that, the other boys have found another level of respect for him and consider him part of the team, despite the fact that he can't hit even a slow-pitched baseball to save his soul. Soul comes not from playing the game, Jonathan has come to believe, but from loving the game.

"What time we leaving?" Jonathan asks.

Jeff lines up his shot. "Game's at 6:30, so 5:30."

Jonathan looks up at Alan, who is the starting pitcher. "Think you're ready to go?"

Alan stands tall and puffs out his chest. "Oh, yeah! Gonna pitch a perfect game!"

Both Jeff and Jonathan laugh aloud.

"Sounds like someone has Sandy Koufax delusions," says Jeff.

"No, I got a better slider," Alan brags.

All three laugh together boisterously.

Jeff watches the 13 ball drop and moves to line up his next shot. Quiet settles over the room, except for the periodic crack of the cue stick, the balls smacking into others, and the Johnny Mathis strains. Jonathan tosses the Pirate album onto an improvised bookshelf beside Jeff's bed and picks up the latest copy of *Sporting News*. With his right arm propping up his head, he flips the page and begins reading more about Maury Wills, his favorite baseball player who is not a Pirate. When playing softball, he pretends he is like Wills, who is the best base stealer in baseball. Jonathan can fly, and once on base, he is an immediate threat to steal the next base.

Jeff sinks the 8 ball on a carom. "Nice shot," Alan says.

"Thanks," Jeff replies as he reaches for a stack of 45 records. He pulls off the Mathis album and puts the stack on the spindle. The first 45 drops onto the turntable and Jonathan begins singing the Essex's latest hit, "Easier Said Than Done," as he flips the page.

Other than the sound of music and pool balls cracking against one another, the room becomes quiet again.

"Eight ball in the side pocket," Alan calls as he lines up the shot.

The 8 ball falls into the called pocket, but the cue ball slowly rolls toward a corner pocket and then drops in. "Shit!" he yells.

Jeff laughs. "Gravity works every time. Guess you should've shimmed up that corner like I told you."

After closing the magazine and tossing it onto the shelf atop the Pirate album, Jonathan jumps up and heads into the pool table area.

Jeff asks him if he wants to play.

"Can't. Gotta cut the grass and water the garden before we leave," says Jonathan as he heads out the door. "Back at 5:30."

Jonathan steps out into the oppressive, muggy heat. It is overcast, as usual. Sweat immediately appears on his skin as he trots up the road. He pulls the power mower out of the garage, checks the gas level, and decides he has enough. After hauling both the mower and himself over the four-foot high sandstone wall, he trudges to the back of the house where he dodges the sheets his mother has hanged to dry.

"Don't cut down my flowers!" his mother hollers through the open kitchen window.

"I won't," he calls back, dragging the mower up the hill behind him, keeping his head ducked to avoid hitting the apple tree branches. Halfway up the hill he turns the mower sideways to prevent it from rolling back down the hill and reaches into his pocket for his transistor radio. He attaches the white wire with the earplug and slips it onto his right ear. Turning it on to KQV, "Candy Girl" by the Four Seasons, his favorite group, comes on mid-tune. Jonathan begins singing loudly in chorus.

Two hundred feet later, the lot flattens out. His mother still plants a garden of tomatoes, cucumbers, zucchini, beets, and a few herbs. It is only a fraction of the one they had when Jonathan's father was alive. Though not much bigger than a toddler then, he vaguely recalls long rows of corn, giants to him then. The rest of the area is now just mowed-down weeds. The new Lawn Boy mower is not nearly as loud as the neighbors' mowers, which he appreciates because it allows him to listen to his music while doing his chore. Jonathan appreciates James buying it because up until the past year, they had to cut the entire yard, over an acre, with a push mower. Ever the perfectionist, James has taken charge of cutting and trimming the portion of the yard immediately around the house, the part that can be seen by all. Andy's task is to rake up the hedge and lawn clippings and trim the grass along the sidewalk while Jonathan mows the rest.

Since the mower discharges the clippings to the right, Jonathan walks counterclockwise around the area, beginning on the perimeter and closing on the center. Thirty minutes later, Jonathan finishes mowing the garden area and begins working his way down the hill. Here he has to simply go back and forth because of the hill's slope, but he also has to mow around the apple and peach trees, some huge rocks that serve as steps, and a concrete set of steps that his father poured to access what was then a chicken coop. The coop has been long gone, but the cement walkway that once sat in front of it still remains as a reminder of those halcyon days for the family Jonathan vaguely recalls. Upon finishing mowing the lengthy hill, he turns the mower on its side and scrapes chunks of wet grass from the casing. Retracing his steps and once again ducking sheets his mother is starting to take down, Jonathan pushes the mower through the backyard.

"Did you cut down my flowers?" his mother asks.

"Every one of them," Jonathan replies teasingly. "Really, Mum, you need to weed them. The weeds are choking them out."

"When I get time. Until then, they'll make it."

After putting the mower back into the garage, Jonathan grabs two metal buckets and heads out to the side of the house to the spigot. He fills both buckets and runs up to the garden where he gives some of the plants an ample drink. He repeats the run another eleven times. As he is watering the last of the plants, he looks up to see his mother approaching with a spray can of pesticide and a couple of garden tools.

There's goulash for dinner, she tells him, which makes him happy. "We got a game tonight, so I'll be down at Jeff's late."

"Be home by 11:00," she says as he turns to run down the hill for the last time.

"Right," Jonathan says to himself, knowing better.

Later that evening, Jonathan and Jeff snuggle in Jeff's bed watching a rerun of *Gunsmoke*. Jonathan feels his back against Jeff's chest, his buttocks against Jeff's now-soft penis, and Jeff's warm breath on his neck. Their legs are intertwined and Jeff's left arm is draped over him.

The thought of it being very late stirs him from his reverie. "What time is it?" he asks.

Without saying a word, Jeff moves his wrist in front of Jonathan's face.

"Nearly 1:00. Mum's not going to be happy. She has threatened to lock me out if I'm not in by 11:00."

Jeff is matter-of-fact. "You can sleep here."

"That would freak her out more. Nah, I better get going. But if she has locked me out, I might be back."

Jeff yawns as Jonathan stands up. "The door's always open."

Jonathan pulls on his briefs, shorts, and T-shirt, slips into his sneakers, steps outside into the stagnant, sultry air, and slowly makes his way up the road, regretting he could not have taken Jeff up on his offer. When he gets to the house, he discovers his mother has finally followed through on her oft-repeated threat to lock him out. While the garage door is locked and the main front and back doors are open to allow at least a wisp of a breeze to flow through should one arise, the screen doors are locked, preventing him from getting in. *Great*, he thinks. *Now what?*

Jonathan sits on the back porch steps and breathes in the humid thick air that is beginning to feel slightly cool on his skin and listens to the crickets chirp. He finds their sounds melodic and comforting and feels he could sit there all night, but he knows better. When he was younger, he slept out in the backyard, and by dawn the army blanket that covered him was soaked with dew. For a moment he reconsiders Jeff's offer, but knowing full well what his mother's reaction to that would be, he decides to attempt breaking in.

Jonathan looks in through the back screen door and can see that the lock latch is visible, ever so slightly, in a tiny gap between the catch-plate and the jamb. Looking around, he spots the grass shears Andy left out and snags them. The blades are just thin enough to slide into the aperture, which he does. In about a minute, he is able to unlatch the door.

Jonathan slowly pulls the door open, steps into the kitchen, and very carefully, eases the door shut. He relocks it and gingerly steps into the dining room in his bare feet. Fortunately, the old refrigerator is humming its usual drone, covering any sound the creaky floors are making. From the dining room, he can see his mother asleep on the living room couch. Exhaling in relief, he steps down the short hallway to the room he shares with his brothers. The door, which swells and sticks in the summer, is slightly ajar. In less than thirty seconds, he is lying abed next to Andy, chuckling quietly in anticipation of his mother's surprise and reaction to his being able to sneak in past her.

In the late morning, he finds her sitting at her usual spot at the dining room table sipping her coffee. She says nothing, but stares right into and through him with a look that says she does not know how he managed to slip in but it had better not happen again.

Keeping a straight face to feign innocence, he laughs silently as he passes her. "Mornin', Mum," he says in a soft whisper as he reaches for a cereal bowl in the kitchen cabinet.

6

November 2, 1995

LOOKING UP, JONATHAN SAW that the archbishop had made his way back up to the altar. He rigidly faced the altar for a moment before stepping back to the book from which he had read the gospel, bowing, and kissing it. Then he moved back to the center and turned to face the congregants. With upraised arms he said, "*Per evangelica dicta deleantur nostra delicta,*" which Jonathan knew meant, "By the words of the gospel may our sins be taken away." He first made the sign of the cross on himself and next, in a sweeping motion, made another over the congregation.

The kissing, intonation, and the blessing confused Jonathan because none of them should have been part of a Requiem Mass ritual according to the guidelines in his missal. The servers too seem befuddled, and after a moment's hesitation said, "*Laus tibi, Christe.*"

"Indeed," Jonathan whispered to himself. "Praise be to you, O Christ."

After blessing the faithful, the archbishop turned back to the altar and began reciting the Nicene Creed, the summary of all what Catholics believe, so ordained at the Council of Nicea during the fourth century reign of Constantine. The small congregation stood in unison, and Jonathan, closing his missal, tried reciting it in Latin from memory.

"*Credo in unum Deum, Patrem omnipotentem, factorem coeli et terrrae, visibilium omnium et invisibilium . . .*"

1967

IT WAS TOUGH GETTING through *Wuthering Heights*. In fact, Jonathan admits he did not get through it at all, the reason for the F on the test. Who cares about a dumb love story in old England, set on the heath? What the hell is the heath anyway? The other guys in the class feel the same. He likes and respects his English teacher, Sister Teresa. In fact, he respects her a lot. There is something about the way she and Sister Marie Joseph, his social studies teacher, approach their classes. They treat and respect their students as young adults, not talking down to them like other teachers.

With the respect the nuns give their students, though, come expectations. To be respected means to be expected of. The root of both verbs, he learned in Sister Vivian's Latin I class, comes from the Latin verb *spectare*: "to look." By his senior year, Jonathan is sensing he is being schooled at a level that will be part of and serve him the rest of his life. The irony is that seeds of disconnection from "the one true faith" are likewise being sown right here in this very Catholic school run by Dominicans who are sharpening his skill to do that which religious institutions hate their members doing: think independently and critically.

So while his protest seems cool and makes him one of the guys, not reading *Wuthering Heights* also stirs within him discomfort because he realizes he is not returning the respect his teacher has shown him. The F has stunned him, and while he laughs outwardly with his cohorts, inside he knows better. Thus, when Kathy Milne, their class's most brilliant and creative student, stands in the front of the class and details the essence of the story—plot, conflict, setting, and characters—Jonathan knows he is hooked. He has fallen in love with literature in general and Heathcliff in particular, so much so he reads the book on his own.

A few weeks later, he tells Sister Teresa what he has done. He expects nothing from her in terms of credit, but with her acknowledging smile, he knows she has forgiven him or at least has reconstituted her respect for him.

It is then that Sister Teresa declares the next reading assignment to be a personal choice, with some restrictions of course. From the rack in the case she has wheeled into the room and opened wide, a plethora of classics abound. As much as he loves Heathcliff, he does not see himself falling in love with another English novel. None seem appealing or stir within him a passion to dive in. A number of his friends choose *Crime and Punishment*, but he chooses *Moby Dick*.

When he carries *Moby Dick* to Sister Teresa, her nod and smile seem to tell him that she is confident he will actually read the book because he will see its relevance to his own life. Her affirmation confirms his choice. As Captain Kirk proclaims at the beginning of his favorite TV program, *Star Trek*, Jonathan feels he is about "to explore strange new worlds . . . to boldly go where no man has gone before."

While countless others have delved into the great mysteries of the great works, this will be a first for Jonathan. More than stepping his toe in to test the waters, he is doing a full swan dive and will swim to the depths of the Idea Ocean.

The opening line, "Call me Ishmael," instantly grabs him. After school, he takes time to visit with Sister Anthony, his ninth grade religion teacher, to get the full story of Ishmael, the rejected son of Abraham. She, of course, gives the story a definite slant—God's—but he is, nevertheless, intrigued.

Jonathan pours through Melville's masterpiece and realizes just how much he wants to know things. That, he decides, is why we are here: to learn. Life is school. It never ends, doesn't close at 3:00 p.m. or take a summer or Christmas break. He wants to know everything that can be known, even what cannot be known . . . yet.

That evening, lying abed with his head propped atop his right arm, he begins reading "Loomings," the first chapter.

> Call me Ishmael. Some years ago—never mind how long precisely—having little or no money in my purse, and nothing particular to interest me on shore, I thought I would sail about a little and see the watery part of the world. It is a way I have of driving off the spleen and regulating the circulation. Whenever I find myself growing grim about the mouth; whenever it is a damp, drizzly November in my soul; whenever I find myself involuntarily pausing before coffin warehouses, and bringing up the rear of every funeral I meet; and especially whenever my hypos get such an upper hand of me,

that it requires a strong moral principle to prevent
me from deliberately stepping into the street, and
methodically knocking people's hats off—then,
I account it high time to get to sea as soon as I can.
This is my substitute for pistol and ball. With a
philosophical flourish Cato throws himself upon his
sword; I quietly take to the ship.

As he reads through the work, sometimes rereading longer passages and entire chapters he finds particularly obscure, Jonathan finds himself reading aloud characters' lines that speak to some stirring passion deep within him. From Captain Peleg to Ishmael about Ahab: "He is a grand, ungodly, god-like man."

"Yes, he is," agrees Jonathan aloud, considering the power of Peleg's observation and the most effective use of consonance by Melville of the hard g, which adds to the power of the insight. Jonathan sees the description of Ahab as a contradiction, yet complete within the context of polar opposites. That ungodly, god-like aspect of him is what makes him grand.

Jonathan views Melville's description of Ahab's countenance and physical deformity and countenance as chilling.

So powerfully did the whole grim aspect of Ahab
affect me . . . that for the first few moments I hardly
noted that not a little of this overbearing grimness
was owing to the barbaric white leg upon which he
partly stood. It had previously come to me that this
ivory leg had at sea been fashioned from the polished
bone of the sperm whale's jaw . . .

There was an infinity of firmest fortitude, a determinate, unsurrenderable willfulness in the fixed and fearless, forward dedication of that glance. Not a word he spoke . . . . And not only that, but moody stricken Ahab stood before them with a crucifixion in his face; in all the nameless regal overbearing dignity of some mighty woe.

As for the white whale, Jonathan easily sees how much he has in common with Captain Ahab. Like Ahab, it is deformed and powerful. Like Ahab, it reacts to its wound. Starbuck argues to Ahab that the fundamental difference between Ahab and the whale is that Ahab is capable of rational thought and making moral decisions, while the whale operates from instinct, but Jonathan believes that Starbuck is selling the whale short. The whale's intelligence might not be rational, but it is, nonetheless, present in much the same way as there is intelligence to those humans with a fervor or passion for something that cannot be proven with evidence.

When Starbuck goes so far as to suggest that it seems blasphemous for Ahab to desire vengeance against such an instinctual creature, Ahab's retort is jaw-dropping to Jonathan: "Talk not to me of blasphemy, man. I would strike the sun if it insulted me."

He is god-like, even if delusional, like every other mortal who dares to speak in such grandiose terms, concludes Jonathan. Ahab's mindset is no different than those who believe they are the arm of God, the arbiter and administrator of his justice on earth, and Ahab's consuming bitterness is frightening to him.

Jonathan is riveted by what Ahab says to the whale's head, which, before he speaks, is likened to the Sphynx. "'. . . speak mighty head, and tell us the secret that is in thee. Of all divers, thou hast dived the deepest. . . . O head! Thou hast seen enough to split the planets and make an infidel of Abraham, and not one syllable is thine.'"

"What is that inscrutableness?" Jonathan mutters to himself. "Is ultimate knowledge possible, and if it is, is it so profound, so beyond human comprehension that it is unspeakable?"

But it is Ahab's last words to the whale—"'Towards thee I roll, thou all-destroying but unconquering whale; to the last I grapple with thee; from hell's heart I stab at thee for hate's sake; I spit my last breath at thee'"—that make Jonathan surmise that despair, anger, and bitterness consume the essence of one's being and propel him to a question he ponders for a long time: How much hatred can one man hold within himself?

November 2, 1995

THE ARCHBISHOP NOTICEABLY SHIFTED his weight on and off his deformed leg, grimacing as he did so. He reached under his vestments and pulled out a white cloth that served as a handkerchief and wiped the sweat from his wrinkled brow, causing a pause in the profession of faith. It struck Jonathan as odd given the church was chilled and damp. After a few seconds, the archbishop resumed stating the creed, which as translated in Jonathan's missal, read, "He was also crucified for us, suffered under Pontius Pilate and was buried. And on the third day he rose again according to the scriptures."

He thought back to the conversation he had before leaving home to come to the funeral. *Am I unwilling to forgive or simply incapable of forgiving?* The first construct made sense if he was consumed with anger and bitterness, but he truly believed he no longer was. The second made more sense, but how and at what point had it come about? Was there a precise moment or could it have happened over a period of time with a string of events that, strung together, caused that outcome?

Was it during the process of stepping from the world of faith and delusion into the world of illusion, of reason, thought, and ideas, stoked and fueled by curiosity? *At what point did I step across that threshold and set forth on this journey to end up in a place vastly different from this of my birth?* And now that he had returned, looped back to this moment of time and place, what had he brought back?

After all, that was part of the deal, wasn't it?

June 2, 1968

JONATHAN'S MOTHER SITS AT the dining room table spreading cards for a game of solitaire. She looks up at him inquisitively. "What are you all dressed up for?"

"My graduation."

She stares a moment with a confused look. "Oh."

After being dropped off by James at the ancient public high school where the Catholic graduation exercise would be held, Jonathan enters the school's auditorium and surveys the familiar faces looking to see if there are any that might be present for him. He sees several of his favorite teachers, including Mr. Perkins and Father Reginald, sitting together and chatting among themselves. When he walks across the stage and accepts his diploma from the school's headmaster, he quickly steals a glance at those teachers who became his mentors and guides and finds reassurance and approval from them through their applause and smiles.

Seeing no celebration awaiting him when he returns home, Jonathan quickly goes to the bedroom and changes into his summer garb of cutoff blue-jean shorts, sleeveless T-shirt, and sneakers.

He finds his older brother watching television and asks if it is okay for him to take the car.

James looks up and stares for a moment. "Where you going?"

"To the bowling alley to hang with Gary for a bit. I won't be long. I have to work tomorrow morning."

James gives him an understanding nod and the keys. Jonathan backs the car out of the garage, but when he gets to the main road, rather than turn right to go to the bowling alley, he makes a left. He cranks the window down and cranks the volume up. Everyone has already gone to bed when he returns home later that night. James and Andy are both snoring softly as he enters their bedroom. Lying in bed with eyes cast up to a darkened ceiling, his mind goes to his lost brother.

"I miss you, Christopher, despite all. I'm sorry you're missing in action. They'll find you. I know they will. I hope Paul's okay. This crazy, fucked-up war."

Jonathan allows his mind to come back to himself, taking a deep breath and exhaling. Slowly, tears flow down his cheeks as he recalls the events of the day.

"It really happened that way," he whispers, then rolls over on his left in the direction of his balled-up little brother.

"There's nothing to be said or done. Face it. You're on your own."

November 2, 1995

WITH A CLEAR VOICE, the archbishop concluded the Nicene Creed. "*Et exspecto resurrectionem mortuorum. Et vitam venturi saeculi. Amen.*"

With the prayer ending, Jonathan sat back in the pew, took a deep breath, and looked over to the casket and to his siblings.

None of them came to my graduation, he thought. *That makes me wonder which of them will have the courage to stand with me. Or will they all flee as the disciples did when the Romans came for Jesus in Gethsemane?*

The archbishop turned to the seated congregants and with full voice said, "*Dominus vobiscum.*"

The servers replied, "*Et cum spiritu tuo.*"

"*Oremus,*" said the archbishop.

Jonathan found the Offertory prayers and turned his attention once again to the activity on the altar. The archbishop began to recite the prayers as he uncovered the bread he would soon consecrate into the body of Christ.

∾∽

1969

DRIVING ACROSS THE FORT Duquesne Bridge on his way to see Father Reginald at St. Francis of Assisi Catholic Church, Jonathan reflects about his relationship with Father Reginald. It was during high school that Jonathan began to develop a relationship with Father Reginald, his senior class religion teacher. The priest is ten years older than Jonathan, and all the while Jonathan has been coming to lean on him for guidance, he has dreamed about what it would be like to have sex with him. He never asks or suggests or even hints, but during their sessions Jonathan keeps hoping Father Reginald will make a move, touch him softly, stroke his hand or, better yet, stroke his leg. To his disappointment, the priest never does, which causes Jonathan to assume Father Reginald is either straight, asexual, or a paragon of self-discipline. Whatever it might be does not matter. Jonathan has become infatuated with him.

Jonathan understands, though, that their relationship is built on a more substantial foundation: Father Reginald has become the one person he can trust, a confidant with whom he can share his most private thoughts without fear of judgment or condemnation. The only others he trusts as much as he does Father Reginald are Jeff and Alan. He remembers the time when he, Jeff, Alan, Tim, and Robby went for a swim at a mountain lake on a particularly muggy summer day. He had no desire to do so, but that was what the other guys wanted to do, and besides, he would not pass up the chance to see Alan's cutoffs glued to his legs. Cutoff, skintight jeans were the style, in or out of the water. But just out of the water made them even more exciting and alluring.

To Jonathan's relief and bewilderment, the guys were really cool when he told them he could not swim and was panicked when it came to being in water. Maybe that is why he came to love being with them. While his brother Christopher could be unmerciful, teasing him about his disproportionate limbs, acne-pocked face, and large head with protruding ears, not one of his friends taunted him. Being sixteen was a lot better than being fourteen. Everyone was growing up.

Alan tried coaxing Jonathan. "Come on, we'll hold you up. You won't drown."

But Jonathan remained nervous and scared. He was okay in calm water up to his neck, but if he could not touch bottom with his toes or could not at least hold on to the side of a pool, he panicked. There was nothing to hold on to in a lake, and the soft sandy bottom gave way quickly.

"Okay," Jonathan agreed, inhaling deeply while trying to hide his misgivings. He could not say no without losing face and, thus, the respect of the only ones he felt truly cared for him. If he at least tried, he would hold their respect. But if he did not try at all, he could never look them in the eyes again. Besides, if he failed and drowned, it would not matter at all.

That thought had crossed his mind more than once. Jonathan remembered how great it felt when Alan, Tim, Robby, and Jeff had buoyed him in the water. They had started in water only four feet deep. Alan and Jeff held him under the arms while Robby and Tim each had one hand under a thigh and the other under his waist. His shaky confidence held as they glided to deeper water. He never trusted anyone as much as he did these guys. And right then, he was trusting them with his life.

As they neared the boundary rope with buoys, Jonathan glanced to his side and saw the water up to Tim's nose, and at that instant, he began flailing. Tim lost his balance and grip and went under, taking Jonathan and the other three guys with him. He fought for air but kept swallowing water. Floundering, he lost all sense of up and down, and the familiar panicky fear burst within him as it crossed his mind that what was actually happening was what he had thought of doing to himself. But then, almost as quickly as he had felt sure he was drowning, his face was above water. Gasping and coughing, he felt himself being pulled by someone who had his arm under his chin. The arm let go in the waist-deep water. Once he could see, he looked into Jeff's dark brown eyes.

Jeff laughed hoarsely. "You're not drowning, but you fucking near drowned us."

More embarrassed than scared at this point, Jonathan shook his head and pushed through the water to the beach. Sitting on the sand with his head in his hands, the last thing he wanted to do was to look at any of them.

"Hey, it's okay," Jeff said.

Feeling intense humiliation in every cell of his body, Jonathan kept his head in his hands. Then he felt a bare knee bumping his. He shivered, just a tad, but not from a chill. Before he heard the voice, he knew it was Alan.

"Hey, it's no big deal. It's cool. Robby's a little pissed, but he's a dumb fuck anyway."

At nineteen, the events at sixteen are a distant past. Jonathan never sees the guys, the ones he once thought he could never live without. Jeff joined the Air Force before the draft could get him, but it was too late for Robby and Tim.

Both were in Vietnam. Alan and Jonathan both got 2-S deferments for college. Jonathan managed to enroll at the University of Pittsburgh, no small feat given the family's financial status. Alan, though, was off to Princeton and had a girlfriend, both of which disappointed Jonathan to the bone.

Jonathan loves coming to Father Reginald's study since he is the only one Jonathan can open up to and trust. Father never judges him. On occasion, he accompanies Father to some gathering. One time, it was to Father Reginald's parents' house, where he not only got to meet them, but also Father's older sister and younger brother. They all doted on him, but the den at the rectory is still the best place to be because it is just the two of them. There Jonathan has Father Reginald completely to himself.

"Bless me, Father, for I have sinned, again," Jonathan says to Father Reginald as they open the confessional session of their meeting

How many times has Jonathan whispered those words knowing he would be doing it again? From the time he was in the sixth grade and began to realize something was happening to his body with the sprouting of hair around his frequently hardening penis, he has enjoyed the pleasure of his own body. Now the biweekly appearance in the confessional has become a joke of a ritual. With a little luck, he will make it to Sunday Mass without having had pleasured himself, but no guarantee.

Jonathan sighs. "I don't know, Father. It's the same story. I'm unable to stop my attraction to guys. God must simply hate me."

"Don't be stupid. You know better. You're playing the victim. It's time to quit feeling sorry for yourself and begin to appreciate the gifts God has blessed you with."

"Then, why can't I be normal? I like being with Peggy and try to do it with her, but I can't. She likes to kiss, and I can't stand it. I don't even get a hard-on when she pets me, but when I think of Alan, even though he's hundreds of miles away and has a girlfriend, I'm as stiff as a board in a second."

Father Reginald reaches over for his Bible. "Saint Paul writes about God's discipline in Hebrews."

The priest begins leafing through a few pages and after finding the precise passage reads, "'My son, neglect not the discipline of the Lord, neither be thou weary when thou art rebuked by him. For whom the Lord loves he chastises; and he scourges every son he receives. Continue under discipline. God deals with you as sons; for what son is there whom his father does not correct?'"

Jonathan smirks. "Sheesh, okay, I got it wrong. It's not his hate but his love that's busting my nuts."

Father Reginald ignores Jonathan's sarcasm. "His point is that we all need discipline, and a good father always corrects his children when they're out of line."

Jonathan thinks for a moment. "I don't get it. Having the hots for men is supposed to be the problem, and this says it's a punishment. If it's a punishment, what did I do to deserve it? And if wanting to have sex with guys is what's bad, then it can't be a punishment, which logically can't be bad in itself. Which is it? Is it the act that is causing me to suffer or is it the consequences of it, like feeling guilty or having to tell you that I jack off when feeling lonely because I can't talk to any of my guy friends the way they do about their girlfriends? Besides,

I don't see my brothers being punished, but I guess that's because they're perfect, especially Saint Theodore. He doesn't suffer; he's just insufferable."

"Focus on you," Father Reginald, says as he skims down the page a bit. Then he continues reading. "Now all discipline seems for the present to be matter not for joy but for grief; but afterwards it yields the most peaceful fruit of justice to those who have been exercised by it."

Jonathan shakes his head in disgust. "So, good times are ahead. Just suck it up because after God gets done knocking me around, it'll feel good. I'll feel good. Maybe I'll even want to thank him."

For a few moments, silence falls upon the men, allowing space for Jonathan to regroup. "I've been sneaking into the psycho section of the Pitt bookstore and reading about sado-masochism. Getting beat up or beating yourself with a belt doesn't seem like fun to me. Been there on the first part, and I can tell you pain hurts. And self-flagellation I'll leave for religious freaks."

"Let me remind you, you're not alone. Do you ever think about all the pain and suffering millions of others deal with every day?"

"All the more reason to believe in a just and caring God, I suppose."

Father Reginald's stare bores right into Jonathan's soul, and he squirms in the chair. After a moment, he drops his eyes to the floor, unable to withstand the wilting pressure of the priest's fixed look.

"Okay, maybe I'm becoming even more sarcastic and cynical, but I'm beginning to wonder why any god gets his kicks watching people suffer." Jonathan looks back up into the priest's gray eyes, fighting to hold back his tears. "Honestly, Father, I don't feel guilty about sex. I feel guilty if I miss Mass or eat meat on Friday, but I honestly don't feel guilty about having sex! What I guess I feel guilty about is not feeling guilty in the first place. I'm just sick of the whole fucking thing." He casts his glistening eyes down at the floor. "Sorry."

When he looks up, Father Reginald is standing directly in front of him. He reaches down and puts his right hand on Jonathan's right shoulder. "It's okay. No need to say you're sorry here. Maybe you can begin, though, by forgiving yourself."

After another moment of silence, Father Reginald makes the Sign of the Cross over Jonathan: "I absolve you of your sins, in the name of the Father, and of the Son, and of the Holy Spirit."

Jonathan closes his eyes and works to regain his composure. Thoughts race through his head of his old friends and his new adult one. He begins to inhale and then exhale slowly and audibly, thinking of the irony of him sitting here opening up to and trusting a priest. A few minutes later, he opens his eyes to see Father Reginald still standing immediately in front of him.

Jonathan looks up into the kind face of his friend and mentor. "Any penance?"

"I think you've already done it, Jonny."

Jonathan nods allowing tears to roll down his cheek unashamedly.

He smiles through tightened lips. "Thanks."

He stands, and Father Reginald pulls him into an embrace. Jonathan, a few inches shorter, burrows his face into the man's shoulder and begins sobbing softly, then uncontrollably. The priest pulls Jonathan in tighter and softly caresses the back of his head. After a minute, Jonathan lifts his head and pulls back.

The priest relaxes his embrace and smiles into Jonathan's eyes. "You know you're loved," he says softly.

"I do," Jonathan whispers, and after a moment's pause says, "Father, I'm doing my best."

Father Reginald smiles and nods his head. "I know."

Jonathan slips on his blue cotton Air Force jacket, zips up the front partially, tightens and ties the drawstring around his waist, and then turns back to Father Reginald. "I have to tell you this, Father. You don't know how tough it was for me to open up to you, to trust you. I had a pretty bad experience with another priest Mr. Perkins took me to see, and it really shook me. The funny thing is that you became my religion teacher then, in my senior year. I guess I would've never thought we'd . . ."

He looks into his friend's eyes again and then continues. "Even though I think I still love the Church, and I think I still believe in her, sometimes, I wonder. I'm finding it harder and harder."

They stand quietly, the priest waiting for Jonathan to continue.

"You're not like the rest, though. I wonder at times if my faith is really in the Church or in you."

Jonathan pulls open the door to the rectory and turns back to his friend, mentor, and only confidant.

"See you next month?" the priest asks.

"I'll be here."

Jonathan runs down the concrete steps from the rectory, taking two at a time, jumps into his 1963 Falcon, and cranks the engine. After a moment's hesitation, the car fires up. He thinks of the other priest and a strange thought comes to mind. *I wonder if he wanted to fuck me.*

Jonathan turns the engine off and sits in the car, remembering the incident. It was his senior year and his favorite teacher and mentor, Mr. Perkins, had taken him to see a priest assigned to a nearby parish who was also a trained psychologist.

The priest's office had been stark, with nothing but a desk and two chairs. On the wall behind him was an enormous crucifix, graphically detailing the bloodletting Jesus suffered. He did not rise to greet Jonathan and Mr. Perkins when they came in, just sat behind his desk as they took seats in front of him.

Jonathan recalled that the priest's skin had been an unnatural ashen gray, likely from not getting sun, which had prompted him to wonder if that was the general condition of all priests. He had leaned forward on his forearms to listen attentively to the background Mr. Perkins offered of Jonathan's issues. When Jonathan's teacher finished, the priest made no comment, just turned to Jonathan and waited for him to start.

Scared and nervous with his voice faltering and cracking, Jonathan said, "It's as he says, Father. I keep thinking about having sex with boys in my class. I know it's wrong, but I cannot help it."

The priest addressed him with an accusatory tone. "Do you masturbate thinking about them?"

"Yes," he replied.

"How often?"

"What? Like how many times do I do it in a day or in a week?"

"Yes. How often?

"I don't know. Sometimes a lot, sometimes just once in a while. But what's that got to do with it? I can't help it. I get hard and I think about guys. I think about guys and I get hard. What am I supposed to do? Wait for it to go away?"

"Yes, that's what you do," the priest had said in a straight-forward monotone. "You work to strengthen your soul, to become stronger, more resolute. What about older men? Do you entertain fantasies about men in their twenties and thirties and perhaps older?"

Jonathan had been dumbfounded. "You mean guys your age?" he finally stammered.

The priest said nothing, keeping his dark eyes riveted on Jonathan as if boring into his soul. Jonathan had imagined the look to be like that of Roger Chillingworth in *The Scarlet Letter* prying into the heart of Arthur Dimmesdale. After stealing a glance towards Mr. Perkins, who remained mute as if being obediently quiet, Jonathan replied, "Yeah, I guess, but this is crazy!"

From that point, the meeting had become a blur. His head swam in some toxic stew as words echoed in his ears: perversion, depraved, sordid. When his head stopped swimming, the priest was beginning to wrap up the meeting.

"But I can help you," he had said. "First, you will need to see me in the confessional booth for a formal confession of all your sins and do the penance I give you. After that, we will set up regular sessions during which we'll explore the reasons for your disorder and help you find peace and comfort in our Lord, Jesus Christ."

Jonathan sat in a daze, feeling helpless, shamed, and humiliated beyond comprehension. He stole another glance towards Mr. Perkins, who nodded his head at the priest. Then Mr. Perkins stood, as had Jonathan, taking the cue. The priest remained seated.

On the ride back, neither Mr. Perkins nor Jonathan said anything immediately. After a few miles, Jonathan turned to his teacher, pointed his finger at him, and yelled, "If you ever try to take me back there to that awful man, we're done! I won't speak to you again! I can't believe you just sat there and didn't defend me! The guy's a fucking idiot, asking me all those embarrassing questions and telling me I'm simply a nut case, but with prayer, I can be cured! And you just sat there! You said nothing in my defense."

After a few moments, he saw and felt Mr. Perkins's hand lightly resting on his left knee. "Sorry," his teacher said.

Jonathan said nothing, just stared out the side window. When Mr. Perkins pulled to the curb at the school, they sat quietly for a while until Jonathan turned to him.

"I don't know if I can trust you again, Mr. Perkins. I needed your help, and you didn't give it. You let me down. I feel betrayed."

"Sorry. I thought he could help you. As I listened to him, I realized I should've talked to him more before taking you to see him."

Without looking over to him or acknowledging his apology, Jonathan opened the door and got out. He stood for a moment with his head and eyes downcast holding the door open. "And I guess I need to understand you did your best," he said softly. Then he straightened up and closed the door without slamming it.

Shaking the sickening thought from his mind, Jonathan restarts his car, turns on the radio already set to KQV, and eases out the clutch to back out of the driveway and heads towards the boulevard. As he drives up the ramp to the boulevard, Creedence Clearwater Revival's recent hit "Fortunate Son" comes on. Thoughts of Robby, Tim, and his brothers sweating it out in the jungle of Nam swim through his mind, and he wonders about the disconnect between the carnage taking place a half a world away and the day-to-day life of President Richard Nixon's silent majority. He rolls his window down and yells to the traffic, "Are you people fucking clueless, or are you so wrapped up in your Pleasant Valley lives that the thought of Americans napalming babies can't invade your conscience?"

As Fogarty repeats the refrain of not being a fortunate one, Jonathan wonders if he will be the unfortunate one in a couple of years. When the song ends, he flips off the radio. "You poor fucks. I wish I had your strength and courage."

After a few moments of being disconnected from his present reality, Jonathan glances at the Sun Drug store on the right as he turns onto Fifth Avenue. He starts to drive by it, but at the last minute pulls into an empty space with a meter. He pulls coins out of his pocket, fishes out a dime, which he inserts into the meter, getting him thirty minutes, and walks briskly into the store keeping his eyes averted from everyone. He heads towards the back corner and breathes a sigh of relief when he sees that no one is using the pay phone and no one is even nearby.

He steps into the booth, pulls the folding glass door as tightly closed as he can, deposits a dime, and dials the memorized number.

Four rings later, the familiar alto voice answers, "Your dime."

Jonathan chuckles. "It is. How you doin'?"

"Nice. And jou?"

"Okay, I guess. Hey, wondering if you're alone. Just need some time with you."

"Always for you, my sweet young man."

Yeah right, thinks Jonathan. Since meeting Boyd the previous summer at the construction site he works at to pay for college, he has come to understand that he is not Boyd's only visitor. "Thanks. Be there in about twenty minutes."

"Don't make too much noise coming up. Old Mrs. Witch-Bitch has been keeping her door ajar to peek at whoever is coming to my room. Guess she's been hearing the springs squeaking through the wall."

Knowing Boyd's penchant for drama, Jonathan smiles, understanding that Boyd would like for her to hear the springs squeaking. "Yeah, sure," he replies.

"I'll leave the door unlocked."

"Okay. Bye."

With his erection already throbbing, Jonathan pushes to get there, even nearly running a couple of yellow-to-red lights. Eighteen minutes later he sees the Maple Street sign. He makes a left on to the one-way cobblestone street and immediately spots an open parking space on the right, a half-block from Boyd's apartment building.

"Perfect. This will let me practice my parallel parking skills," he murmurs. With one swing, he backs perfectly into the spot four inches from the curb and laughs aloud. "Fuck, you're good."

As he crosses the street, he sees no one out and decides to risk it by walking directly to Boyd's apartment rather than taking his usual circuitous route that insures no one connects him and his car with Boyd's building. Starting up the crumbling concrete walkway to Boyd's building, Jonathan tries, to no avail, to avoid crunching the dry maple and oak leaves abundantly lying about. The stiff hinge protests as he pushes open the door, and despite his best efforts, the stairs announce his presence. At the top, he turns right to 207 but glances quickly at 209. He notes the slight beam of light shining through the jamb and mentally hisses an expletive.

As gently as he can, he turns the knob and pushes the door open to 207. As usual, the room is darkened save for a dozen or so flickering candles. Stepping through, he feels a warm hand reach from behind the door fondling his crotch. He turns into the naked, hirsute, muscular body and opens his mouth.

After allowing his mouth probed and body stroked, Boyd whispers, "Let's give old Mrs. Bitch-Witch something to imagine as she masturbates her cunt."

Jonathan melts into his embrace. "Yeah, let's," he replies.

8

November 2, 1995

RAISING HIS EYES, THE archbishop blessed the offering. *"Veni, Sanctificator omnipotens aeterne Deus: et bene dic hoc sacrificium tuo sancto nomini praeparatum."*

As the archbishop continued on, Jonathan realized he could translate without referencing the text in English: "I wash my hands in innocence and I walk around your altar, O Lord." Sister Valentina had apparently done a masterful job of teaching him Latin.

He glanced over at the English, nodded his head, and continued to read the rest of the prayer in Latin, only occasionally needing to kick around in his brain for the English word.

". . . speaking thanks and recalling your many wonderful deeds. O Lord, I love this place in which you reside, which is the place of your glory . . ."

‿◦⌣

1971

THE YOUNG AMERICANS FOR Freedom group is gathered in the University of Pittsburgh student union waiting anxiously for the arrival of William F. Buckley, their founder and the founder and editor of the *National Review*. In short order, Buckley and his small entourage arrives, and the exuberant students swarm around forming a circle and shaking hands. Buckley greets each in his imperial tone and says how happy he is to be there.

After introductions are done, Jonathan thrusts forward his hand, which is holding his draft card. "Mr. Buckley, will you sign my draft card?"

"Yes, even though it might be illegal," the Brahmin replies.

Jonathan is anxious to demonstrate his newfound conservative credentials and intellectual acumen. "I watch *Firing Line* every week. It really helps me construct counterarguments with other students in my poli-sci classes."

With his head cocked back, Buckley grins widely, treating Jonathan to the full array of his famous teeth as he signs the card. "It is good to know I have at least one viewer in this hotbed of liberalism. Have you read any of my books?"

Jonathan points to his Young Americans for Freedom colleagues. "Oh, you have a lot of fans here. I have *Up from Liberalism* next to my bed. And I know I'm not the only one here who does."

"What about *God and Man at Yale*?"

"Sorry, Mr. Buckley, no, but I've read *Did You Ever See a Dream Walking* and *Inveighing We Will Go*, and I'm now reading *Quotations from Chairman Bill*. I call you and *National Review* my answer to Mao's *Little Red Book*."

Buckley turns his gaze and smile to another YAF member but continues dialoguing with Jonathan. "Good, good. Do you read other conservative writers?"

"Sure, I've read *Suicide of the West* by James Burnham and *Edmund Burke* by Russell Kirk. Professor Keefe was not real happy when I referred to them in our class discussion. He called them intellectual lightweights."

"Burke, of course, is the founder of modern conservative thought," Buckley says. "He wrote in reaction to the excesses and horrors of the French Revolution. Today, we must keep his words in mind with the drumbeat of statism at the expense of personal liberty. The New Deal, with the programs it spawned, has been the greatest attack on our liberty and our republic since its founding."

Buckley gestures to his admirers, who are clinging to his every word. "It's important that all of you not only understand that but also take action to stop the tide of statism and reverse its encroachment."

Jonathan is anxious to reinforce what Buckley has said. "That's what I say to my mother, but the last time I did, she waved her Social Security check in front of my face and said, 'This is the reason you have food in your belly, a roof over your head, and you can go to college.'"

Jonathan notices Buckley wince and pause as he hands a book he just autographed back to one of Jonathan's friends, a fellow YAF member named Keith. Buckley looks back at him for a moment with his famed arched eyebrow pointed upward, and Jonathan can feel his slate-blue eyes drilling into him. Jonathan glances over at Keith for support, but quickly picks up on the hostility in Keith's eyes, which are telling him what a dumb fuck ass he has just made of himself.

Buckley is now giving his complete attention to another admirer, and something dawns on Jonathan as he looks at the man: He has a long, pointy nose.

Picking up on the coldness that has overtaken the gathering, Jonathan slinks to the rear and listens halfheartedly to the continuing exchange between Buckley and Jonathan's fellow YAFers. Glancing up at the overlarge clock in the recess that has Roman numerals in lieu of numbers, he notes that the time is IX:XVIII and decides to get some work done.

Completely retreating from the group, Jonathan slowly moves towards the overstuffed, coffee-splotched couches where a couple disinterested students lay sprawled with books, notebooks, and loose papers strewn around them. Finding a relatively secluded seat, Jonathan reaches into his crammed tote bag and pulls out his copy of the Douay-Rheims Bible he carries for his history of religion class. Most of the other students use the King James version for reference, but nominally still a Catholic, Jonathan uses that version subscribing to the Catholic position that all other biblical versions are replete with errors, unacceptable to the one, holy, apostolic, Catholic Church.

He looks back towards the group from which he now suddenly feels excommunicated for repeating his mother's emphatic declaration and begins to sense something has changed. A dialogue within himself commences as he tries to process what had just unfolded.

It's not so much about what mum said, it's deeper . . . as if there is no room for another point of view even in a dialectic dialogue. That's not right.

He fumbles through his trove of ancillary reading materials, sorting them haphazardly in an order that makes no particular sense.

Chairman Mao. Chairman Bill. Is there much of a difference?

Jonathan looks across the coffee table at his otherwise disinterested fellow students. One, a long-haired hippy type, is sound asleep, mouth agape, snorting as he inhales. It dawns on Jonathan that the young man is in his comparative government class. The book he was reading until he passed out is one of the required readings on the Soviet system. Jonathan chuckles to himself because the book put him to sleep too.

Pulling out the history of religion class syllabus, he sees that the Gospel of John is the next up for that class. The syllabus says that he is to read the entire gospel and write a ten-page summary of what he discerns is John's primary message, with a minimum of twelve specific events or exchanges to substantiate that thesis.

Jonathan looks back up at the clock with Roman numerals and recalls the time he noted on it as he stepped back from the group: 9:18. That passage in John seems like a good place to start. Leafing through his copy of the Bible, he finds the passage and begins to read it. "The Jews then did not believe concerning him, that he had been blind, and had received his sight, until they called the parents of him that had received his sight."

He continues on to the next verses in John. "And asked them, saying: Is this your son, who you say was born blind? How then doth he see? His parents answered them, and said: We know that this is our son, and that he was born blind; But how he now seeth, we know not; or who hath opened his eyes, we know not: ask himself: he is of age, let him speak for himself."

Jonathan raises his eyes and sees that the YAF meeting with Bill Buckley has either disbursed or moved elsewhere.

Then he returns to the verses from John he has just read and contemplates them. Someone born blind and who now sees, and his parents disavow any knowledge of that possibility. Why? How could they not be excited to give testimony to a miracle? They should be overjoyed, exulting.

Born blind, but not literally. A metaphor. Blind to what? To knowledge? To truth? We're all born that way. The only way out of that is to learn. A teacher is necessary. Who are my teachers? Mum. Sister Marie Joseph. Father Reginald. Dr. Keefe. William F. Buckley. How about Mao? Pope Paul VI? Can you learn what is true and not true from a teacher who proclaims what is true but really isn't? Ironic, but I suppose, yes. How do you know when a teacher is false and what he is teaching is false? How do you know? Can you trust anyone?

Jonathan closes his eyes and listens to the whirring of the ceiling fan, feeling the slight breeze and relishing the coolness it dispenses. He feels himself growing drowsy and hears his own snort, which jars him somewhat alert. He opens his eyes to see Keith sauntering towards him.

"Well, you made an ass of yourself, you dumb fuck," Keith says.

"I only repeated something my mother said. I don't believe it, and that's what I wanted to convey."

"You fucking embarrassed him!"

"Buckley? Embarrassed? Come on. He's got an ego as tall as the Cathedral of Ignorance!"

"He couldn't respond to you because that would've made it seem like he was attacking your mother. He's too much of a gentleman to do that."

"Give me a fucking break. Buckley would go after his own

mother if he thought she was wrong. No, it's not about that, Keith. The man simply had no response. He's been fucking rich his entire life. He doesn't know what it's like to eat cornmeal mush for dinner, what it's like to be poor. For that matter, neither do you!"

"Hey, lay off! I'm your friend. I know life hasn't been easy, but it's not my fault. Quit feeling sorry for yourself."

"Sorry. It's just that I feel every one of you judges me because my family doesn't have money. Fuck, I have to work three fucking jobs just to pay for this. And I'm fucking lucky. At least I can go to college and not get my ass shot off in Nam."

"I don't judge you. You're my friend, my best friend. I don't care about how much money you have or don't have or anything else. You're just cool to be with."

"Why?"

The look on Keith's face suggests he is feeling a bit uneasy. "I don't know. You're just not like any of the other guys. You're honest and caring. That's all."

They sit for a few moments in an uneasy silence.

Jonathan looks deep into Keith's eyes. "There's stuff you don't know that might make you feel differently," he says, feeling his face burning.

"Like what?"

Jonathan lowers his voice to nearly a whisper. "Stuff. Just stuff. I can't talk about it here with everyone around."

"Then let's get out of here. I got some good weed. We can go over to Schenley Park and do a joint."

"What about the Gestapo fuzz?"

With a glint in his eyes, Keith smiles. "Fuck 'em. Guess we're going off the reservation, eh pardner?"

Jonathan stuffs his readings and notes back into his bag and nods once towards Keith. "As young conservatives, we're supposed to be straitlaced, ruddy-faced, and upstanding."

"Yeah, I guess we can only take that proper, righteous, uptight shit so far."

They move through the student union towards the enormous doors that open to a panoply of darkness filled with city lights.

"Do you think Buckley tokes on occasion?" asks Keith.

"No, but he probably jacks off to porn," Jonathan replies.

Both laugh boisterously.

"You're funnier than shit."

Jonathan becomes serious for a moment. "I have my moments."

They make their way across campus and finding a slight break in the traffic on Forbes Avenue, they bolt across, dodging several cars driven by motorists showing no intention of slowing. They scramble onto the sidewalk.

"That was close," Keith says.

Jonathan waxes philosophical. "When you're young, you're invincible." After a slight pause he adds, "And immortal."

"When do you become mortal?"

Jonathan muses. "I think at some point when you get old, when you begin to allow your fear to control you."

"Far out, Jon. Pretty insightful."

They walk through the parking lot between Hillman Library and Carnegie Library and begin the climb up to Schenley Park, where Jonathan has parked his 1968, sea-foam-green Cougar.

"This is a sharp looking car," says Keith.

Jonathan lights up at the compliment about one of the few material possessions he values. "Got it out of salvage, rescued him from potential dismemberment. I love it. Only a 302, but it kicks ass. Can't say what it is, but there's something about this car. It's classy. Camaros and Challengers don't come close."

They get in and begin to slowly cruise through the park. Jonathan keeps his hand on the gearstick, and after a few moments, slides it onto Keith's knee. He feels Keith's leg stiffen but not pull away and, keeping his eyes on the road ahead, he soon feels the soft touch of Keith's hand on his. After a moment, Keith slides his hand onto Jonathan's crotch. Jonathan does the same to Keith, and with one hand, he maneuvers the Cougar into a spot away from the glare of the streetlight.

Keith unzips the side compartment of his tote bag and pulls out a small bag and a pipe. As he works to load the bong, Jonathan shifts his eyes from the action on Keith's side to the area around. He speaks softly. "No one near, so far. But maybe we should find some cover in the trees before lighting up."

"Yeah, good idea," Keith replies.

They leave the car, closing their doors as quietly as possible. The cars parked along the roadway all seem deserted. Jonathan points to the empty cars and whispers to Keith, "Probably doing what we're doing,"

With the moonlight providing sufficient brightness, they steal and grope their way deep into the grove of ancient trees. Keith points to a nook formed by four trees. "Good spot there."

They settle onto the soft ground, where Keith extracts the loaded bong, pouch, and cigarette lighter. Keith deftly brings the lighter to life and begins sucking on the bong clenched between his teeth, drawing the flame into the sweet grass. After several draws and exhalations, he hands it to Jonathan who follows Keith's lead, being careful not to inhale too deeply. When he was fourteen, he had tried to smoke a cigarette stolen from Christopher's pack, and he still recalled the unpleasantness of the experience. The burning lungs and choking, coupled with his fear of being found out because he smelled like smoke, had been enough to make him swear off smoking—at least cigarettes.

He hands the bong back to Keith after several tokes and lies back onto the nest of grass and leaves feeling abundantly warmed. In a moment he feels Keith's hand lightly caressing his left leg and moving up to his crotch. Using both hands, Keith unzips Jonathan's jeans and slides his hand in and through his briefs to feel the hardness. He slowly pulls it free and lowers his mouth onto it. Jonathan allows his head to fall back and his eyes to close, slowly taking in the moist warmth of Keith's lips, tongue, and mouth on his cock. He caresses Keith's neck, then sighs and allows himself to forget all else, telling himself to stay in the moment.

Driving back to drop Keith off at his car, Jonathan breaks the silence. "You okay?"

"Yeah, sure," replies Keith, who pauses then continues. "It's that I never did that before. I always thought it would be gross, something a real man doesn't do."

Jonathan becomes sardonic. "Well, maybe we're not real men."

"Or maybe there's no such animal," Keith replies.

"Far out. Pretty insightful," says Jonathan.

9

November 2, 1995

JONATHAN WAS STARTLED FROM his reverie by the upraised voice of the archbishop saying, *"Orate fratres, ut meum ac vestrum sacrificium aaceptabile fiat apud Deum Patrem omnipotentem,"* which Jonathan's mind translated with little conscious help on his part: "Pray, brethren, that my sacrifice and yours may become acceptable to God the Father Almighty."

Jonathan found the Secret for the Mass on the Day of Death or Burial in the back of his missal and read it, beseeching the Lord to grant eternal rest to the deceased.

"Singular," mused Jonathan. "Ought it to be better expressed in the collective third person?"

The archbishop's voice became loud as he concluded the Secret. *"Per omnia saecula saeculorum."*

The congregants rose at the intonation of the Archbishop. Without having to think about it, Jonathan flipped a few pages to the Daily Mass for the Dead to find the proper preface and read in English. "It is fitting indeed and just, right and helpful to salvation, for us always and everywhere to give thanks to You, O Holy Lord, Father Almighty, Everlasting God, through Christ our Lord . . ."

࿇

1973

THE BONFIRE SEEMS THE perfect ending to what has been a perfect day. Jonathan sits among his brothers and sisters sipping his Scotch over ice. Elizabeth has ice water, and Juliana, Mary Agnes, and James drink root beer from plastic cups. Ruth, Christopher, Paul, and Andy each hold beers, sipping either an Iron City or Rolling Rock except for Christopher, who has brought a good supply of Rainier from Seattle, where he has settled. Having been introduced to the finer tastes of Scotch by his boss, Jonathan no longer finds pleasure in imbibing what he calls "sour water."

It is a perfectly clear night. For once, the dog days of August, pernicious in how they reduce every mammal to a puddle of sweat, have failed thus far to materialize. With three weeks to go before Labor Day, there is still ample opportunity for nature's sauna to kick in.

Thinking of Labor Day, Jonathan tries to find meaning in the fact that for the first time in sixteen years he will not be sitting in a classroom on the first Tuesday of September. Nor does he need fear the draft that has fed LBJ's and Nixon's war machine, which funnels poor and working class young men to the killing fields of Vietnam. A joint in his right little toe that causes a soft corn to form between his toes when he wears tight footwear, such as the cowboy boots he favors of late, has saved him. The pain becomes excruciating and the only way for it to be permanently fixed is through an operation in which the surgeon makes an incision between the toes and shaves the excess bone.

A month after graduating from Pitt, he received his draft notice. From 2-S, student deferred, he was reclassified 1-A.

Despite the drawdown of American troops from Nam, fresh fodder was still needed. Just like three of his older brothers, now all veterans—including Christopher, who had been missing in action—Jonathan would be fresh meat. The draft lottery, instituted as a transition piece to an all-volunteer army, had not been kind to Jonathan. In the initial lottery, his number was eighty-nine. And since the numbers up to one hundred ninety-five were called, he knew his days would be numbered once his 2-S deferment evaporated with his graduation unless his foot problems saved him from the draft.

A simple letter from his podiatrist did what pleas from his mother and common sense could not. It made clear that if the army wanted him, it would need to perform the operation before Jonathan could march in combat boots. Nevertheless, how he avoided the draft would never sit well with him, for it was in the mix of the moral dilemma his generation faced: do one's duty by obediently following the military-industrial complex war machine or refuse to serve, perhaps by permanently relocating to Canada.

Jonathan takes in the scene and reflects on his place in the group. While it is a perfect day and setting, somehow something seems askew, not authentic, as if each of his siblings is, as he is, masking some trauma or secret.

"We have to do this every year," says Mary Agnes as she leans back on her boyfriend and looks at her brothers and sisters, each nestled comfortably on either a lawn chair or hay bale. "It's sad Mum's and Dad's families have not kept together. Heck, I didn't even know Grandma Slovanco before she died. And none of Dad's and only half of Mum's brothers and sisters can be bothered with us."

"I agree," says Juliana. "Nothing is more important than family."

In the background can be heard strains of John Denver singing "Take me Home, Country Roads" from a portable stereo Ruth's husband set up by running an extension cord from their barn to the pasture where earlier in the day, the Slovanco clan pitched horseshoes and played softball using dried cow pies as bases.

"I can't remember ever being all together like this, even at Mum's house on Christmas," adds Ruth.

"Almost all together," Mary Agnes pointedly reminds them. "You would've thought Theodore could've found a couple of days in his busy schedule to be with his family now that he's retired. Even Christopher, with all he's gone through, is here."

"Well, some things have happened," says Elizabeth in his defense. "He asked me not to say anything until everything was arranged, and now it is."

When she does not continue, Ruth prompts her. "What's he got cooking now?"

"He's entering a seminary to become a priest."

"What? Where did that come from?" James asks.

"It's something he seriously considered doing after high school."

"Well, didn't he enlist in 1950 right after graduation?" asks Ruth.

"He did," Elizabeth replies. "He and Dad went around and around on the idea of him going into the seminary. Dad didn't like it. Told him he saw no point in priests and that his future was in the factory like the rest of his family. But then the

North Koreans invaded the South a couple of weeks after his graduation, so he felt that was his duty."

"It was also his ticket out," cracks James.

"No," Elizabeth says, disagreeing. "While he never liked the idea of going to work in a factory, that's not the reason he enlisted. He truly did believe in doing his patriotic duty. He and Dad got into awful arguments about communism. Dad was a big labor guy and strong for Truman and the Democrats, but Theodore liked Nixon. So when the communists invaded South Korea, he believed that's what he was supposed to do."

"When did he contract polio?" Juliana asks.

Andy seems incredulous. "He has polio?"

"You didn't know that?" Christopher says.

Elizabeth clarifies. "He doesn't anymore. He contracted it in 1952. There was an epidemic, ironically just when the Salk vaccine was being developed. Fortunately, it wasn't as debilitating for Theodore as it was for so many others."

Andy's facial expression shifts from doubt to comprehension. "So that explains his limp."

"Couldn't he get a discharge because of it?" asks Mary Agnes.

Elizabeth attempts to clarify again. "He could've, but it hadn't yet progressed to the point where it was causing a major handicap and the war was raging in Korea, so he decided to stay in."

"Mum told me one time he wanted to try out for the major leagues, that he was a great pitcher," Mary Agnes says. "Is that true?"

"It is," says James. "He had a great arm. The Pirates even sent a scout to watch him, but Dad told him he was only kidding himself if he thought he could play along with the likes of Joe DiMaggio and Ted Williams."

"I guess then the polio put an end to that dream," Andy adds. "That had to be rough."

"You're right," says Elizabeth. "I think that was the toughest part. He always said he wasn't bitter and he believed God had other plans for him, but I don't know."

"What about when Dad died?" Mary Agnes asks. "Couldn't he have gotten a discharge so he could go home and support the family?"

"There was some talk about that," says Elizabeth, "but it wasn't something he wanted to do."

Andy frowns. "You would've thought his family would've come first, but I guess God and country did."

"And still do," Christopher interjects. "Probably sleeps wrapped in a flag and eats apple pie three times a day."

Paul and Andy laugh at Christopher's wisecrack, but the rest ignore it.

"So, I don't get it about him now wanting to become a priest," says Mary Agnes. "What's this all about?"

Elizabeth is first to respond. "Well, as I said, he seriously thought about becoming one when we were in high school. He talked about it a lot. When we were kids, Mum and Aunt Margaret took us to see *Going My Way* and *The Bells of St. Mary's*. After he saw Bing Crosby playing Father O'Malley, Theo became enthralled with the idea.

"That's when he started going to Mass almost every morning even before school and during the summer. Whenever we talked over the past few years, he spoke about how upset he was with all the changes made since Vatican II. So instead of entering Saint John's or another mainstream Catholic seminary, he's going to one run by the Society of Saint Pius X, which is in Minnesota, I believe."

Juliana nods. "Well, I agree with him on that. I hate all that guitar strumming and everything in English. That's why I built that altar in my back room."

"I like the changes," Ruth says. "Besides, it doesn't really matter how you pray, as long as you do."

"Or don't," adds Andy.

Christopher lifts his beer. "I'll drink to that."

"Right," says Paul.

Ruth seems unsure about something, maybe even unsure about where the conversation is heading. "But still, hasn't the pope banned the Society of St. Pius X?"

"No," Juliana says. "I think Paul VI ordered Archbishop Lefebvre to stop ordaining priests, but the archbishop refused. I'm not totally sure of his argument, but I think he essentially believes that as an archbishop defending the ancient way of saying Mass, the ordinations of priests are valid."

Christopher sighs. "So, Theodore believes that and plans to become a priest ordained by Archbishop—how do you say his name . . . Lefer?"

Elizabeth corrects him by spelling it out. "He's French, so the b and v are silent. Sort of rhymes with prefer in English."

"Yeah, I get it," says Christopher. "I've read Jean-Paul Sartre and Albert Camus, who was actually Algerian. The French are the world's deepest and most passionate thinkers."

"Didn't Camus write *The Myth of Sisyphus*?" Jonathan asks. "I read it in one of my philosophy classes."

Christopher affirms Jonathan's query with a nod. "I'm

impressed, little brother, that you would dig into such stuff."

Jonathan smiles, appreciating the compliment from the brother he considers the real intellectual giant of the family. "Thanks. The story connected for me because I had just studied the Sisyphus myth in ancient Greece history class. I found Camus's spin on it fascinating—as my hero Mr. Spock would put it. He says so much of what we do in life, like working on an assembly line, is absurd and meaningless."

Mary Agnes seems to be growing agitated. "Well, what's absurd and meaningless is all this talk about philosophy. We're supposed to be having fun and enjoying the warm summer evening and each other, not talking about deep stuff."

Christopher shakes his head, his eyes zeroing in on Mary Agnes. "That's what you don't get. Even this has no meaning. All this religion talk and Theodore becoming a priest! Shit, the man's over forty. What's he trying to prove? Or better yet, what's he trying to hide from? He cannot undo the past. It cannot change. What he did, he did. What happened, happened. I don't think any of us faults him."

Ruth firmly voices her agreement with Christopher. "That's right. It was tough in all kinds of ways, but Mum pulled us through. If she hadn't, we wouldn't be here right now together—well, almost all together."

The group becomes quiet, seemingly uncomfortable about the direction and tone of the conversation. James, looking around at his brothers and sisters, apparently tries to find something they can all attest to. "We're tougher for it all."

Ruth, though, does not seem to want to let her point go easily. "But you deserve the most credit. You weren't even eighteen when it happened, yet you went to work and gave all you earned to Mum. It might not have been a whole lot, but between that and what she got from his pension and Social Security, it kept us fed and in our home."

Christopher raises his beer towards his older brother. "Hear, hear!"

The rest join him by raising their drinks and voicing their appreciation for James while he lowers his eyes and noticeably squirms.

Changing the subject abruptly, Paul asks, "Didn't Dad golf and hunt?"

"He did," Elizabeth says, "but for him they weren't the same. Golf was a game, something he could do with his buddies. But hunting was serious business. When I think of it, hunting was the only thing Dad and Theodore had in common"

Christopher once again shakes his head. "Typical Western Pennsylvanians. Here hunting is religion, more than Catholicism."

In a gentle voice, Juliana chides him. "Don't be sacrilegious."

Christopher looks straight at Juliana. "Again, it's all bullshit. It's absurd. All religions are absurd. They try to explain the inexplicable simplistically—like fairy tales."

"I don't agree," Juliana replies. "But still, I don't think any of that has anything to do with Theodore wanting to become a priest."

It is later that evening, and four of the brothers sit around the fire, which is now dying into embers that crackle and spit. Christopher lies back in a chaise lounge with outstretched legs while Paul sits slouched on a folding chair with a Camel cigarette between the thumb and index finger of his left hand.

In front of the fire, Andy lies sprawled with his head propped up by his left arm, poking and turning the glowing embers with a stick in his right hand. Jonathan also sits on the ground, leaning back onto a hay bale with his legs drawn up to his chest. Each brother has a drink: a glass of twelve-year-old The Glenlivet for Jonathan and beers for the rest. The night sky remains clear and star-speckled and the air is warm. In the distance they can hear voices and engines running from the farmhouse area as the rest of the family packs picnic supplies and children in station wagons and pickup trucks.

Pointing to Jonathan's drink, Paul breaks the silence. "I still don't know how you can drink that stuff."

Jonathan tries to act composed but his tone indicates defensiveness. "It's an acquired taste."

Paul laughs lightly. "Which means it's so bad, anyone who wants to drink it has to torture his taste buds into submission."

"I blame it on or give credit to Glenn. He loves it and always buys when we go down to the bar after work. Since he was buying, I would just sip it. But after a while, I began to like it and found rum and coke and stuff like that too gooey and sweet. Besides, Scotch helps open the mind for deeper thinking."

Andy lets out a light yawp. "I can dig it. Pot works for me."

Jonathan looks at Christopher, who is seemingly sliding into oblivion. "Chris, you mentioned Camus before and the absurdity of everything. I'm trying to get my head around that idea, but after a day like this when we're all together, it's difficult."

Christopher sits quietly, not responding at first. But after a few moments, he lifts his eyes and looks pointedly at

Jonathan. "You weren't in Vietnam. I don't say that to embarrass you or make you feel guilty. I'm glad you were able to duck it. But if you want to experience absurdity, go off to war."

"What was it like being a prisoner of war?" Andy asks.

Christopher takes a draw on his Rainier and looks down at Andy. "More fucked up than not being one." Turning his attention back to Jonathan, he continues. "Camus writes that we become accustomed to the practice of living long before we get used to thinking. We want clarity and familiarity, he says. Well, right here today, you had that. Everything's simple, neat, and tidy. Comfortable. Easy to explain."

He takes another draw and then continues. "All of you are Catholic. Do you know why? It has nothing to do with revealed truth, the Resurrection, or any of that blather. You're Catholic because Mum's Catholic, and she's Catholic because Bubba was Catholic. It's that simple. Your choice of religion is like your taste in meals: based on tradition. Mum fed us kielbasa, fried cabbage, and sauerkraut, so you love it. Your boss introduces you to Scotch and you develop a taste for it. While you might develop a taste for Italian or Mexican food and drink, it's much more unusual for a Westerner to develop a taste for, say, Thai food and sake. It's like how there is little difference between Protestants and Catholics and Orthodox, although they'll argue there is. Compared to Buddhism however, they're pretty much peas in a pod."

The brothers remain quiet as Christopher's drains the remainder of his beer. He reaches into his ice chest for another, pulls the tab from it, and swallows another gulp. "It's as Bertrand Russell writes: Fear is the reason for religious dogma and pretty much all else in human life. Fear of nature especially. He says that in our attempt to control things over which we have no power, we create religion and an all-powerful God so we can get him to do our bidding. Through prayer, sacrifice—whatever—we share in his omnipotence, his power. We can make the rain fall. We can cause others to do our bidding or to be more like us. We can, therefore, control both nature and people. The sad reality is that in the end, there is little difference, if any, among rabbis, mullahs, witch doctors, and priests. Voodoo is voodoo."

Jonathan sits quietly and after a few moments of reflection, addresses his brother. "Chris, I can't and won't argue with you. You're much smarter than I, so I'd lose that argument. But even though I understand logically what you're saying is true, I can't buy it. There has to be more!"

"Why? Why does there have to be more? Is it your fear or your desire for answers to things there aren't answers to?"

"No, I honestly can say it's neither. This is just too complex, and I think either extreme, from an all-powerful creator to chance, is simplistic and, therefore, unsatisfactory."

"William of Occam argues that in a case of unknown, the simplest answer is likely the correct one," Christopher replies smugly.

"So are you saying you could be wrong and the pope, the church, and big brother can be right after all?" Jonathan asks.

"Logically, as your hero Mr. Spock would say, I have to allow for that."

Jonathan not only sees the gaping hole in his brother's thinking, he also knows instinctively that his brother is wrong. "True, if one is forced into an either-or dichotomy, but this isn't either-or. There is more. I know it. I sense it. I'm not sure what the answer is, but I know this: Neither you nor Theodore is correct."

"And you know how?"

"My Aquarius gut tells me so."

"Most illogical."

"As they say in France, where it seems both Theodore and you have found your favorite theologians and philosophers, *au contraire*. That's true only if one operates within the construct of a duality, thus separating the intuition from the mind. It's all one, brother Christopher, and until one separates from that type of dualistic thinking, he's doomed to keep repeating the errors and mistakes of the past."

Later, as Jonathan makes his way down the dirt driveway to the country road in the Cougar, he takes in the shadowy pastoral setting and the star-pocked black sky, trying to make sense of the incongruity of the day's events. Something's not quite right, he thinks, but he is not sure what it is. He punches the radio button to KQV and listens to the strains of "Master Jack." When the song ends, he turns off the radio, the lyrics still running through his mind as he drives through the dark country roads. A colored ribbon from the sky tying up all your problems to make them look neat. Teaching others, not to help them think for themselves, but to use them. Teaching becoming indoctrinating.

The memory of the scene with William F. Buckley comes to mind. Jonathan enumerates his list of teachers. As he does, the list grows, and as the list grows, Jonathan's breathing becomes more rapid and shallow. He looks up through the cracked windshield at the speckled sky and seethes, then thumps the butt of his right hand on the steering wheel and shouts, "Fuck you, you bastard!"

10

November 2, 1995

JONATHAN LOOKED AROUND THE church, breathed the sweet incense in counts of eight, and exhaled slowly. The breath of the Holy Spirit. The choir's singing imbued him with a sense of wonderment and comfort that carried him back to the earliest days of his boyhood when he sat nestled in the comfort of his mother's warm, soft cloth coat. Jonathan breathed the cadence of each note.

"*Sanctus, Sanctus, Sanctus, Dominus Deus Sabaoth.*"

His mind jumped to *Macbeth* and Macbeth's contention that life is nothing more than walking shadow, a tale told by an idiot. Feeling himself sliding slowly forward onto his knees, he folded his hands in a cup, closed his eyes, and placed his forehead in the vessel. He breathed in again, this time his breath in rhythm with the cadence of the choir, and allowed the strains to wash over him and his tears to moisten his buried face. *Who am I?* he asked himself in meditation. *What have I become?*

The faithful slid to their knees, and the archbishop whispered readings from the Canon, the most sacred of prayers in the Mass. His words echoed from the expanses of the vaulted ceiling. He bent and kissed the altar, then made the sign of the cross over the unconsecrated bread wafers.

Jonathan turned his gaze to the dome. Memories wafted upward. He looked to the casket and wondered when he had cut the umbilical cord that tied him to this: his family, church, and community of old.

He looked back at the reading: ". . . in the first place, we offer for Your Holy Catholic Church . . . "

∽∘∾

1975

THE BEER MUG THUMPS as Brad sets it down hard on the bar and turns to Jonathan with a frustrated look. His eyes are bloodshot, though not from drinking. He and Jonathan have only had two drafts apiece. His voice is strong and his head shakes from side to side. "I . . . still . . . don't get why you feel you need to go, man" he says.

"That makes two of us," Jonathan admits. "I don't know. Ever since I made that trip to Colorado last summer and climbed out on that snowfield at twelve thousand feet, I cannot get it out of my head. Since then I've had this sense that I'm part of the mountains and belong in them."

"We got mountains here too. Maybe not as high, but still pretty rugged."

"True, but the Rockies are very different than the Alleghenies. These are like foothills. Besides, Brad, I don't belong here."

"*Whaddaya mean you don't belong here?* Of course you do. We're a team, man. It'd be like breaking up the Steelers, like us trading Mean Joe Greene or Lynn Swann. Hey, you know we're going to win the Super Bowl this year."

"Well, maybe, but Colorado has a team too, the Broncos."

"Bunch of sissy cowgirls. Never be a team as tough as the Steelers. They're like our town, man: hard as steel. Shot and a beer. That's who we are."

"You are. I'm not."

"That's crazy and you know it. Look, is it something one of us did or said? Cause if it is, I'll kick his fucking ass. You know I'd do that for you."

"I know you would, Brad, but no way! It's been cool hanging with you, CJ, Burke, and the other guys, and I love Kristi. You're lucky to have her as your wife."

"Yeah, sometimes I wonder, though, if you two don't have a thing going behind my back."

"We don't and wouldn't ever. You can trust me on that."

Brad nudges Jonathan's arm with his elbow and jokingly laughs. "Too much of a good buddy to hit on his friend's wife even if she's gorgeous and has big tits?

"She has big tits? I hadn't noticed."

"Yeah, if you haven't, you're the only guy within fifty miles who hasn't."

"Well, let's leave it at that. I'm not interested in your wife, believe me. No, Brad, ever since that day in Rocky Mountain National Park, I knew Colorado was to be my home. Something about it. When you're up that high and you look around and see nothing but mountains and snow and trees down below. And you inhale the crisp clean air. Now I know what John Denver means when he sings 'Rocky Mountain High.' It's different, Brad. It's not like here. I can't put my finger on it yet, but somehow I feel that's where I'm to go. It's where I can be free to be me."

"You're free to be you here."

Jonathan swivels his stool to look directly at Brad. His eyes focus and his tone becomes firm. "No, I'm not, Brad. Someday maybe I can tell you about it, when I understand it. But this isn't home. Not for me. Oh, maybe it will always be home in the sense that it's where I grew up and where the family and all you guys are. But, no."

He pauses for a moment and then continues wistfully. "I don't know, Brad. It's like something's calling."

Brad puts a wry look on his face. "You sound like Tony in *West Side Story*."

"Didn't know you were into musicals, Brad. But, could be."

1976

JONATHAN TOSSES THE FOOTBALL to Adam during their lunch break. "So, what's the plan for happy hour?" he asks.

"Same as last Friday. Fifty-cent beers at the Broker, then the discos. Aaron and Dave said they'd meet us there. How's that sound?"

"I like it. I never went to a disco until I moved here. All we went to in Pittsburgh were dive bars with old women dancing to "Roll me over in the Clover" shit. I'm not big into disco music like the Bee Gees and Abba, but I liked the Lift. It was pulsing big time."

"Yeah, it's a cool place."

"I like how they've hung skis on the walls and the poster that says 'Keep your tips up.' Sure glad you and Aaron taught me how to ski . . . well, sort of."

"You'll get the hang of it. If you stay with it, you'll be better than any of us."

"I doubt it," Jonathan replies laughing lightly at the suggestion but liking the idea.

"You did okay, especially when we went to Mary Jane in Winter Park."

"But not before I nearly broke my neck getting down that first run. You were such a jerk taking me up a blue-black on my second day."

"Well, you didn't break your neck and you managed to get down it. It's no big deal, Jon, no big deal. The only way you're going to learn is to go for it."

Later that afternoon, Jonathan and Adam meet up with Aaron and Dave at the Broker for happy hour. Aaron sucks in some foam off the head of his beer and looks to Jonathan. "So, when do classes start?"

Dave looks surprised. "Classes? You going back to school?"

"Yeah, I decided to become the only thing I ever wanted to become: a teacher."

"Great! What kind? What level?"

"I have a BA in English and a minor in American history. I'm thinking of getting a master's in American literature."

Another guy standing to Jonathan's left steps into the circle. "Teach English? I teach high school English, and I've discovered that if one is a natural, he can teach pretty much anything."

Jonathan is doubtful. "I don't know. I think it would help if a teacher has a strong body of content to draw on."

"True, but as I said, you can always get that. By the way, my name's Cress."

They shake hands. "Jonathan. This is Adam, Aaron, and Dave." They each shake hands in turn.

Cress takes a sip of beer and turns his attention back to Jonathan. "A bright person can research the content on his own. You just need to read the works and criticisms and study the author's background. And you're on your way."

"What about style and literary periods and genres?"

"Same there. At first it's content. You already have a background in American history, so if your focus becomes American lit, you're further ahead than those who don't. Writings invariably reflect the times in which they're produced.

"As for style, it's one thing to intellectually know about writers and their works but quite another to understand them. That might sound vague, but I've seen many who teach Faulkner and Hemingway and Morrison but can't appreciate the complexity and mystery of their writings. Great teachers are like great writers: they're born, not made."

Jonathan considers Cress's insights while sipping on his Budweiser draw. Cress sips his as well and then continues.

"Don't get me wrong, all greats, whether artists, musicians, or teachers, can have their skills honed and learn new tricks. But that's part of what makes them great; they're not afraid to look at something new. And they're not so arrogant that they believe they have all the answers."

Jonathan shakes his head. "I don't know about that. Hemingway was pretty cocksure full of himself and then blew his brains out. I love his writing but I loathe his persona."

"No doubt, but what's also true is that they're filled with quirks and foibles. That's because artists don't operate in a box, in confinement. They don't recognize what others see as requisite boundaries. They see boundaries as artificial restrictions and limitations imposed by a society or culture intent on getting compliance and conformity."

Jonathan looks intensely into Cress's eyes and nods his head. "I like that. I like how you're making me think and pushing me to think beyond my boundaries."

Cress smiles and stares directly into Jonathan's eyes. "Well, cool."

For a moment, Jonathan stares back, but then lowers his eyes in embarrassment. When he looks up again, he sees Cress sipping his beer and looking off into the crowd of young men and women all jostling and bumping into each other. He realizes his friends have moved off somewhere. Scanning the crowd, he sees Adam and Dave talking to two young women and Aaron chatting with another off to the side.

"Looks as if you're friends have abandoned you," says Cress.

"Nah, they're out exploring, probably bored with our conversation."

"Were you bored?"

"Me? No way. I'm intrigued." Jonathan pauses and then says, "Was intrigued."

Cress seems to pick up on Jonathan's embarrassment. He smiles and looks deep into Jonathan's eyes. "It's okay. I'm intrigued too."

The two young men quietly sip on their beers and listen to the throbbing music blaring in the background. The Bee Gees are singing about life going nowhere and staying alive. Cress tips his mug upward to sip the last of his beer and turns to get another. "Buy you one?"

"Sure. I'll get the next round, though I have to watch my budget."

Cress orders two mugs, slips two one-dollar bills into the tip jar, and makes his way back to Jonathan. "New to town?" he asks as he hands Jonathan one of the beers.

"Thanks. A little over a year, but I love it."

Jonathan tells Cress his story beginning with the day he pulled into Colorado. He tells about finding work at Sears, meeting Adam and Aaron in separate circumstances though they are brothers, learning to ski, and then coming to the conclusion that he not only wanted to live the rest of his life in Colorado, but he also wanted to do that as a teacher.

"How old are you?

"Twenty-six."

"I'm thirty-three." Cress begins telling his story beginning with his arrival in Colorado in 1970.

As Cress speaks, Jonathan cannot help focusing on his thick dark brown hair and almost coal-black eyes. A hint of beard gives Cress a rustic look, indicating a hirsute body. Jonathan's eyes slip to the tuft of hair puffing out from Cress's T-shirt. Just as Cress finishes, Jonathan feels a soft jab in his back and turns to see his three friends.

We're heading over to the Lift," says Adam. "You coming?"

Jonathan takes a final swig. "Oh, yeah." He turns to Cress. "Why don't you join us? I still owe you one."

"Sure, if it's okay with you all."

Dave hoists his near-empty mug in a toast. "Hell, yeah! The more the merrier." After draining the rest of his beer, Dave turns to Jonathan. "By the way, you never answered Aaron's question about when you start back to school."

"I have a big meeting next Thursday, and then classes begin the following Tuesday, the day after Labor Day."

Aaron lets out a whoop. "Well, I guess we'll have to celebrate tonight. Party!"

Jonathan notices the buzz he's feeling. "Oh, yeah! I'm all about celebrating."

Cress smiles and places his hand on the small of Jonathan's back. "Me too. Let me be the first to welcome you to teaching."

"I'm not there yet."

"A year from now, you will be."

Jonathan laughs. "Then I'll be a rookie."

"For sure. Right now you're a fledgling, but it won't take long before you're a grizzled, battle-scarred veteran."

The five of them begin elbowing their way to the door. Jonathan shouts over his shoulder to Cress. "You don't look grizzled."

"Thanks. I'm Dorian Gray. My picture ages while I stay eternally young."

"*Puer aeternus?*"

As they reach the door, Cress leans into Jonathan close to his ear. "Of course. I don't intend to ever grow old."

On the following Thursday, Jonathan picks his way across the Boulder campus of the University of Colorado using a sketched map as a guide. Nestled into the cradle of the Flatirons, the rustic rock-face mountains that serve as the entrance to the Rocky Mountains from Boulder contrasts against the deepest blue sky he has ever seen. The campus fills him with a sense of awe and inspiration, and the pinkish-brown sandstone exteriors and terra-cotta roofs of the buildings mesmerize him. Energetically adding to the scene are the crowds of young people. Some saunter while others hurry to get their final pre-semester stuff taken care of. The strains of The Hues Corporation's recent hit waft through his brain and Jonathan begins singing "Rock the Boat" inside his head.

A young man brings Jonathan back to Boulder. "Excuse me, but do you know where the Education Building is?" The young man's shoulder-length hair is pulled back in a ponytail and he is dressed in standard attire: tie-dyed T-shirt, cutoffs, and sandals.

His green eyes penetrate into Jonathan, briefly stunning him. *Twenty-one, twenty-two tops*, he thinks. Jonathan lies. "Uh, yeah, it's right up here. On my way there myself."

"Cool. Mind if I walk with you?"

"Not at all. Name's Jonathan."

"Zach." They shake hands. "Decided to go into education, so I need to do a late registration to take the crapola methods classes. And you?"

Apprehensive that he tells too much too quickly, like how he is probably more than a couple years older than Zach, Jonathan confesses the truth. "Actually, I'm coming back to school. I've already earned my BA, but I need to go through the methods gauntlet same as you. I'm not thrilled about it, but I decided teaching is what I want to do."

"Excellent! I like to see older guys who are willing to regroup and not get caught up in a lifestyle not for them."

Jonathan winces as Zach continues.

"Guys end up either in dead-end careers or the soulless corporate world where they lose sight of the meaning of life in the pursuit of big money. I'm thinking of three possibilities:

an Indian reservation, an inner-city school, or with troubled kids in alternative ed, maybe a group home setting."

"You hit it right on. My mother keeps encouraging me to become a lawyer. I think I'd be very good at it because I love the law and, as she says, love to argue, but the idea of getting caught up in the corporate money thing, as you say, is not for me."

"Have you thought about becoming a public defender or an advocate for those who can't afford lawyers?"

"No, but that's a great idea. I keep picturing lawyers in those big paneled offices behind twelve-foot oak desks with pert young paralegals and uptight executive secretaries."

Zach laughs as he shakes his head. "You sound like you're still caught up in Perry Mason's world."

A frozen smile comes across Jonathan's face as he looks down at the flagstone. A moment later, he feels Zach jab his arm. "Hey! There's my girl. Thanks for the guide. Nice meeting you, and, hey, maybe catch you at the Dark Horse for a beer. Either way, good luck."

"Yeah, you too."

Jonathan sighs as he watches Zach drape his arm over the shoulder of a dark-haired coed also clad in a tie-dyed T-shirt, cutoffs, and sandals. He quickly reverses direction and heads towards the meeting for returning students and groans. "Older guy."

Inside the ancient theater of the University Memorial Center, Jonathan joins the swarm of youth making its way to the assembly. With his age now fresh in his mind, he takes note of a few older adults, several, in fact, apparently in their late thirties and forties. He looks over to two older women who look as if they might be returning to earn their certifications to teach after having raised their children. An image of Theodore going back to school—a seminary no less—flashes through his mind. He was over forty, he thinks. Good for him.

Seeing the rows in the back of the room filling like in church, Jonathan makes his way to the front. Sliding across the nearly empty row towards the center, he sees the same two women he espied a few minutes earlier. Leaving one seat empty between him and them, he sits awaiting the din to dim and order to arise from the chaos. The doubts he had that morning about the wisdom of going back to school and becoming a teacher return until he is brought back to reality by a loud voice asking everyone to quiet down so they can get started.

During the exchange between the professors on stage and his fellow students in the audience, Jonathan realizes that he is not actually enrolled in the fall program. He completed the preregistration in the spring, but did not follow up with the formal one in the summer. Major blunder. Confused almost to the point of panic, he races to the office of the School of Education after the meeting, where Marcella, the older and kind department secretary, confirms for him after searching through his file that he is not officially enrolled.

Jonathan is frantic. "What do I do?"

"You'll have to find your advisor, whoever he is, and see if he can open a few doors for you."

His frantic descends into dejection. "Great. Jack Taylor is officially my advisor, but I have yet to meet him. John Houser has been handling all my stuff for him while Taylor's been off somewhere."

Crestfallen, Jonathan begins retracing his steps to the University Memorial Center where he happens upon the two professors who led the meeting earlier. Stepping in the front of them to get their attention, one asks if he can help him.

"Yes, sir," Jonathan says and explains his conundrum.

"Who's your advisor?"

"Some guy by the name of Jack Taylor, but I've never met him. It seems he's always off on some fishing expedition whenever I try to contact him, so John Houser has handled it all for me."

The professor puts his arm around Jonathan's shoulders. "Well, Mr. Slovanco, it's a pleasure to finally have met you. I'm Jack Taylor,"

While Jonathan stands amid a pool of embarrassment, face reddening and throat tightening, Dr. Taylor goes on. "You're right, son. I haven't been here for you, and I take responsibility for that. Having said that, it still leaves you with the problem. But, here's what we can do."

Dr. Taylor, arm still draped around Jonathan's shoulders, begins laying out a game plan as they walk to the Education Building. Once in his office, Dr. Taylor types, signs, and hands Jonathan a letter he is to carry to each of his potential professors the next day. On Friday morning, he arrives at the campus before 8:00 a.m. and resolutely sets out on his expedition. Each professor gives Jonathan permission to be added to his class roster.

A few weeks later, while sitting in Dr. Taylor's class, the enormity of the crazy way he got enrolled dawns on Jonathan. All doubts and fears were waylaid at the moment he realized he was not enrolled. He glances around at his twenty-three fellow students, nearly all older than him, yet each on his or her path to becoming a teacher. He looks up to the man who has become more than his professor and a twinge of gratitude overtakes him. The fact that Dr. Taylor was at first a source of frustration but then his rescuer percolates in Jonathan's mind. Irony, he thinks. No, it's as if it had to happen the way it did.

The magnitude of the way his life is unfolding begins to play out in his mind. He pictures the Flatirons and imagines scaling them. Under his breath he utters a thank you to someone or something.

11

November 2, 1995

THE ARCHBISHOP'S VOICE ROSE as he concluded the prayer for the commemoration of the living. ". . . *tibique reddunt vota sua aeterno Deo, vivo et vero.*"

With his hands raised but separated in front of his chest, the archbishop began reciting a list of saints beginning with Mary who, Jonathan reminded himself, belongs with them and not with her son, despite the fact that she is called the Mother of God. He recalled the fierce debate that took place in his history of religion class about Mary's status. Protestants insisted that the Roman Catholic Church's special emphasis on Mary elevated her to a goddess. His friend Levi had listened to what he considered to be a pointless debate.

"The rest of the world really doesn't care. It's an internecine theological battle," Levi had said. "We Jews have similar types of theological arguments among the Orthodox, Conservative, Reformed, and who knows what. You Christians not only don't care, you are hardly interested in our debate. Which makes sense. Same for non-Christians about your petty squabbles. They're irrelevant."

Jonathan sighed as he plowed through the Commemoration of the Saints prayer, which, to him, was a who's who listing of early Christian males. No women, of course, other than the "ever virgin" Blessed Mother. There were two Johns and two Pauls. The first martyr, Stephen, didn't make it, but twins Cosmos and Damian, who died two hundred years later, did. It depended on whether you had an influential and powerful advocacy group after you croaked, he thought. Money talked then, too.

∽◊∾

1977

JONATHAN NOTICES THE SWEAT from his mixed drink seeping through and soaking the napkin. He reaches across the bar, pulls a few more napkins from the stack to wipe the area dry, and tosses the mushy blob into the trash can behind the bar. Slowly, he runs his hand across the surface of the bar, carefully feeling the wood's impressions, carvings, and scars. Then he stirs his drink with two red straws and takes a long sip. Carefully, Jonathan sets the glass in the center of the fresh napkin, pulls the straws out, and begins intertwining and folding them around each other, tying a semi-tight knot.

From his perch, Jonathan gazes over at the pool table area where four boisterous men challenge competitors in a partners' match. Their bravado, fueled by several hours of alcohol consumption, reverberates. To the left of the table, two more men toss darts more quietly, which changes without warning when one of them makes a particularly accurate toss. When that happens, their clamoring reinforces the shouts from the pool players, which makes conversation challenging, if not impossible.

That is fine with Jonathan. He has frequented the Quadrangle off and on since he arrived in town two years ago. He reflects on that and how the reasons for coming to the Quadrangle have changed in just that brief time span.

Ron, the bartender, makes his way to Jonathan. "Ready for another?"

"Sure. With no place to go and nothing to do, it's going to be a long evening. So I need to take it easy."

A grin creases Ron's face. "That's what cabs are for."

"Oh, for sure, but it's the morning after that's the killer."

Ron replaces the once-again soggy napkin with a fresh one before setting Jonathan's fresh drink down. "Sign of premature aging. I used to be able to do shots throughout my shift, but now it hurts to do more than three or four."

"Three or four? I'm only twenty-seven, but I'd be on the floor in a fetal position moaning incoherently and viewing the world of sneakers and boots if I did three or four shots. Besides, it's more than gauche to do shots while sipping good Scotch."

Jonathan likes Ron. He has had an extraordinary longevity at the Quadrangle, going on six years. Even in the short time Jonathan has been coming in, he has seen a number of other bartenders come and go. Ron, who appears to be a few years older than Jonathan, seems to enjoy his job a lot. He is deliberate in his action, never hurrying even when the crowd begins to pack in. His facial expression is sardonic, as if he knows everything about you, which he probably does. It works and no one bullshits Ron.

Jonathan studies Ron as he saunters back with the change. "You see it all."

Ron wipes the bar with the towel he carries on his shoulder between uses. "Pretty much, but I still learn something new every day. Tending a gay bar will do that for you."

Jonathan takes a sip, pulls the two fresh straws from the drink, and begins interweaving them into and through the two he has already twisted and tied. Next, he reaches farther down the bar and grabs a small handful of black stirrers from a canister. These he slides over the tips of the red ones and begins attaching them in a freestyle manner, intricately bending and tying them off.

A man two stools to his right watches the artwork unfold. "Bar origami?"

Jonathan laughs. "No, just something I do to keep from getting bored."

"Well, I think they're pretty creative. I've seen you make them before. A few weeks ago you left one and a guy asked Ron for it. Said he'd put it in his living room."

"If that made him happy, I'm glad he did. I guess some can find meaning in them, like modern artwork. I guess one could call it 'bar impressionism' or 'drunken surrealism.'"

Jonathan recognizes the man though he does not know his name. He has seen him off and on at the Quadrangle, but other than a few nods, they have not communicated until now. Jonathan finds him appealing. The studs in his earlobes and left nostril work well, enhancing his sexuality. He is taller than Jonathan, maybe six feet two, and when he leaves the bar and strides purposefully to the restroom, Jonathan notes his slim, long legs with tight hamstrings and muses that he might be a runner. Jonathan has been considering taking up distance running.

The man keeps his slightly silvering hair cropped and is blessed with a generous smile. His teeth are small, even, and nearly pure white. When talking to others, he gets animated, and Jonathan loves to watch his warm, dark brown eyes grow when he is excited. Even when noise and din from the crowd and pulsing mix of disco and rock prevent conversation, Jonathan sneaks peaks at him. In return, he notices the man stealing a quick glance back at him, which at first embarrasses Jonathan and makes him wonder if he is being voyeuristic. But then, what guy in a gay bar is not checking everyone else out?

Over the next several minutes, he interconnects a dozen or so red and black straws and then weaves four larger green ones through the configuration, slightly bending them at about their midpoints to provide a set of unsteady, but somewhat functioning legs. In the background, Billy Joel is singing "Piano Man" on the jukebox, and Jonathan sings softly with him, the irony about it being a Saturday night and men all around him making love to their tonic and gins. The last line of the verse, which speaks of wearing a younger man's clothes, prompts him to wonder how much longer that will be true for him. Thirty is only two years away.

The man slides back onto his stool and he eyes Jonathan's creation. "Tyrannosaurus?"

Jonathan refocuses his eye and attention on his project. "You can call it anything you want. Maybe a four-legged spider. It depends on how it strikes a chord in your psyche. Someone else might simply see it as a mass of straws stuck together."

"That's true, but that would only show how dull he is. To

me, imagination is the most vital of our mind processes. I enjoy watching you create those. It's like you're telling a story through your hands. Your face becomes so intense, a bomb could go off and I don't think it would faze you."

Just then, loud voices erupt from the pool table area and a stick crashes on the surface of the table. Jonathan lifts his eyes and looks over at the action. Two men are lifting their mugs in a toast to their victory while one of the vanquished escapes into the restroom and the other weaves his unsteady way back to his stool at the far end of the bar.

The man empties his drink and shouts as the din reaches a temporary crescendo. "Gotta go. Gotta get up at 4:00 for work. But I wanted to say hi and introduce myself before leaving. I'm Edward."

"Jonathan," he replies.

They shake hands and Jonathan turns his head as the man passes behind him. "What do you do?" Jonathan asks him.

"Pediatric nurse at Denver General. Love it, although I see lots of sadness. Kids can really tear your heart out when they're suffering."

"Good for you," he replies and lifts and offers Edward his creation. "Want it?"

"Sure. Thanks. I'll take it to the hospital. I bet one of the kids would love it. Maybe cheer him up."

They shake hands again and this time Jonathan feels the ring on the man's middle finger and notices his firm but gentle grip. Jonathan gazes at Edward as he walks to the door. "Wow!" he says under his breath. Before stepping out, Edward holds the door for another and glances back at Jonathan. "Yep, a runner. That would be some marathon. I could do that for four hours," he says under his breath.

As he shifts his weight on the stool, the paperback copy of *Jonathan Livingston Seagull* in his hip pocket reminds Jonathan of its presence. He pulls it out and sets it on the bar, again taking note of the wood grain. It was recently refinished by one of the Quadrangle's regulars, a professional carpenter who diligently failed to remove the deep scratches and etchings engraved over its half-century life. The bar has a rich legacy, having served, among other incarnations, as a speakeasy during Prohibition and a cabaret of sorts during the Eisenhower administration. The dark pine counter—the one original piece that has survived every redesign effort—carries the bar's memory. Each carving is an anecdote, a strand of the fabric of the bar's story, which a careful observer can decipher much like an Egyptologist reading the history of that ancient land and culture does through a careful study of its hieroglyphics.

Holding the book in one hand and lifting his drink with the other, Jonathan muses about how books have been important to him from the time he was in Sister Bernadette's first grade class. He still remembers how he loved reading the John and Jill stories, especially the ones about sledding. When he was a teenager, he came to dislike winter because he constantly seemed to be fighting off a cold or the flu. Ironically, since his move to Colorado, skiing is becoming his new wintertime adventure. It has been a convoluted line from sledding down the long hill in his mother's backyard to skiing steep mogul runs, but a line there is. Connections between what at first seem to be disparate events have come to intrigue him.

He has also become intrigued by how books play a critical role in his life, even when it comes to connecting with guys, which happened for the first time quite unintentionally. Arriving a couple of hours early at the Quadrangle a few months ago, he had with him a copy of Herman Melville's short stories, figuring it would help him pass the time until the crowd filtered in. After ordering his usual, he pulled out the collection from his hip pocket and began reading "Bartleby."

As the elixir entered his bloodstream and began working its magic, the narcotic effect warmed and comforted him. Lifting his glass for another sip, he noticed a man sitting around the curvature of the bar three stools to his left intently staring at him. Jonathan did not recall seeing him before, but was pleased with what he now saw. His light chocolate skin was enhanced by the glistening sheen of a silver shirt. The slight angle upward that Jonathan needed to lift his head to look at his face indicated he was taller than Jonathan. His dark brown hair shaved to almost a half-inch length accented the regal shape of his head. His nose was thin, as were his lips. But they gave way to a wide smile that revealed immaculate large, perfectly straight teeth.

When the man nodded at him, Jonathan smiled. "How's it going?" he asked.

"Good," the man replied warmly. "What're you reading?"

"A short story by Herman Melville. He's one of my favorite authors." Unsure of himself and fearful of embarrassing the man, Jonathan nevertheless clumsily asked, "What about you? Do you read?"

"I used to when I was in high school. My favorite class was English. I struggled and didn't get very good grades, but I always liked the class discussions about the books we read, especially about the ones I hadn't." He laughed lightly and lifted his drink, tipping it to Jonathan. "My name's Luthor."

"As in Martin Luther King?"

"No, though he's certainly a personal hero, being a brother. I'm more Lex Luthor, you know the arch-villain in the Superman stories. It's spelled with an *o*, not an *e*."

Jonathan, in turn, laughed lightly. "Well, you hardly seem villainous to me. But even if you are, I'm still glad you're here. My name's Jonathan."

"Glad to meet you. Let's just say my mother had a perverse sense of humor. But I also have to confess to a personal villainous side," he said, winking.

Over the next few minutes, Luthor had casually moved one stool to his right and Jonathan had reciprocated by moving one on his left. From their perches, they discussed the subtleties and complexities of writers from William Faulkner to Tom Wolfe.

"What about modern fiction?" Luthor asked.

"I seem to be more connected with the classics like *Moby Dick*, which to me is one of the greatest pieces of fiction," Jonathan replied.

"Well, when I read, I prefer writers who help me understand my story better. When I was a boy, I discovered Langston Hughes and James Baldwin. They were once huge for black kids because if you think it's tough being a white gay boy, you should feel what it's like being a black gay boy."

Jonathan nodded. "Or Hispanic, I understand."

Luthor took a draw on his 7 and 7. Yeah, it's all that macho bullshit. Some cultures emphasize it more than others."

Becoming conscious of the fact that his mind has trailed off to that experience a few months ago, Jonathan opens the copy of *Jonathan Livingston Seagull* to the chapter with the bookmark. But memories of Luthor's lean, brown body come back to him. He reflects on how, through Luthor and other gay men, he is coming to learn and appreciate gay culture in its myriad of distillations and how distinct it is from straight culture. A gay bar, he has concluded, is akin to the quantum universe, and the men in the bar are like quantum particles. Movements are unpredictable and erratic with infinite potential outcomes. Gay men come and go as particles leap from one universe to another, seemingly existing in two or more places at the same time.

He shakes his head, crunches an ice cube, and once again turns his attention to Bach's short but intricate work, periodically sipping his Scotch as he reads. It is a story with which he can connect, especially the scene in which Jonathan finds himself alone on a cliff, having been banished from the gull society for working at perfecting his flying rather than squabbling over food scraps with the rest of the flock.

Jonathan reads a while and then, as he reaches down for his drink, he glances to his left to where the guy who liked his art had sat. His eyes fall on a treasure trove of a person who in turn is looking directly at him.

"What're you reading?" the man asks.

"*Jonathan Livingston Seagull.*"

"Any good?"

"Love it."

"I've heard of it but haven't gotten to it yet."

Pulling his jacket from the back of the stool on which he's sitting, he moves to the empty one next to Jonathan. "Mind?"

"Not at all," says Jonathan as the man drapes his coat and settles in.

"My name's Nicholas."

"Jonathan. I've seen you here before, but it's been a while."

"Well, what can I say? Life happens, and lately a lot of it."

Jonathan probes into Nicholas's deep green eyes. "Care to share?"

"Not really. At least, not yet. Maybe later."

Sensing he has hit a sensitive nerve and is moving along too fast, Jonathan looks up at the TV hanging just inside the entrance to his right on which some football film clips are running. He feels Nicholas' body heat, and it warms him even more.

Leaning back and pretending to stretch, he catches a glance of Nicholas looking down at and stirring his drink. Italian or perhaps Greek, Jonathan surmises hopefully. Mediterranean men are almost always an immediate turn on for him. It is not just their physical beauty but their demeanor as well. They can be passionate yet compassionate, rough and sometimes coarse, but gentle at the same time. He understands he is stereotyping, but they seem universally to be great cooks or at least experts in their family's cultural cuisine. Any combination of cheese, olives, and tomato sauce melts him. Add a touch of Chianti, and he's easily putty.

Nicholas looks over and breaks the brief silence. "So, tell me more about that book about a bird."

"Well, Jonathan is a seagull and a member of a flock, which is an interesting term in that *flock* takes on a subtle *double entendre*. His job is like that of all the others: to scavenge for food primarily from human trash, dumps, and landfills.

But Jonathan finds that lifestyle mundane and absurd, kind of how many of us see the rat race and the mechanistic, soulless *modus operandi* of modern society. So, he decides to pursue his passion, which is to fly faster than any gull ever has. In reality, he wants to transcend the mundane and truly live. And for that he's made an outcast, ostracized first, then finally banished from the flock for daring to be true to his nature.

"From there, alone and forlorn but with an undying belief in himself and his life's purpose, he flees from the flock and begins his adventure. On his journey he encounters a guide or mentor who not only validates him, but also encourages him to be undaunted by the flock and his own shortcomings, failings, and missteps. There's much more, but I don't want to ruin it for you."

Nicholas good-naturedly jabs him. "So you want to tease me?"

"No, I just want to whet your appetite."

"Well, that you've done, and I'm not just talking about the book."

12

November 2, 1995

THE ARCHBISHOP CONCLUDED HIS prayer. "*Per eundem Christum Dominum nostrum.*"

"Amen," the servers responded.

The ringing of the altar bells by one of the servers signaled the essence of the Mass was at hand—the reenactment of the sacrifice of Calvary in which Jesus Christ offers himself as a most acceptable victim to the Eternal Father for man's salvation. The worshipers' focus, prayerful concentration, and quiet became more pronounced. Jonathan alternated between reading his missal and observing the archbishop as he blessed the unconsecrated bread and wine five times.

Jonathan's mind drifted, but the perfect stillness in the church brought Jonathan's attention back to the scene on the altar. The archbishop, holding the bread and praying, was consecrating the Host.

Holding the Host aloft, the archbishop said, "*Hoc est enim Corpus meum.*"

Reverberating through Jonathan's mind was the English translation: For this is my body . . . for this is my body . . . for this is my body . . . for this is my body . . .

∽∽∽

1979

JONATHAN LIES DREAMILY SEARCHING the inscrutable face of Daniel who snores gently, rhythmically, his chest expanding in harmony with his breaths, much as it does when he does yoga.

Though a Jesuit priest, Daniel is often more connected with Buddhist practice, Jonathan has come to believe, than ritualistic, structured, and dogmatic Catholicism. Daniel's deep brown eyes and shaggy mane give testimony to his Leonine character: energetic, courageous, and very much willing to go where angels fear to tread. Though orthodoxy no longer remains an aspect of his belief structure, Father Daniel remains a loyal Catholic, a puzzle to Jonathan.

In one discussion with Jonathan, Father Daniel questioned whether the Resurrection was literal. "Why is it so critical that Jesus rise from the dead? The important thing is that he taught us the way. We're all divine given we're aspects of the Divine. What is so incredibly incomprehensible is how in this age of discoveries and knowledge light years beyond the comprehension of ancient peoples, so many still buy in to the literalness rather than the symbolism of an act, which is so much more powerful."

The first to awake that Saturday morning, Jonathan gazes at Daniel sleeping. No one has a more beautiful body from Jonathan's perspective, and it is a body he has intimately explored numerous times. Daniel slowly stretches, eyes closed. Jonathan burrows into the tuft of hair on Daniel's chest and the cave of his heart hidden beneath it.

His mind travels back to his most unpleasant life events. He reflects on the first grades of elementary school when he wandered aimlessly through the schoolyard, friendless, not invited to join in the other children's games, being too shy, timid, and embarrassed to invite himself in. A sense of unworthiness and detachment took hold in his late teen and early adult years. Later, he navigated the shoals of the subterranean side of gay sex life, with its risk-taking and sometimes even life-threatening behavior. It seemed an inevitable circumstance he and every other gay man faced.

Jonathan has come to understand that he had to experience every moment of it to get where he is today. Growing up Catholic in that community at that moment of history and in that geographical space gave him little choice than to be immersed and indelibly infused with its culture, strictures, and values, save one, which left him one alternative: flight. After crossing the River Styx and entering underground gay culture, the choices he made, though not always safe, were inexplicably necessary. He shudders recalling a fist he took in the eye out of the blue and the knife held to his throat as he cruised through the brush of a city park after dark.

November 2, 1995

THE ECHOING STILLNESS ONCE again brought Jonathan's attention back to the altar. The archbishop was holding the chalice of wine and pronouncing the words that transformed it into the blood of Christ. The words also reverberated within Jonathan: the chalice of my blood . . . shed for you and for many . . . .

1979

"FAGGOT!" HIS ATTACKER YELLED as his fist found its target. The knife wielder quickly released his grip and ran off in search of other victims, but not until he nicked the skin below Jonathan's Adam's apple and drew blood. If it had been a bit deeper, Jonathan knew he would have been dead.

On another occasion, Jonathan had met a guy named Kevin in a bar, an airman from Lowry Air Force base, who was more closeted than Jonathan, hiding a secret for which he would have faced dishonorable discharge. He had a wife and two teenage sons. Jonathan had gotten to know him quite well after several encounters and felt comfortable driving close to the base's gate to pick him up. That last night though, Kevin became upset to the point of paranoia, convinced his superiors were figuring him out. He blamed Jonathan, seeing him as his personal tempter and seducer. Kevin scratched a blade along Jonathan's jugular vein.

"I'll just tell them you picked me up hitchhiking and made a move. They won't convict me for defending myself against a pervert."

Jonathan attempted to plant doubt in Kevin's mind about the credibility of such a tale. "So, why were you hitchhiking when you could've called your wife for a ride?"

Keeping his cool, Jonathan talked reassuringly while he drove, telling Kevin that no matter what, even if found innocent, everyone would have it in the back of their mind that he might have been out philandering. He had to think of his sons. It was not textbook methodology to calm someone bent on violence, but Jonathan had developed a way with words and tone that seemed to calm those who became extremely agitated and upset.

Lying on his back and staring at the ceiling, Jonathan wonders about how he has become adept at using that same skill to redirect the focus of those curious about his sexuality. It works with nearly everyone, but Jonathan is coming to especially love and hold dear the two with whom it does not: his mother and Daniel. Jonathan senses that his mother, bless her heart, sees into and through him. He dreads the day she dies. Daniel immediately saw into and through him when they met during a teachers' conference in San Francisco. His ability to do that was one of the reasons Jonathan fell in love with him.

That evening at dinner with Daniel, Jonathan knew he had found his life mate. That Daniel was a Jesuit priest who taught religion was ironic, to be sure. But Jonathan viewed that circumstance as a mere surmountable obstacle.

Daniel's hirsute body with its tawny chestnut-colored hair had worked to seal the deal. Playfully, Jonathan imagines that in another life Daniel was a king of the jungle. If it is true owners often share the looks or personalities of their dogs, then why not humans and animals in the wild? If Daniel were to sit outside a male lion's enclosure at the San Diego Zoo, as close as he could get, anyone seeing him and the lion would likely surmise that they were bonded as closely as any man and his dog are. And when Daniel gets going on issues about which he is passionate such as war, poverty, social injustice, and a bad ref call, he roars.

After showering, Daniel and Jonathan towel each other off. "I can't spend the day because I'm saying a special Mass this afternoon for the poor and homeless. Plus, we have a food and clothing drive afterwards."

That part of Daniel, that abundant, compassionate, and sacred heart, helps keep him burning in Jonathan's own. After being ticketed by an undercover cop he had made a move on in a bookstore, Daniel attempted suicide when the story became the lead on a local TV station. Fortunately, the housekeeper discovered him in time and was able to call 911. Several months later, having endured countless counseling sessions within a "monastic retreat," Daniel emerged a new man, shaky but accepting of his homosexuality. The sham of his conservative attitude about Catholicism in particular and religion in general lay in ashes within the crucible of his transformation. His therapist, Father Patrick, who had drop-dead good looks and killer ice-blue eyes, portrayed himself as a traditional Catholic. Daniel, however, told Jonathan he was convinced the priest was more closeted than him, which explained the reason they connected so well.

Jonathan gently chides Daniel as they dress. "There's no doubt that between your efforts at the school and for the poor, you're doing noble work, but I wonder. After all you've gone through and the dogmatic line still coming down from corporate headquarters, how you can still remain so intimately connected with the Church."

Daniel good-naturedly pokes his finger into Jonathan's ribs. "You're a cynic."

"I am when it comes to life in general, but not about this. In ancient Greece, I was an epicurean. In this incarnation, I'm a skeptic and rationalist, albeit one who subscribes to some sort of transcendent power and who believes dogmatic religions ultimately bring about havoc, harm, and ruin. They're about preserving their self-interests including power, influence, and money.

"Christianity, especially the Catholic Church, is the greatest scam ever perpetrated on humanity. The Church fathers figured out the key to corporate success: create a product they convince people they need, in this case salvation. No other business has been able to match that message. If I don't use Crest three times a day, my teeth might get cavities and hurt, but all that could ultimately happen is that they will rot and I'll need to have them pulled with great pain or crowned at great expense. But my soul? That's forever. If I don't go to Mass or if I sleep with a man, even one I love for his inner beauty as Jesus loved John, I'll suffer eternally."

Daniel pulls up his trousers. "You know that's nonsense. That's where Christianity has gone wrong. That's not what Jesus was about . . . is about."

Jonathan buttons Daniel's shirt, his intensity softening to a wicked smile. "Oh, really? Do you think Jesus was hot for John? I was when I was a kid and still was until you sidled up to me on that boat." The glint from Daniel's eyes gives Jonathan the message he might be going too far. "Okay, seriously, what did Jesus really say? We don't even have absolute proof he actually lived. Besides Paul and his band of fellow travelers with their anecdotal accounts, the only historical reference to him is by Josephus, and that is more in passing. It's like the *Rocky Mountain News* noting the execution of some revolutionary in a remote and minor country—except that event, faithfully recorded, is forever emblazoned in the historical account. Unfortunately, the *Jerusalem Times* wasn't in business yet to give those of us living two thousand years later a solid accounting of that day's news."

Daniel and Jonathan move to the kitchen where Jonathan begins preparing breakfast while Daniel boils water in the kettle for tea. Jonathan slices homemade bread he baked for their toast and cracks eggs into a bowl for omelets.

"You have to admit, there were some real loose screws who got the whole thing going, like Origen who castrated himself. But I'll give them this: Madison Avenue could not have come up with a better product or selling strategy. And let's not get going on the Inquisition, the burning of heretics and Jews, the slaughtering of so-called infidels, and the repression of women."

Slightly irritated, Daniel pecks Jonathan on his lips. "Yes, let's not. But I guess that's why I love you—that always processing mind of yours."

Jonathan points to his crotch. "Oh. All along I thought it was because of this."

Daniel reaches down and cups it, then gives Jonathan another peck. "Yes, that too."

As Daniel works his way through the *Rocky Mountain News*, Jonathan sets their places at the breakfast bar and thinks about how much he had come to hate cooking. During his teen and young adult years, he never minded cleaning up even the worst kitchen disasters if someone else prepared the meal, but the idea of cooking up a four-course meal bothered him.

That was different when he was a boy. He loved to bake until the day Theodore came home for a visit, learned he had baked cookies, and castigated him for doing woman's work. In hindsight, Jonathan realizes that was when he began to feel ashamed of who he is and ashamed of many things about himself—the love of being in the kitchen for one.

The punch he took and the knives to his throat were strangely more humiliating than frightening in comparison. At neither time did he truly feel his life was endangered. But the shame heaped upon him in those exchanges was real, and it took control of his life. While the potential of his death did not bother Jonathan, the multiple bouts with psychos did.

The incident with Kevin had happened when Jonathan was rereading *Moby Dick* for his masters-level class on the transcendentalists. The story's opening line, "Call me Ishmael," always moved him. Short and succinct, it got right at it. From the time he read it in high school, Jonathan identified with Ishmael. He loved Starbuck for his cool dispassionate ability to reason, that is, with anyone except Ahab. Kevin, he concluded, was as obsessed with being wronged by the universe as Ahab was with the white whale. Nestling into his pillows after ridding himself of Kevin, Jonathan sipped his bedtime cocktail of single-malt Scotch over rocks and immersed himself in Melville.

"Vengeance on a dumb brute!" cried Starbuck, "that simply smote thee from blindest instinct! Madness! To be enraged with a dumb thing, Captain Ahab, seems blasphemous."

"Hark ye yet again,—the little lower layer. All visible objects, man, are but as pasteboard masks. But in each event—in the living act, the undoubted deed—there, some unknown but still reasoning thing puts forth the mouldings of its features from behind the unreasoning mask. If man will strike, strike through the mask! How can the prisoner reach outside except by thrusting through the wall? To me, the white whale is that wall, shoved near to me. Sometimes I think there's naught beyond. But 'tis enough. He tasks me; he heaps me. I see in him outrageous strength, with an inscrutable malice sinewing it. That inscrutable thing is chiefly what I hate; and be the white whale agent, or be the white whale principal, I will wreak that hate upon him. Talk not to me of blasphemy, man; I'd strike the sun if it insulted me."

As Jonathan read on, his mind roamed, making connections. Ahab. Theodore. White whale. Inscrutable malice. Pasteboard mask. What tasks him? Heaps him?

As Daniel wipes the last smear of syrup from the plate with his toast, Jonathan reaches over and takes hold of his left hand. Daniel inquisitively looks at him.

"Thanks, Daniel."

"For what? You're the one who made the omelet."

"For being my teacher. For showing me what being true to yourself really means."

Daniel nods and the two men sit in silence. Daniel clears his throat, stands, and pulls Jonathan up into an embrace. He holds Jonathan tightly and then peers down into his eyes. "You have to tell them. That is the only way you'll find peace with yourself."

Jonathan nods in turn and smiles faintly. "I know. I'm just not ready. The time's not right."

Watching Daniel through the window as he backs out of the driveway, Jonathan wonders about how his family will react to his inevitable confession. *Mum will love you,* he muses. *Theodore will despise you. And the rest? What about Dad? Would he have loved you? Would he have accepted Daniel?* He will never know how his father would have taken it. As for the rest, he is not quite sure he is ready to know.

13

November 2, 1995

SWEAT HAD FORMED ON his forehead. Jonathan reached up and touched it, then pulled a handkerchief embroidered with a gold *J* out of his hip pocket. It was one of the few personal items his mother could afford to give him. He wiped his forehead and began his slow eight-count breath work. Eight in, eight out.

He looked up to see the archbishop concluding the prayers for the offering. The archbishop kissed the altar and made the sign of the cross twice. ". . . *sacrosanctum Filii tui Corpus, et Sanguinem sumpserimus omni benedictione coelesti et gratia replamur. Per eundem Christum Dominum nostrum. Amen.*"

This was a prayer that all those receiving the body and blood of Christ be filled with grace and heavenly blessing.

The family members remained kneeling. Jonathan did the same and began reading the prayers commemorating the dead. He included the names of his mother and father. He paused and looked at the archbishop and then at his brothers and sisters, reflecting on the degree that their lives had been altered by death and how much had changed since their father's departure, years earlier. In that moment, Jonathan finally realized the enormity of not only what had happened so long ago, but also how they, as a family, had failed to deal with the devastating emotional and psychological toll the tragedy had taken, especially given its suddenness and the fact their father's death had resulted from the hand of one of his own while they hunted.

Jonathan looked at the casket, staring intently. "Mum," he whispered, "you were our heart, our strength, and our rock, the foundation upon which we sat. You saw us through. We survived. Now you're gone. What now?"

1981

DANIEL AND JONATHAN DRIVE through Denver in Daniel's new red Escort, making their way to a restaurant. Traffic seems light even though it is a Friday rush hour. They head northwest on Speer Boulevard and cross Broadway. The radio is tuned in to KIMN where Blondie's recent hit, "Rapture," plays.

Jonathan reaches and turns the volume down and turns to Daniel. "I'm not sure what to say to him. I haven't seen him since I can remember. I'm in a very different place than I was . . . something he can never understand or want to understand."

"He's still your brother. Just be honest. Speak your truth."

"It's not that simple. He's an egocentric monomaniac, which I'm sure sounds redundant. When I think back to our family days and how whenever he came home it was all about him, I'm able now to finally put it in perspective. Even when he wasn't around, his non-presence cast a shadow. The power he had over the rest of us was mesmerizing and profound and strangely enhanced by his non-presence. It's as if he was the victim, as if some great wrong or injustice had been inflicted on him by some mysterious power, which in his thinking couldn't have been God because that would mean he deserved it. No, he could only conclude that whatever attacked him came from the source of ultimate evil."

"But he's a priest now, an ordained minister of the gospel. That might have a salubrious effect on him."

"The gospel is the last thing on his mind. For him, what happens in the Church is all about ritual, dogma, and judgment. That's the reason he studied under and was ordained by that reactionary archbishop who won't budge a scintilla when it comes to Vatican II and the new order of the Mass. For him, Jesus will always be that traditional caricature of a king sitting at the right hand of God, dispensing heavenly justice. Messages Jesus delivered like love thy neighbor as thyself and forgiveness and compassion are meaningless. In fact, if Jesus came back and re-taught those same messages, Theodore would nail him to the cross again for heresy."

"Overstatement?"

"Maybe, but I'll get back to you on that. I understand he likes Mexican food. That's the reason I chose Las Margaritas. Maybe that can be our common ground. At least I'm hoping it will be. I just hope he doesn't say grace with a special plea to Our Lady of Guadalupe since we're enjoying her peoples' ethnic cuisine."

Jonathan pauses in thought.

"There's something else though, something that happened to him—from what I gather from my sisters. He was always quite conservative and a strong Catholic. Legend has it he attended daily mass throughout the year. But then, *most* of my siblings are traditionalists. It seems, though, that over the years he became more so, which is hard to believe anyone can be more rigid and unbending."

"Perhaps it was the military culture and the war. He helped drop bombs in Vietnam, after all."

"Yeah, but from his point of view he was doing his duty as a good American—all that John Wayne, God, and country shit—as if God picks sides and must be an American. I doubt it was a matter of conscience for him."

"Probably not, but doing stuff like that can make fanatics even more fanatical, hardened. Soldiers, even those not in hand-to-hand combat, can become so inured to the violence around them that they crash badly and begin to dehumanize their enemy. Think of William Calley and My Lai."

"I try not to. I shudder when I do. It reminds me of the Sand Creek Massacre. Same story: innocents, primarily women, children, and elderly man, gunned down or bayoneted. Then it was American Indians; one hundred years later it was Vietnamese. Same story, different characters, same outcome. I'm not saying that's not it, but my gut says something happened that was far more personal."

"Maybe," says Daniel.

Reaching over and taking Jonathan's hand, he offers, "I can still join you if you think it would make things easier. Maybe it'll keep you from getting into heavier stuff."

"No, but thanks, Daniel. It means a lot for you to offer, but it would be more difficult, I think. He's no dummy. He's earned a PhD, which is something I wouldn't do. He'll get suspicious and begin to probe."

"So, let him. He's going to find out sooner or later."

"True, but for now, I'm opting for later. I know . . . I'm a coward, but once again my gut says this is not the time. There will be a time, but it has to be when I'm ready. Besides, this is his time. He's now Father Slovanco, officially or unofficially in the eyes of the Church. Either way, it's no sweat off my back."

Daniel pulls into the restaurant's drop-off lane and after coming to a stop, turns to Jonathan. "You're no coward."

Jonathan looks deep into Daniel's eyes and nods.

"I'll be back by 9:00. If you're not out, I'll wait. So don't feel rushed, unless you want to, of course. Now, give me a kiss and venture forth, Young Skywalker. Your father awaits you."

Jonathan laughs as Daniel gives a peck on his lips. "Thanks, Obi Wan. I love your perverse sense of humor."

As he enters Las Margaritas, Jonathan espies his brother sitting in the first booth, eyes fixed on the menu clutched in his hand. Despite its Mexican fare, the restaurant's decor reminds Jonathan of an old English pub. Juxtaposed with the English pub furnishings are paintings depicting Mexican scenes. The one in the center, dwarfing the others, is of a broad and ornate cathedral and its square with worshippers making their way to it. White-laced cloths cover the tables. At the table where Theodore sits are a bowl of chips and salsa, two place settings, and two glasses of ice water.

Theodore is dressed in the traditional priestly garb: black shirt and trousers with the white Roman collar. His thinning jet-black hair is beginning to be laced with gray, which accentuates the pasty appearance of his skin. Wire-rimmed glasses sit prominently on his aquiline nose. His jaw seems set and his vision looks focused, as if he is reading an encyclical or other serious work rather than a simple menu.

Jonathan muses as he allows himself a moment to take it all in before heading over to the booth where his brother sits. It seems a bit surrealistic to him, as if he has seen his brother dressed like this once before.

Purposely, he walks towards his older brother, and at that moment Theodore looks up to see him approaching. Theodore tries to stand, but has trouble negotiating his way out of the booth. Seeing that, Jonathan picks up his pace. At the table, he takes Theodore's extended hand and shakes it.

"Brother, it's good to see you. Please don't get up."

"Thank you, Jonny. This bum leg seems to be giving me more and more trouble, but it's a burden I need to carry. Still, it's good to be here. I cannot remember seeing you since you were a boy. You've grown into a solid man."

"Thanks, Ted, or should I call you Father Slovanco? I think the last time I saw you I was just starting high school."

"You're probably right. If I recall correctly, that was in '64 when the communists attacked our ships in the Gulf of Tonkin. When we essentially declared war with the Gulf of Tonkin Resolution, I assisted the pilots flying sorties from our aircraft carrier, day and night. After that, I didn't find time to get home."

"All for naught."

"Nonsense. We would've won if Nixon had kept the pressure up, but he got hamstrung by the Democrats in Congress who caved to those long-haired bums."

"You think so?"

"Agnew was right when he said that they were effete

nattering nabobs of negativism. The liberals were not only selling out our country, but also our church."

Jonathan avoids the reference to the Catholic Church. "So I take it you like Reagan as president."

"He doesn't have the intellectual acumen of Barry Goldwater, but he has charm and a sense of class that will help dealing with the Soviets as well as the Democrats."

"So his being divorced is not an issue for you? I thought that was a death nail for a politician, especially a conservative one."

"I don't like it, but we had no choice. Carter was a joke. The Iranian hostage situation proved that."

The waiter approaches, which helps save the moment for Jonathan. He breaks from his customary Scotch and orders a margarita while Theodore orders a glass of Chablis. After ordering their dinners, fish tacos for Theodore and the chile relleno platter for Jonathan, the conversation promptly moves to Theodore's ordination.

"You asked if it would be more appropriate for you to address me as Father rather than brother. In time, I suppose I will get use to that, but for now, Theodore or Ted is fine."

"So what made you want to become a priest?"

"From the time I was little, I knew I would become one. The Korean War was raging when I got out of high school, and I knew I had to do my duty. I stayed in longer than I had initially planned, but I never gave up on the idea of becoming a priest. When I saw the havoc wreaked upon Holy Mother Church in Vatican II by the liberals, I became increasingly alarmed. But God, in his omniscience, sent Archbishop Lefebvre to save the Church, and I knew our prayers were answered. It was the greatest personal blessing to have been ordained by the archbishop himself."

"Well, congratulations. I'm sure you were quite honored to be ordained by the archbishop."

"It's not about man's honor, but God's, and doing his work. His Church is facing mortal danger if she is not defended. The modernists are doing Satan's work. In 1907, Pope Pius X condemned those insidious maneuverings in his encyclical *Pascendi Dominici Danielis*. He saw it coming."

"But this is a new age, don't you think? One that requires a fresh way of looking at the way we do stuff. After all, we don't practice medicine or run our finances like we did two thousand years ago."

His brother the priest thunders as he slaps his hand down onto the table with such force that it rattles the plates and silverware. "No! That's what the sainted Pope Pius X wrote about. History and science are irrelevant to God. What he wrought when he sent his only begotten son to be sacrificed can never change. The Mass is inviolable. The Council of Trent settled that. The words the priest utters, as well as the ritual itself, must be followed to the letter with no deviation. This *Novus Ordo*, Paul VI's new Mass, is a sacrilege, an anathema, and must be exorcised from the liturgy."

Jonathan takes a sip of his margarita. "I see."

"Modern society is coming undone. Look at what has happened with the war protests and race riots."

"You don't think, despite the violence, some good stuff has happened because of them?"

"Absolutely not! We have lost a war for the first time in American history, a war we could've won had we been resolute.

That's only the beginning of what the liberals have done. Have you been following the news about how some of those queers are dying? It's God's wrath. Oh, they think they started a revolution in 1969 in their Stonewall uprising, but what they don't realize is they have provoked the hand of an angry God." Theodore pauses to take a sip of his wine, and then sneers, "Those queers."

Jonathan feels his throat constricting and heart palpitating. Sweat beads form on his brow and his hands begin to feel clammy. He reaches for his margarita in the hope that it will disguise his discomfort and calm his heightened emotions. In so doing, he notices his brother's flared nostrils and heavy breathing. The classic sermon "Sinners in the Hands of an Angry God" by the Puritan preacher, Jonathan Edwards, flashes into his mind. The stirring images Edwards creates about God's wrath become vivid: great waters dammed for the present, a bow and arrow aimed for the sinner's heart, and, Jonathan's favorite given its very vivid imagery, a spider God holds over the Pit of Hell.

Jonathan scans the room, shaking his head, as if searching for someone or a thought he is unable to grasp. He looks across the table at his brother, whose eyes are downcast as he stares at his glass of wine, and studies him. His eyes squint and then what he was searching for dawns on him. *That priest. I've seen this man before. I'm there again.*

Theodore takes a sip of his wine and looks up to Jonathan. "One night when I was in training camp, I awoke and felt this hand on my private area. I froze, at first paralyzed by what was happening. I opened my eyes and in the dim light, I saw my lieutenant kneeling next to me. Disgust ran through me. I wanted to yell, but didn't."

"What did you do?"

"I reached for his arm and grabbed it firmly. I could see the fear in his eyes. I held his arm and stared at him for a moment and then pushed him away. I rolled over onto my side, and he got up and crept out."

"Did you report it?"

"No. It wouldn't have done any good. It would've been my word against his, and with him outranking me, I knew I'd be ruined."

"I'm sorry that happened."

Theodore bores directly into Jonathan's eyes. "Men touching each other is disgusting, a perversion, something God hates more than anything else. I hope, Jonny, you never have to deal with that."

14

November 2, 1995

WITH THE CONGREGANTS REMAINING on their knees, the archbishop uncovered the chalice and genuflected. With his right hand, he took the Host, which was no longer a wafer of bread but the literal body of Christ, and with his left hand, he took the chalice, which was no longer wine but the blood of Christ. He made the sign of the cross with the Host above the chalice five times, then elevated the chalice and the Host and placed them back on the corporal, the blessed cloth, and covered the chalice. He genuflected and after rising in a loud voice said, "*Per omnia saecula saeculorum*," to which the servers responded, "Amen."

With those words concluding the Minor Elevation, the archbishop intoned, "*Oremus.*"

In unison the family, including Jonathan, stood to recite the Lord's Prayer, which Jonathan had committed to memory in Latin as a boy. As he listened to the others, Jonathan pulled from his journal pocket a letter he had written to his dad.

∽○∾

1983

Dear Dad,

We've never had a real conversation. After all, I wasn't quite four years old when you died. So we never had the opportunity to get to know each other. From where you are, you might know who I am, what I've become, and what I've accomplished, but I know so little of you. Of course, that's not your fault. I'm sure that if you had your druthers, you would have stuck around a lot longer. But fate has its ways, and it wasn't to be.

Still, whatever I do know is within the context of your role as father and provider. You seemed to have provided for our large family relatively well on a minimal salary, and you died tragically, far too young. What I don't know is who you were as a person, as a man, what you liked to do besides hunting and golfing. How did you smile and laugh? What made you smile and laugh, or did you? What made you angry? Or sad?

Given your life experiences, what great wisdom floated around in that mind of yours? What was it like growing up in the early twentieth century? As you grew into a young man, how did it feel to know how your father died? You were only five years old when he got nailed in the factory. I guess that is something we both share: losing our dads at an age when we really couldn't grasp the idea of fatherhood and what a father does.

Do you remember the incident at all? What went through your head about it as a five-year-old and later, as a young man and an adult? Did you even give it a thought? I think you would've, but then, blocking out painful memories seems to help some people go on and function, even if it means they don't really live.

I don't consciously recall anything about your death, but nevertheless, images are in here, in my head. You're lying on the ground surrounded by dry dead weeds, dressed in your hunting garb with a pool of blood oozing from your chest. I suspect you weren't in pain though you might've been. Somehow, still, you knew it was your time to leave. If that was the case, was your spirit hovering above the scene, looking down at your body, still physically alive but really gone because your spirit had already fled?

You came of age during the Roaring Twenties. How exciting was that? Speakeasies, prohibition, the Jazz Age. Wow! To be a teenager and then to turn eighteen during that epoch had to be crazy. And baseball! The 1925 Pirates winning the World Series. You were sixteen. Then the 1927 Pirates losing to arguably the greatest team to play on the diamond: the New York Yankees. Babe Ruth, Lou Gehrig. It couldn't have gotten any better.

Then the Stock Market Crash. 1929. The end of an era. You went into the army. I never did find out your rank. I guess I could, but does it really matter? You served. Besides, in my book, to be a private takes far more courage than to be a general. But then, I was neither.

I still have a copy of yours and Mum's wedding picture. I have to say, you were quite the stud. Dark eyes and hair and a killer smile. No wonder Mum was smitten. And you were a stud: ten children. Today ten is a perfect score, like in Olympics gymnastics. Some might say, though, that your ten wasn't perfect, that you produced an anomaly. I'm the anomaly among your children, the different one. I'm okay with that, but are you? I suspect the others, most of them anyway, will have a problem with that once I tell them.

I wonder, though, why you returned to Western Pennsylvania after your enlistment was up. Did anything happen during your enlistment that caused you to return and settle down? Or was your life journey simply dictated by what was expected of that same culture I found repressive and stultifying? When I was getting ready to leave home and move to Colorado, Uncle Henry got in my face and said, "You were born here, you live here, and you're to die here!"

"Like hell!" I retorted, and off I went, more determined than ever to make it elsewhere.

The stories I wish you could tell me. I'm not sure which I'm sadder about, the fact that your stories were lost before I could hear them or the possibility that the story of you and who you were will become lost by not being told. Stories die with the teller, but the teller's story can still be told. Perhaps I can do that. Perhaps I can tell your story. Of course, in large part, it would have to be through the perspectives and memories of your children. But, so what? All memories are flawed. We create memories to align with our story. One's version of a past event is only one version, as distorted and valid as others.

I wonder, too, about our relationship. From what I've been told, you were a very traditional male, and the few details I know of you seem to confirm that. How would you have dealt with me? I doubt you could've understood. I sure didn't. I just knew that I was the way I was, and it's taken me a lifetime to sort it out. I guess I am still sorting it out and always will be. *Nunc et semper*—now and always.

Would you have loved me, Dad, as I am for who I am? Or would you have disapproved and perhaps knocked me around? Is there a difference? Is knocking around one's child a sign of love or is it an expression of frustration played out through violence because of the parent's inability or refusal to come to know and understand their child? And does that arise in part because the child does not fulfill the preconceived image or follow the path his parents define for him?

I recall Father Reginald reading me passages from Saint Paul's Epistle to the Hebrews about God's discipline. One passage stated, "For whom the Lord loves he chastises; and he scourges every son he receives." He goes on to say that all discipline in the present is not received with joy but with grief. Yet afterwards, one finds peace in it.

Perhaps that's true in principle, but it does have a caveat: the discipline needs to have been warranted for actions, not for being who one is. My bet is that Theodore—Father Theodore—would greatly dispute that. He argues that one is who he chooses to be, not as he is born to be. For him, only physical traits and mental capacity come with the package at birth. All the rest is choice. From his point of view, one cannot be born gay any more than one can be born Catholic, which brings up another conundrum when one thinks about it. I wonder when he chose to be heterosexual and a Catholic and if he did some serious experimenting before making his final decision?

I wonder, too, how we would've gotten along with you being Virgo and me Aquarius. Virgo is earth, grounded and practical and relating to the harvest, while Aquarius is an air sign and can be given to flights of fantasy. It might've been a conflict of energies, but then, maybe not. From what I was told about you, our home and all that related to it were aspects of your essentialism. In ancient Greece, Hestia would've been one of your personal goddesses. The chicken coop and your huge garden, which had shrunk to a mere fraction of its grand size by the time I grew up, were expressions of that. It's interesting thinking about it. They went away when you did. The harvest died the day you died.

Books and ideas have always been most important to me. There is something energizing in them: new ideas and forms. But while my astrological key phrase, according to Isabel Hickey, is "I know," yours is "I analyze," and my sense is that through your analytical mind, you would come to accept a reality even if it was not something you approved of.

I left the Catholic Church, which to me has become a superstitious, power-hungry organization that achieves its goals by promising the worst form of outcome—eternal damnation—if you don't live in accordance with its strictures. Great product to market. I could no longer endure the repression. How ironic that I found safety and security in the Church as a boy! But things began to happen as I matured, things I couldn't understand. Over time, I've found liberation in them, and that's the reason, I feel, I receive such opprobrium and condemnation.

One can argue, I suppose, that I replaced one set of superstitious beliefs with another, a maddening mixture of paganism, Buddhism, and Western astrology. Carl Jung and Joseph Campbell have become two of my gurus. Being Aquarius, I like to point out—tongue in cheek—that I cannot subscribe to taking things on faith. Evidence in conjunction with reason must be one's guidance system. But then that leads to atheism, which in itself is not bad, for I have found atheists to be more civil, thoughtful, and peace-loving than Christians. But I sense, deep within myself, that there is a transcendent power or energy unifying everything. However, our energy—what some call soul or spirit—does not emanate from out there, beyond the reaches of our planet, but from here, from our Mother Earth.

Of course, here I go, going off on something philosophical, as I'm prone to do, avoiding doing or going to places that make me uncomfortable. What can I say? As a family, we were not taught to say 'I love you' or to even hug one another. We were taught to stoically keep our emotions in check and to focus on accomplishing tasks at hand. I suppose that made sense because we had to focus on surviving, especially after you had left. But as a little boy, none of it needed to make sense. It was the way it was, and that reality was, therefore, normal. That's not good enough anymore, and it hasn't been since I came to realize who and what I am.

Sure, life hasn't been particularly easy or joyful for me, but I've learned that it rarely is for others, either. When I look around at the problems others face and burdens they carry, I am reminded that my load is relatively insignificant. I hate whining and I hate playing the victim. Those who whine send me up a wall, so I avoid dealing with my stuff for fear it will come across as neurotic whining. I keep it all inside, putting on a happy face but descending into the dark abyss when I'm away from those who know me, or think they do. And that dark abyss is not just inside me, it is also there in my actions. It is the reason I haunted dank and dark bars, Dad.

But thanks to my therapist, my meditative practice, and my friend Daniel, who is a phenomenal man,

I think I'm getting my arms around this. At least I hope I am because the alternative is not good. Going into that shadow region of one's psyche has been most painful, mentally as well as physically. Recalling that experience with the priest psychologist while in high school was excruciating. But I survived it, and with that, I've broken its power. If crushing truths perish when acknowledged, as Albert Camus has written, that truth took some time to perish. But I have learned that I don't need to give it power by allowing it to control my life, that I don't need to use it as an excuse to play the victim.

I'm surprised and grateful I'm still here, in one piece physically and only a bit scarred mentally. I'm grateful that I caused no one lasting harm, at least as far as I know. I shudder to think I might have. But then, haven't we all?

I guess, Dad, what I want to know is whether you loved me, or would have loved me had you been around to see how I turned out, which I've been told is quite different than what you would have approved of. I used to wish it could have been different, but I no longer do. I've come to accept who and what I am and offer gratitude each day for my many blessings. Because of who and what I am, I'm coming to know the world, coming to understand the immensity of existence, and in so doing, I am marveling at the mystery of it all.

I'm saddened, though, to see that it has not turned out so well for the entire brood you sired and Mum gave birth to. But I have come to understand that our family is not so different from others, that many families are dysfunctional and disintegrate because there is nothing cohesive to keep them together. I used to wonder why it had to be that way with us, but then learned the importance of process. Our experiences are not just part of us as individuals, they are part of our interpersonal relationships. I've learned we have to put all of our stuff in the context of those interpersonal relationships: family, friends, community, culture, and society.

I have no regrets, but honestly, that doesn't make it any easier. Like every other human being, in the end, I want only happiness. In that pursuit, I've come to realize that happiness can only be achieved through love, beginning with self-love and then love of others and love from others.

The big question, the unanswerable one remains: Dad, did you love me? Do you love me?

∽०∾

JONATHAN SCROLLED THROUGH THE letter to the line, "Perhaps I can tell your story," and shook his head ruefully. That is where the trouble began, he thought. I dared write his story, our story. I had to be silenced, shamed, so that that story would not be told.

He folded the letter and stuffed it back into his hip pocket, then settled back in the pew, allowing the incense and strained sounds of the organ filter into his senses. He closed his eyes and let his mind go, wishing he could pray but knowing that escape was no longer an option. Instead, he just allowed himself to remember trying to make sense of something impervious to being made sense of.

The church was again enshrouded in silence following the Our Father until the archbishop's low voice and rustling vestments cut through it and echoed from the domed ceiling. Holding the gold paten between his first and second fingers and praying, he made the sign of the cross with it on himself, kissed it, and placed it back on the altar. He then reached into the ciborium and took one of the consecrated Hosts, now the body of Christ, broke it, and placed half on the paten. He then broke off a particle from the other to drop into the chalice of wine, now the blood of Christ, saying, "*Haec commixtio et consecratio Corporis et Sanguinis Domini nostri Jesu Christi, fiat accipientibus nobis in vitam aeternam.*"

Jonathan knew that it was a prayer for the body and blood of Christ to help those receiving them find life everlasting.

The archbishop genuflected, turned towards the faithful, and with spread arms as if in supplication said, "*Agnus Dei, qui tollis peccata mundi, donis eis requiem.*"

Jonathan murmured in English, "Lamb of God, you who take away the sins of the world, grant them peace."

15

Spring, 1985

JONATHAN LEANS INTO THE wind as he makes his way up the bluff overlooking the Pacific near Fort Ross. It is spring break, and he has decided he needs some personal time and space. Things with Daniel have been a bit tenuous of late, and the wild Pacific Coast promised to provide the elixir and refuge needed to process. He could not pass up the opportunity to explore San Francisco, from the bay to the breakers, on his own, even though he is not much of a city person, preferring the outback to challenge and find himself. But for as long as he could remember, San Francisco, is one of three cities—New Orleans and Boston being the other two—that have held a fascination for him, causing him to wonder if he didn't have a previous life in each.

San Francisco did not disappoint. In fact, it gave Jonathan more than he had hoped for. From Fisherman's Wharf to the bars in the Castro, he absorbed every ion of energy, inhaling magical air he found curiously enervating. Three days of the magical elixir were enough though, so he rented a car and headed north on Highway 101 through the Napa Valley and past Santa Rosa to the Guerneville exit. From there he followed the Russian River down and west to the small enclave where he discovered an open culture and community of men to his liking.

Finding lodging at a gay-oriented resort, he decided to hold off on the venture into the village and donned his running shoes for a trot up to a nearby redwood cove. It was late afternoon and warm, so he was surprised at how few others were present. That was okay because while their voices did not reverberate, the few wandering through or sitting on benches still cracked the silence of the tree village. It was the first time he saw the enormous trees in person and walked in awe among them. Noting how soft and cushiony the ground was, he removed his shoes and walked barefoot. The sensations he felt through the nerve endings in his feet were intoxicating and brought back boyhood memories of running barefoot through the woods, the soles of his feet coarsened and tough as leather.

A natural seat between two of the protruding massive roots provided a place for him to sit, and he settled into its embrace, then stretched his legs out to feel the ground through his bare skin. Pulling his left leg up to allow his sole to caress the ground, he focused all his thoughts on the feelings of the stones, the tiny branches, and the root to feel every indenture, bump, and sharp edge. He switched feet and sat meditating on the experience.

After slipping his shoes back on, he ran back to his cabin, showered, and dressed for the evening. He decided on dark gray casual trousers with a lavender pullover top and slipped into his cordovan penny loafers. For a second, he panicked, thinking he had left the matching belt at home, but found the belt curled and nestled between his boxers and socks. Thankfully, disaster was averted.

The bars were hopping, which surprised him given the size of the town. In the first one, he beamed when he saw a shuffleboard table. Jonathan is good, able to slide the puck along either rail with the right amount of spin and just enough velocity to let it sit snugly at the farthest edge of the board. If his opponent failed to knock him off, he unfailingly "put pants on it" by placing the next one a few inches in front to prevent it being knocked off the next time. He decided it was going to be a fun evening, and it was.

His name was Joseph, and he was as gorgeous as his last name, Rose. He was the bartender and after several shots and increasingly more personal banter, he asked Jonathan to stay after closing. The next day they spent hours of endless touching, fondling, caressing, and entering in Jonathan's cabin. Two days later, Jonathan took a scenic drive along the coast on Highway 1, hoping he would not plunge into the ocean, not because the road was precarious, but because he could not help gaping in awe at the power of the waves.

Now he finds sitting atop the bluff this Friday afternoon to be exhilarating despite the powerful surf winds pounding the shore. Jonathan's fear of water might prevent him from going to see what Moby Dick saw in the deep, but he can sit transfixed near the ocean for hours exploring in his mind what he is fearful of exploring with his body.

Dressed in his standard casual attire of hiking shorts, runner's T-shirt, and running shoes, Jonathan sits on the ground with his knees pulled up in front of his chest, zips up his windbreaker, and wraps his arms around his legs to give him stability. Spring break could not have come at a more perfect time. He rolls "more perfect" over in his mind. The phrase irritates him despite it being in the Preamble to the Constitution. Precision in expression, written or spoken, has become an obsession with him. Less than perfect is what we are, yet ironically, it is in our imperfection that we are perfect, he reasons.

In an ongoing battle with the wind, he wraps his windbreaker tighter, pulls his baseball cap down, and pulls the hood of the windbreaker up over it. As a tern swoops overhead, he reflects on the last reading he did with his honors American lit class before spring break. British lit is not his strength, but he enjoys reading *The Rime of the Ancient Mariner* after wrapping up *Moby Dick*. He tries to get his students to understand that the ancient mariner, along with Ahab and the rest of the sailors, serve as archetypes. He has found it is easier to get a concept across when it is discussed in context. In one quarter, his students will be seniors in his friend Denise's class, and she appreciates the idea of his giving them a taste of her curriculum before they enter their last high school English class, which will be advanced placement level. Then they will stand a fighting chance of doing well with her demanding expectations.

One of the challenges he enjoys most in the classroom is moving his students to a deeper appreciation of fiction. "Well-written fiction," he explains, "is truer than nonfiction because it deals with universal truths. Your truth and my truth always conflict because each person filters everything through their personal senses and the lens of their socialization."

Universal truth; personal truth. At what point will he own up to his? When will he act with courage and finally be true to himself. Coming out will more than likely cause the fabric of his family to be irrevocably torn. He thinks about the Islamic revolution in Iran and correlates the culture there to that of his own tribe. Both are led by an ayatollah, different only in matters of faith. Dogma, the art of codifying the will and mind of God, knows no singular tradition. Across the globe, people live in worlds defined by such inanities, some on a grand scale and others in their tribes. The Greeks fought to the death at Salamis 2,500 years ago to defeat that notion. And here we are again, progressing towards that same theocracy because we insist, as Camus held, on placing history on the throne of God.

Fixing his gaze on the tumultuous waters of the Pacific with the windbreaker drawn tight and his knees to his chest, Jonathan notices his mind darting from one story, one allusion, to another. It is okay to him. It might be chaotic to others, but he finds an interconnectedness among the stories that makes sense to him. Unlike the ancient mariner, Jonathan has not committed some unforgivable act. He has shot no albatross, though he is fully aware that when Theodore learns his truth, God's wrath will descend.

Jonathan's eye is caught by the sight of a gull landing on a rock formation to his right. Turning his attention to it, he says, "You tried to fly faster than any gull, and for that you're condemned and ostracized. You asked the right question when you wondered why it is so hard to convince a bird that he is free and could prove it to himself. Well, Mr. Gull, I don't know myself. Is it because we're full of fear that we will be humiliated, demeaned, and degraded? Shame is a most powerful tool to get someone to submit to another's will.

"You tell your disciples that their bodies are nothing more than thought and that they can break the chains of their bodies by breaking the chains of their thoughts. But here's my conundrum, Mr. Gull. If I live my life according to a lie and deny my truth, I'm a coward. That's not honorable. But if I speak my truth, I am shamed.

"The tribe, with its strictures and taboos, has power. To break the chain of thought, conditioned and hardened in that crucible of one's youth, is the tough part. No wonder Jesus sweated bullets in Gethsemane, anticipating his crucifixion. I don't believe that was fear of his impending torture. He had the advantage of being the Son of God, for God's sake. Surely he could endure the pain, as excruciating as he knew it would be. It had to be something more.

"To be shamed—that's the crux of it. You were ordered to stand in the Center for Shame because you violated the Gull family rules. The ancient mariner shrives his sin to the hermit. But to whom do I confess my truth? Confess it, as if I'm sorry for being what I am? No, proclaim it!"

Lowering his head onto his knees, Jonathan closes his eyes to allow the sensation of the gale to swirl through him. He feels the hair on his lower legs ripple and listens to the wind reverberate in his windbreaker hood, which reminds him of the story of Job in the Old Testament listening to God in the whirlwind. When he lifts his head, he sees that the gull has flown off. "Who am I kidding? Deny as I will, I have an albatross around my neck and only I can remove it."

Jonathan pushes himself up, hesitates, and settles back to a seated position with legs outstretched. He removes his shoes and inspects the soles of his feet, looking for cracks and abrasions in the skin that he has been told is a symptom of infection. "None," he says and breathes a sigh of relief stretching out each leg to full length. He wiggles his toes and stretches both feet outward and after several moments, puts his shoes and socks back on. Rolling over, he settles back on his haunches and faces down in a yogic child's pose, feeling tiny stones, grains of sand, and vegetation pressed against his brow. His legs and upper body are warmed not only from the weight of his upper body covering them, but also from the ground's radiant heat.

The wind continues to howl, but Jonathan feels strangely secured to the ground, like a huge boulder that even hurricane force winds cannot lift or even budge. While the wind ruffles his windbreaker, he remains as still and solid as the large boulders he passes on climbs to the tops of Colorado's peaks. He is as much a part of Mother Earth as the massive rock outcropping upon which his new friend the gull sat a few moments ago. He breathes deeply and slowly on counts of eight, and with each inhalation, he begins to process and distinguish the various smells around him: the soil, grass, and subtle whiffs of seawater that seep beneath his human cave.

Empty the mind. Let it all go. Focus on your breath.

He refocuses his energy on his breathing and gently brings his wandering, wondering mind back to the present, to the here, to the now. "I shrive not to Almighty God, but to That I Am, that I Am."

Summer 1985

WITH APPREHENSION, JONATHAN PULLS into the driveway. He notes the well-manicured grass, neatly edged between the two cement runners. The sandstone retaining walls are perfectly aligned, arranged in a coordinated pattern that at first misses the eye of the casual observer. He steps out of the 1968 Cougar he has kept in mint condition since college and surveys the scene. It is a warm day and the morning dew still gives the grass and the other vegetation a soft texture. They glisten as the warming rays of the filtered sun splash across them. Jonathan inhales deeply, feeling the moist air fill his lungs, as if he has inhaled a mountain spring. Unlike the dry air of Colorado, which he has come to love, the air here is usually heavy and stifling. But today it is not.

The long row of hedges has been trimmed in a perfect ninety-degree box. James, the engineer, has recently put his usual angular and symmetrical touch on the foliage, which Jonathan knows will immediately begin to resist James's efforts and grow as it will. Jonathan smiles and shakes his head. So Republican, he says to himself.

He surveys the old house, a simple construction built, ironically, in the midst of the Great Depression, and allows a sense of homesickness to wash over him. He begins to recall how, after Dad's death, Mum had used some of her death benefit money and put aluminum siding on it. What a great idea, he reminds himself. The original wood siding was in constant need of maintenance with the chipping white paint demanding scraping, regular touch-up, and a periodic fresh coat of paint.

The upgrade had its problems, initially, because she worked with two different companies, one for the siding and the other for the awnings. She wanted a cream color for both, but failed to closely look at how each company defined cream. The company that put the siding on saw it as more brown, while the awning group gave it a more yellowish hue. At first it was a cause for consternation, but once everyone came to realize there was nothing to be done—the other possible awning shades were even more different—acceptance set in. Over time it has given the place a distinguished look, one which most people find intriguing. Without a doubt, no other place looks remotely like the Slovancos'.

The house retains its original footprint, slightly wider than deep, thirty feet by twenty-four feet, resting atop a cement block foundation that encloses a garage, barely wide and long enough to house a car, and a basement—actually a cellar—that once seemed spacious, even cavernous, but now seems tiny and cramped. He looks admiringly at the recently scrubbed awnings, which stand in contrast to the siding because it remains in need of scrubbing. James will have that done by the end of the weekend.

Jonathan inhales deeply once again, allowing the dew-scented air to bathe his lungs, and fingers his ring of keys, finding the one for the garage door. He chuckles as he recalls the time he broke in. It was not all that difficult. A good kick on the garage door handle was enough to pop it inward and release the catch. James was furious with him and tried to rework the setup, but it was never really secure, not that it needed to be. After all the years, the neighborhood still maintains its original character with many of the same neighbors. Besides, now as it was then, there is really nothing valuable enough to be worth a thief's time and effort.

After unlocking and pulling up the lumbering vintage wooden door, he notes that the garage is empty. James, his only sibling remaining at home, is at work. The garage is swept clean and quite organized. The left side is bare, other than the window that allows light to penetrate from the well that surrounds it. Jonathan recalls the baby bunny that got trapped in it when he was a boy. It could not hop out on its own, and it took him a good hour to get it to hop into a shoebox with which he lifted it to freedom. His mother seemed sardonic and unimpressed with his feat. "He'll just eat my beets," she had said.

On the right hangs the ancient bulky wooden ladder that weighs a ton. Below it hangs the heavy black rubber garden hose draped around the spigot and beyond hangs an assortment of lawn and garden tools, each on an 8d finish nail through the hole James has precisely drilled through the center four inches from the top of its handle. The hand tools are hanging in their proper places above the wooden bench their dad made. On the left is an intricately made tool chest, about thirty inches wide and eighteen inches high. The cherry finish emits a soft satin glow and the dark metal handles tastefully protrude. Jonathan is familiar with it, having frequently opened the green felt-lined drawers and curiously and admiringly fingered their dad's instruments as a boy. It was not his bailiwick, but Jonathan understood that his dad was not an ordinary mill worker but a skilled craftsman. It is something he remains proud of.

The green door into the cellar, hand constructed with a series of planks joined together by three others forming a Z, still serves well. It swings open smoothly when he lifts the latch, and he is surprised by how bright it is when he enters. The concrete floor James painted a grayish blue some years ago shines immaculately, and the concrete blocks that make up the foundation, painted a softer blue, gleam as well. Sitting mute in the back right corner, dominating the room is the gas furnace. The rope clothesline hanging from the floor joists waits to be assigned its next load from the same Maytag wringer washer Jonathan recalls from his childhood. He takes in the moist, warm, sweet scent of the Fels-Naptha soap his mother faithfully uses and listens for a moment to the chugging of the machine's agitator and the sloshing of the water. The Maytag maintains its special place of prominence in front of the two washtubs and the window that looks out onto a little sidewalk that accesses the outside spigot.

He kicks off his shoes and checks out the array of coats no one will likely wear again, still hanging from hooks attached to the same two-by-six, also now painted. His eyes move to the ironing board and white upright freezer that sit opposite the furnace. The old oak dining room table that had once hosted many feasts now holds a small stack of shirts to be ironed

He looks up the wooden stairs covered with black vinyl treads and sees it is dark at the top, which likely means the door is closed because the door to the porch is open. Ninety degrees to each other in the tiny kitchen, they both swing inward, which permits only one to be open at a time. As he climbs the stairs, he detects another pleasant welcoming odor, fresh bread, and knows that warm homemade bread with melting butter and canned blueberry jam awaits him. It does not get any better than that in his mind.

Once he has arrived at the top of the stairs, he pushes the cellar door open just enough to reach through and gently push the door to the porch enough to allow him to squeeze through. He steps into the kitchen and spies the bread cooling beneath towels. On a window sill above the stove sits the same radio he listened to as boy. Then it blared early sixties rock 'n' roll; now it softly emanates some classical piece. Looking out the back window, he sees white bed sheets flapping ever so gently in the gentle breeze.

"You're here," his mother says as she steps through the door with her laundry basket.

"Yep. It got too late to push through last night, so I slept in the car at a rest stop near Zanesville."

"You should've gone to Martha's. You could've slept there."

"No big deal. I don't remember where she lives. It's been so long since you and I went there to see Butchie. Besides, I really don't know your cousins very well. I'm not like James, who knows everyone and how everyone relates."

"You want some tea?"

"Yeah, I'll make it," he replies as he reaches for the old kettle.

While he fills the kettle with water and sets it on the stove to boil, his mother goes down to the cellar to finish the load of laundry. The familiar sounds of her movements and the running washing machine evoke memories of this most basic of household activities, repeated by her so many times in his childhood that he thinks he could perform it himself, though he never has. First, she stops the washer, runs the sheets through the wringer, and puts them in the rinse tub. Then she drops the hose to allow the soapy water to empty and once done, refills the machine with warm rinse water. She runs the sheets through the wringer again, puts them back into the machine, and lets them slosh a bit. She turns off the machine and runs them through the wringer again before putting them into the laundry basket for hanging.

While she hangs them on the clothesline, Jonathan makes his tea. After coming back into the kitchen, his mother puts a heaping tablespoon of Nescafé instant into her cup and pours the remainder of the hot water from the tea kettle, which nearly fills the cup. She reaches into the refrigerator, pulls out a glass quart bottle of milk, and adds some to her coffee. As usual, it spills over the top of the cup onto the stove. She slurps it down, adds a teaspoon of sugar, and stirs it. Again it sloshes over, and again she sips some to get it below the brim. Jonathan watches with bemused wonderment and awe, and when she looks up and sees him, she asks, "What?"

"Nothing. Just wondering why you don't put a saucer under it."

"It just gets dirty."

"So does the stove."

"So, I just wipe it."

Jonathan shakes his head, smiles, and concedes, knowing that once again, she has won the exchange. They carry their cups of brew into the dining room, which like the living room and kitchen, is painted a soft pink.

"So, how's teaching?" she asks after sipping more coffee.

"Great. I'm mastering it. I no longer need to create an intricate lesson plan. I know what I want to do—reading, grammar, etcetera—so I just make sure I have all the materials I need to do it. I'm really beginning to read the kids better, more aware of what is happening among them and which ones are in need of tutoring or a hug."

"Humph. I told you you'd be a better lawyer. Any thought about going back to law school?"

"I used to think about it, especially after a long night of grading papers or sitting through parent conferences, but not anymore. When I was first hired, I taught both English and American history. When they hired another teacher the next year, I got to teach English full-time, with an emphasis on American lit, and have been since."

"What grades?"

"Ninth and eleventh. I love them both. The freshmen can be fun, but juniors have become my favorite. I love the discussions we have. There's something magical about sixteen- and seventeen-year-old minds. They're past hormones, at least the raging ones, and begin to focus on life. It's as if they're opening their eyes for the first time intellectually and abstractly. So when Thoreau says, 'Simplify, simplify,' they get it. They don't do it, of course, but at least it's a seed planted in their fertile imaginations that one day might bear fruit."

"Good. How's everything else? Got any friends? Get close to anyone?"

"I do," says Jonathan nodding his head, "and I have."

They both sit quietly for a few moments, and Jonathan begins to feel his throat constricting and aching. He swallows and notices his breath becoming shallow and his skin warming. His mother sits quietly, staring out the window at the laundry as if she senses something is coming and wants to give her son space. He lifts his cup and sees it trembling ever so slightly in his hand. After taking a few sips, he sets it back on the table, takes a deep breath, and says, "Mum, I met a guy. In fact, I met him a few years ago. He's a priest, and I love him." And then after a long pause, he adds, "I'm gay, Mum."

His mother reaches down, lifts her mug, and takes a long sip. "I know. I've known it from when you were a little boy."

"Really? How come you never said anything?"

"Why? It's your life and you had enough to deal with without me embarrassing you any more than you were."

"How about the rest? Do they know?"

She takes another sip of her Nescafé and stares at the table as if she is trying to decipher a mystery ensconced in it. After a long pause, she looks back up at Jonathan and with a flat voice says, "No, probably not." And after another pause adds, "In fact, I know they don't."

Jonathan tells her all about Daniel while she listens attentively, breaking eye contact only to lift her cup.

"Well, when I was a little boy, I thought you expected me to become a priest," he says after his summary.

"No," she replies. "I didn't want that. I only wanted you to be happy . . . and be a lawyer."

"Well, how's one out of two?"

"I'll take that, but I do worry about you."

He tries to assure her. "I'm fine, Mum, honest. I don't go where I'm not safe."

"That's not what I worry about. Have you read about Rock Hudson? I don't want that happening to you."

"It's a scary time for us. I know. I think about it every day. I have friends who are sick, and it's put a real strain on Daniel and me and our relationship. But for some reason, I think we're both okay and will be okay. But if one or both of us is infected or gets infected, we'll have to live . . . or perhaps die . . . with it. We simply cannot change who and what we are, and we cannot live in fear under a rock, Mum.

"Ironically, I learned one of my most important lessons at my high school graduation when no one came. It was apparent I'd be on my own. That's okay. It wasn't pleasant, but I'm much stronger and better for it, that and being gay. To be honest, every once in a while I think of Ted and offer thanks for being gay, because without the grace of being gay, there might I have gone."

They sit in silence for a minute.

"Now, can I have a slice of bread with butter and jelly? That is the reason I drove fifteen hundred miles, after all."

She nods, goes to the kitchen, and brings back the slightly warm loaf of bread, along with butter, jelly, and utensils.

"Smells great, Mum," he says as she slices the bread. "I remember how you made sure to slice the bread very evenly so we'd all get the exact same size when I was a kid. It's a lesson I've carried over into my life and classroom. Fair is fair."

"Good," she says. "But now you can have as many slices as you want and as thick as you want."

"I like that, Mum, and extra blueberry jam, please."

She hands him his buttered and jellied bread. "Jonny, sorry I wasn't there."

"It's okay, Mum. You had a lot happening, and I've come to understand that it was the first step of a walk I'd have to do alone. It was good prep. No regrets."

"Never have them. Do your best and be satisfied knowing that you have."

"Sounds like something some guy sitting under a Bodhi tree said twenty-five hundred years ago."

November 2, 1995

AS THE CHOIR FINISHED, Jonathan looked up and saw the archbishop stand and ponderously limp back to the altar as if he were carrying an additional burden that tasked his crippled leg. Seemingly incapable of taking each of the three steps in a normal step up, he first raised his right leg and set his right foot on the lower step. Next, he slowly drew up his crippled left leg and placed his left foot next to his right. He repeated the process onto the second step, and then after a brief pause to catch his breath, he labored up onto the third and the main altar platform.

He whispered the prayers before Holy Communion, omitting the first as per the ritual of a Requiem Mass. Upon concluding them, he leaned forward and took the paten with both parts of the sacred Host into his left hand and raising his voice enough to be clearly heard, he said three times while striking his breast, "*Domine, non sum dignus, ut intres sub tectum meum, sed tantum dic verbo, et sanabitur anima mea.*"

"Lord, I am not worthy that you should come under my roof; but only say the word, and my soul will be healed." Jonathan recognized its allusion to Mathew 8:8 and recalled the biblical story of the Roman soldier who asked Jesus to heal his manservant. He wondered why a commander would plead for the life of his lowly servant . . . unless there was more to the relationship.

After making the sign of the cross with the sacred Host over the paten, he consumed the Host slowly and deliberately. Next, he uncovered the chalice that held the blood of Christ and after genuflecting, gathered the remaining particles and put them in the chalice. With the chalice, he made the sign of the cross again and then reverently drank the blood of Christ.

For what seemed several minutes, the archbishop stood in prayer facing the tabernacle, slightly bowed. The church remained perfectly still, and Jonathan could hear his own breath flowing, which caused him to concentrate on it, inhaling deeply on counts of eight and then exhaling in the same slow, deliberate pattern.

The archbishop genuflected slowly, seemingly in pain, as he struggled to raise himself back up. He opened the tabernacle and removed the ciborium, the chalice-like vessel that held consecrated Hosts to be distributed to the faithful who were free from sin. Taking one of the sacred Hosts in his right hand, he turned to the congregants, and while holding the sacred Host over the ciborium, said, "*Ecce Agnus Dei, ecce qui tollit peccata mundi.*" Then in synchronicity with the bells the server rang, he recited thrice the words he had said earlier, the words so similar to those spoken by the Roman soldier: "*Domine, non sum dignus, ut intres sub tectum meum, sed tantum dic verbo, et sanabitur anima mea.*"

∾o∾

Wednesday, October 28, 1987

Dear Brothers and Sisters,

As I approach the midpoint of this earthly sojourn, assuming I live long enough to reach my mid-seventies, I am sensing it is time to "officially" acknowledge something you might already have suspected: I am gay.

When back East last time, I was asked why I had not as yet gotten married. My response was, "That's a long story for another time." Well, I was wrong on both points. The story is not long, although it constitutes a major aspect of my life, and it should not have been saved for another time. The moment was there, but I chose not to seize it.

As a boy, I felt connected and had a sense of belonging to our home and to our church. But after entering puberty, I began feeling a pervasive sense of discomfort about my being and place. My feelings and desires and interests were not the same as those of my friends. They talked about girls and being with them, which was of no interest to me.

Ironically, I wanted to be with them, not just for friendship and fun times, but also to be intimate with a few. In fact, my first sexual activity began when I was not quite sixteen with one of them who will remain nameless for obvious reasons.

It was then that I began to explore what that meant. In an effort to understand, I reached out to a couple of my male teachers, which I realize now was a cry for help. Each did his best to support and guide me, but in the end, they could not resolve my conflict, and the turmoil wreaked havoc on my psyche. Over time, I came to understand that there was only one person who could resolve that conflict: me. What I have also come to understand is that my conflict was not with myself or nature but with others: individuals, groups, society in general, and the Church.

Since that time, I have known I am homosexual. I had, however, bought in to the Catholic belief that homosexual practices are sinful, and if I lived my life actively giving attention to my inclinations, hell would be my final destination. That debate naturally compounded my angst. Something was out of whack, was askew. With work, I was able to understand it was not me. That led to the journey, which in brief has led to this: I no longer believe in the Catholic Church, the communion of saints, the forgiveness of sins, the resurrection of the body, and all else related to the Church's teachings. What I do believe in is my Self and the goodness of my Being, being a part of the Godhead, the Eternal Source: Great Spirit and Mother Gaia.

In addition to the Catholic Church, I had family, friends, and society with which to deal. The term "queer" was bandied so routinely, I felt I could never admit to being one in those years. In addition to the derogatory, demeaning language, I received endless messages—both subtle and overt—suggesting I would be less of a human being for admitting I was gay. Essentially, I was shamed into compliance.

Sisyphus Wins | 215

In my young adult years, I tried opening up to a couple of close friends but got little support. They suggested I "change." In response, I wondered if it was possible that they could become homos. The answer is no, of course, given that this essential part of being comes with birth. On that note though, I do not blame them or any of you. We were all operating within a cultural construct predicated on fear, power, and compliance. Many of you still do and likely will continue to operate in that mindset. So it goes.

I sensed that if I stayed in Pittsburgh, an unhappy life and/or early unpleasant demise would be my destiny. So I moved to Colorado and, wouldn't you know, the very first friends I made, still my deepest friends to this day, accepted me without reservation or qualification. How different from there! Over time, I have developed many other friendships in Colorado with both men and women who have been nothing but accepting and supportive. In the process, they have become a virtual family for me.

One reason I remained closeted over the years from you but not them was the lingering compelling need for approval from my birth family. There was still that element of insecurity. It has taken me all these years of spiritual and psychological processing to get to this point. As a result, what I have come to understand is that I am a Being of the Eternal and that what I do, thus my character, is a large measure of That I Am. In other words, I now accept the totality of my Being, love who I am, and walk forth each day in a sacred way, intent to live from my higher self and to do what I can to make Earth a better place for all the Beings of God and Nature.

When I was at the reunion two years ago, I felt out of place. Partly that was due to my new life as a Coloradan, but the rest was due to me believing I had to continue with my charade of being someone I'm not. I felt compelled to be dishonest to be accepted among you without judgment, to be loved unconditionally.

In this plane of dualities, ironies, and contradictions, I am the same guy—boy, man, and brother—you knew, but who has, over time, morphed into a very different one by letting go of his fear. I was born gay with a deep spiritual aspect to my being. That has not changed. What has changed is how I see that and all the rest of this "reality." I blame no one for the manner in which my life is unfolding and work to find no fault or hold anger, for it is the path I chose to travel before I was born into this incarnation.

My journey has taken me along a completely different path. Politically, I have evolved into a social/political liberal and a spiritual Child of Nature, something you might call pagan. I do not worship God, but I work to feel identification with the divine through "right living," as Buddhists say, and meditative practices.

On this journey, I have also come to understand that there is no such thing as a coincidence. What happens is a synchronicity of events. I am excited about where the journey will take me next. My intention is to be with that man who will help bring personal happiness to me as I to him. In fact, there has been one with whom I have connected. Ironically, he is a priest. His family is fully aware of his orientation and for the most part rejoices in it—for, you see, they almost lost him. He has acted with courage to exorcise his demons, and if I am to be worthy of his love, I can do no less.

My worldview, defined more and more by the discoveries made by quantum physicists, holds that the possibilities are endless! This I believe, along with one other thing that gives me hope: Mum knows. We talked about it when I was there last, two years ago. When I opened up to her, I found I hadn't needed to because she said she knew it all along. I believe that. Good mothers know their children and accept them for who they are without reservation. Good fathers do as well, but ours didn't live long enough for him and me to get to know each other.

This letter, which I am sending to each of you, is simply about giving you new information or confirming something you may have suspected and whispered about. What you do with it is your choice. The only favor I ask is that you spare me the promise to pray for me in the sense of "saving my soul." What I will appreciate are prayers in the form of loving, compassionate, and supportive energetic thoughts. In the meantime, I have the rest of my life to live as a free spirit learning what I can of the Great Mystery and doing what I can to make this wondrous Earth a better place for all of the Beings of Nature.

Now that I have dropped that bombshell, I would like to propose something that I hope can bring us together.

This might sound crazy, but I would like to tell our dad's story. It would be about the man who sired us, who helped give us life. I have been researching his history and that of his time, and I have been putting it within the context of the stories I have heard mostly from you older ones. I am overwhelmed by the fullness of his life, the richness of his character, and the blessing each of us has from being one of his children.

I'm not sure what the biography will look like when all is said and done because it will undoubtedly take on a life of its own and unfold as it will. His energy/spirit has been my guiding force since that profound moment when driving to Mum's, I felt a "tap on the shoulder" and heard a "voice" say, "Drive to the cemetery." It was then and there that he and I began the conversation we could have had no other way because of his untimely death. That was new. From the time I was little, I felt despair and a sense of abandonment. "My father is dead, so I have no father" became my mental fallback and mantra. That, I am sure, is another reason I felt different: I was the only boy my age I knew without a father. But now, I sense he is not dead, but alive in each of us whether through his genes or the stories of him remembered and told.

For his story to be told, the participation of all his children is required. Within each of us, especially you older ones who were blessed to grow up when he was alive, is a remnant of fabric that, when woven together in story form, will be the tapestry not only of an amazing man, but also of his family.

This is, of course, the thirty-fourth anniversary of
his death. Sunday is All Saints Day and Monday, All
Souls Day. I mention this because, as I wrote earlier,
I no longer believe in saints, a heaven that is "out there,"
or the resurrection of the body. But I do believe in a
heaven on Earth where our spirit resides before and
after our physical life.

I'm sure Dad was no saint in the sense of having
lived a pure life. Who has? Nonetheless, when it comes
to getting the job done and right living, he was a saint
of this Earth. I like to think that he did his best. Have we?

In the end, this project will look like what it needs to.
It is the teacher and Aquarian in me. It is part of who I
am: a son of Isadore Aloysius Slovanco.

Namaste,

Jonny

November 2, 1995

JONATHAN LOOKED OVER TO his siblings, several of
whom were whispering while striking their breasts. When the
third recitation was finished, the four sisters, along with James
and Paul, stood, moved to the center of the aisle, and sidled
past the black-draped coffin, making their way to the front.
They knelt at the Communion rail as the archbishop carefully
descended the steps, limped to the Communion rail, and
stood in front of Elizabeth. She opened her mouth and stuck
her tongue out to receive the body of Christ.

The archbishop held the Host in front of her and prayed that the body of Christ would bring her to everlasting life.

Elizabeth softly said, "Amen," and the archbishop placed the Host on her tongue. As the archbishop stepped to his right to repeat the ritual with Ruth, Elizabeth stood and with eyes barely open, walked slowly back to her pew where she knelt and buried her face in her hands.

Jonathan remained kneeling and stayed with his breath work. He watched the archbishop after completing the ritual with Ruth and then with James, Juliana, Paul, and Mary Agnes. Each in turn returned to his or her place lost in prayer, either with closed eyes and head cast down or with faces buried in their hands.

Recalling the prayer he once had memorized and said silently after countless Communions, Jonathan turned pages until he found it and read it. "Behold O kind and most sweet Jesus, I cast myself on my knees in your sight, and with the most fervent desire of my soul I pray and beseech you that you would impress upon my heart lively sentiments of Faith, Hope, and Charity . . ."

As Jonathan read the reference to Christ's five wounds, he remained kneeling and visualized the scene on Golgotha in all its horror. He tried to meditate on it, but found he could not. The vivid depiction of the human bloodletting was incomprehensible, but no more than the thought that so many needed it to believe in a transcendent being. ". . . *having before my eyes that which David spoke in prophecy of You, O good Jesus: They have pierced my hands and feet; they have numbered all my bones.*"

In that moment, he realized that the mystery of faith had, over his lifetime, itself become mysterious. When he finally looked up, the archbishop had completed the post-Communion rituals and was once again struggling down the altar steps. He limped to the bench, the hobbled leg seemingly more painful as the Mass continued. The servers each took a side of his vestment and pulled it wide and the archbishop sank to the bench. The servers bowed to him, turned and bowed to the tabernacle, and sat, as did the congregants.

November 2, 1987, All Souls Day

Brother:

I have read your letter announcing your "coming out," as you homosexuals call it, with considerable consternation and dread for your soul. While the news is most disturbing, becoming a homosexual is your choice, one you will eternally rue. What is more disturbing, however, is your idea of writing a biography of our father. As paterfamilias, naturally and spiritually, I am forced to respond.

Sadly and calamitously for your eternal soul, you have decided to lead a life of perversion. If your goal is to find some sort of consolation in the notion our father would have approved of that decision, I can assure you he would have been neither proud nor tolerant. Not only would he have not accepted and approved of you and your choice, his wrath would have descended upon you in a fury, much like how the God of the prophets punished his chosen people when they strayed afar. I felt his swift arm of justice, and while I found no pleasure in feeling it then, I now profoundly appreciate his discipline. I am very much the man I am due to it.

Know this: If our father lived for you to benefit from his wrath and discipline, you would not be prancing in your soft effeminate world and being in danger of losing your immortal soul. He would have meted out a most severe discipline, which would have been nothing compared to our heavenly Father's wrath and the damnation awaiting you.

In his encyclical *Pascendi Dominici Danielis*: On the Doctrine of Modernists, Pope Saint Pius X recognized the danger and pitfalls of the diabolical work of Satan in modern thinking and anticipated its pervading influence. Even Holy Mother Church, he foresaw, would not be immune to Satan's work. Unlike the liberal modernists who seized control of our Church in Vatican II, I know the will and mind of God. Accordingly, I clearly recognize the hand of Satan in his perverse attempt to undermine the Kingdom of Heaven on earth.

With regard to you, not only am I most concerned for your soul, but I also question your mental state. You bizarrely claim you have been in psychic communication with him. That indicates you are not of sound mind and, thus, not a person to be trusted with such an undertaking.

Life was not easy after the tragedy that befell our father, but we stood strong. Our sainted mother has been our rock and beacon. You claim you told her about your perversion, and she said she was aware of it from the time you were a child. While I question that, I, nonetheless, accept your word, knowing it could have arisen only from a mother's most tender heart who was giving solace to her aggrieved child.

As to the proposed biography, I counsel you to reconsider. It would be most unwise. It would not only bring you ridicule and shame, but that same ridicule and shame would also be assuredly heaped on the rest of us. In like manner, I am imploring our brothers and sisters to not contribute to or support it in any way. Doing so will lead to one outcome: the disintegration of our family and the smearing of our great name.

My humble prayer, which I offer daily to our Lord and Savior Jesus Christ, is that you are not lost and that there is still within you a grain of guilt for your aberrant and disgusting behavior. Further, my hope is that this project is your way of clearing your conscience. If so, I kneel with humble gratitude before our Lord and Savior. Nevertheless, until you ask for forgiveness, atone for your sins, and return to the arms of Holy Mother Church, no good will come of it or to you.

Know, Jonathan, that I am here for you. Come to my church, confess your sins, and receive the Holy Eucharist, the body and blood of Jesus Christ. Only then can you save your soul from eternal damnation and confound the prince of evil and all his reprobates. Yours in Christ,
Theodore

November 2, 1995

JONATHAN BREATHED IN SLOWLY, noting the sweet abundance of incense pervading the air. The lacquer on the ancient pews came alive. He slowly began to take in the sights of his childhood, the statues of Saint Joseph on the right side of the altar and of the Blessed Mother on the left side. Along the sidewalls were statues of Saint William, Saint Patrick, and two others whose identities he had forgotten. The alabaster reconstructions of the stations of the cross that depicted Christ's final journey, carrying his cross through the streets of Jerusalem to Mount Calvary, had been hand painted to depict vividly the bloody horror of that day. Christ's torture and agony, along with the terror and hysteria of the women, could be seen on their faces.

Jonathan counted them in his mind as he reviewed them, beginning at the front left of the church and ending near the front of the right side, where he sat. There were seven on each side, fourteen in all: being condemned; accepting his cross; falling once; meeting his mother; assisted by Simon with his cross; his face being wiped by Veronica; falling a second time; speaking to the women; falling a third time; being stripped to his loin cloth; nailed to the cross; dying; being taken down from the cross; and finally being laid in the tomb.

Tilting his head back, Jonathan uplifted his gaze to the ceiling and took in the heavenly scene that prompted him as a boy, in all of his innocence, to reflect, *I'm no longer innocent, yet I AM. I'm no longer that boy, yet he's still here.*

He scanned the four evangelists and recalled how he was so fascinated and in love with their stories, especially Luke's depiction of the nativity. It was now myth for him, but it was still a beautiful story in its symbolic majesty. Peace on Earth, to men of good will. Craning his neck, he took in the balcony where the choir sat in their black robes. All men, even though the Church had, in a very tiny step towards inclusion, allowed women to sing. But not in this time and at this place.

He turned his gaze back to the front to the sanctuary and the little red light that hung in the front of it signaling Christ's presence. The pulpit stood stark on the left side, the great altar in the center, and the bench upon which the archbishop sat on the right. Jonathan could see only the left side of his face, which was focused resolutely on the pulpit. He closed his eyes and reflected on why it had come to this. When he opened them, he saw that the archbishop had ascended the altar and completed the ritual of washing the chalice. Jonathan turned his missal to the post-Communion prayer and read about beseeching God so that he would grant forgiveness for the souls of the departed and give them the bliss of eternal light because of this sacrament being performed.

The archbishop turned to the congregants and said, "*Dominus vobiscum.*"

"*Et cum spiritu tuo,*" replied the servers.

"*Requiescant in pace,*" said the archbishop.

∾o∾

Midnight, December 21, 1987

"HI," SAYS DANIEL.

Jonathan's voice is weak. "Hi, yourself."

Jonathan slowly scans the room as if he needs to be reminded that he is in a hospital. Everything is in order, from the bed with rails he is lying in to the intravenous drip attached to his arm.

"Sorry," he says.

"No need to be sorry. I'm happy and relieved you're here and going to be okay."

"I guess."

Jonathan lifts his arms and stares at the bandages on his wrists. He forces a half smile. "Did I make a mess?"

"Nothing a little soap and water couldn't clean up."

"Good. Thanks. Thanks for saving me."

"I think maybe something greater was at work here. I was supposed to be at the church for Christmas Mass rehearsal, but Father Roberts became concerned about the storm intensifying, so he sent us home. Otherwise, we might not be talking now or ever."

Jonathan nods his head. "I know. After you left, I sat watching the snow swirling around. I kept thinking about my graduation. No one from my family was there for me then either. I remember asking James for the car after I got back and saw there wasn't going to be a party or a gathering of any sort. I told him I was going to hang out at the bowling alley. Instead, I drove into Pittsburgh to the point where the three rivers meet. I walked along the banks of the Allegheny River, staring into its murky waters, then up onto the bridge where I stood and looked into the middle of the river. The dark, gray water was mesmerizing, gently flowing by. I was feeling sad and lonely. And lost.

"Then, out of nowhere, some guy tapped me on my shoulder. He completely startled me. He wasn't a bum or a drunk, just a decent looking older man. It was weird because few people walk along that bridge. When I turned and looked at him, he asked if I was okay. I lied and told him I was and was just out getting some fresh air. I remember the smile he put on his face, as if he understood and knew I was lying. So he said, 'Yeah, me too, but it's time to go back into town. It's getting late.'

"So we did. Neither of us said a word. He walked me to my car as if he knew exactly where I had parked. He shook my hand and said it was really important for me to go straight home and get some sleep because I would have a big day tomorrow. When I said it wasn't likely, all he said was, 'Of course you will because it'll be the first day of the rest of your life,' and then he just walked away.

"It sounded so trite, but somehow I sensed he was right. Something new was about to happen. But I still felt very sad."

"Maybe he was your guardian angel."

"I've wondered about that possibility."

They sit in silence, both reflecting. After a few moments, Jonathan looks up into Daniel's eyes and with a slight smile, nods. He looks back at his bandaged wrists and continues.

"After you left for choir practice, I kept thinking about that day and how I didn't feel worthy. And then I thought about the stretch of time when you and I split, and how lost I felt, and how I don't want to be alone anymore, and I thought, *No more. I'm tired of this shit.* Then I thought about the lunatic in the park who put the knife to my throat and the airman who flipped out and pulled his knife too, and maybe how I might've been better off if one of them had finished the job. So I drank some more and decided I could easily finish what they didn't.

"It was eerie, and I guess I finally snapped. Next thing I knew, I was lying here. When I saw the bandages, I knew what I had done. I asked the nurse, and she just smiled sweetly and said, 'You're gonna be okay, love.' And here you are."

Daniel pushes the blue sheets inward and sits on the bed. He reaches down and takes both of Jonathan's bandaged wrists in his hands. He looks into Jonathan's eyes and smiling softly and warmly, leans forward and kisses Jonathan on the forehead. "Jonathan, I love you," he says. "I know that what you did wasn't something you planned or wanted. I guess I can say I know exactly how you felt and are feeling. I was there too, remember?"

"Yeah, I remember."

"Do you also remember how filled with joy you were, how you felt after I told you about it, and that despite it all, I made it?"

Jonathan smiles more strongly. "Yeah."

"Well, that's how I feel now. So . . . thank you for being here and staying with me."

A larger smile forms on Jonathan and his eyes glisten. "Okay, I get it. Me too."

Daniel's voice becomes wistful as his eyes bore into Jonathan's. "Another thought comes to mind about your visitor that night. Maybe he was more than your guardian angel. Maybe he was your . . ."

Jonathan's eyes grow larger as he stares at Daniel trying to comprehend the magnitude of what his lover has just implied. "My dad? You think?"

"No one knows ultimate reality. Everyone creates and lives in a myth about what reality is. You were at your most desperate moment, consciously or unconsciously considering performing the ultimate act that night. Someone or some form approached and spoke to you. You weren't hallucinating. Not only did he talk to you, but he also walked you safely to your car. It sounds as if he knew everything about your circumstances and he wanted you to be safe."

Jonathan allows the possibility to percolate in his mind. After a few moments, he looks back up into Daniel's eyes. "And maybe he arranged for the storm to hit so you could get to me in time too."

Daniel nods.

"Maybe he hasn't left me after all. Perhaps he's been with me my entire life, protecting me the whole time. God knows I've needed it. It's crazy to think, but—"

"No, it's not crazy to consider. At least, it's no crazier than belief in the resurrection."

Again they sit quietly, allowing Jonathan to ponder the possibility and the strength of this new insight. Daniel reaches down for the cup of water and puts the straw up to Jonathan's lips. He takes a couple of sips. After setting the cup back on the tray, Daniel's eyes narrow as if he is focusing to make a statement that might not be received well.

"I haven't contacted your family yet, but I think they should know."

Jonathan becomes agitated. "No! I don't want them to know. If they cared, they would've reached out by now. But they don't. Even if they care, they've been silenced."

"At least your mother should know."

"No, especially not Mum. I don't know what this would do to her. She's the toughest woman I have ever known, but she's been pretty fragile since her stroke. And after her closest brother, Uncle Leo, took his life, the last thing she needs to hear is that her own son tried to do the same. No, she's had enough to endure."

Daniel sits quietly.

"No, Daniel, please. I'm going to make it. What I did was stupid, but as you know, I get so down anyway at this time of year. I hate these short days. I get depressed. But now it's Solstice and the days will get longer. I know my spirits will improve. I promise."

Daniel nods his consent. "Okay. But you have to promise me also you'll start seeing your therapist again. You have to talk about this. You can't keep it all inside. If you keep repressing it, my fear is something like this will happen again."

"Okay, deal. But you have to promise me something in return."

"What?"

"You'll never leave me again."

Daniel takes Jonathan's two bandaged wrists and leans forward to kiss him again. "Deal," he says.

∽o∾

November 2, 1995

THE ARCHBISHOP TURNED BACK to the altar as the congregants remained seated and knelt, rapt in recitation. Jonathan read from his missal the prayer asking that the tribute of the archbishop's worship and the sacrifice he offered be pleasing to God.

18

Saturday, October 28, 1995

JONATHAN SITS AT THE BREAKFAST bar sipping a steaming cup of green tea and gazing at the denuded aspens in their front yard. The suns shines brightly and the wind is blustery, but without leaves, the branches merely tremble and quiver. Stoic in their stances, the aspens demonstrate their resilience and strength, remaining resolute despite the infernal buffets with which nature's wind pounds them.

"Checking in," says Daniel.

Jonathan winces, startled. He nods as he looks up at Daniel. "I'm doing okay. Mary Agnes's message wasn't unexpected. To be truthful, it's a relief."

"Did she leave any details?"

"No, it was straightforward. Basic facts. No emotion. Funeral will be Thursday."

"Have you decided whether to go?"

"I'm back and forth. On the one hand, she gave me life and will always be my mother. On the other, she's basically been dead these past eight years."

"I know how difficult it has been for you knowing how incapacitated she was."

"There was no point going back to see her with her being comatose since her stroke. It's as if we collapsed when she did.

Other than an occasional call or letter from Ruth or Andy, as you know, there's been little communication between them and me since."

"Sad."

"The power of a fatwa. Salman Rushdie isn't alone."

"How about we go for a nice drive? Maybe up Wolf Creek Pass. We haven't been there for some time and the road should be clear. It's early, so we'd be there by lunch."

"That's a great idea. Get the truck ready and I'll pack us a lunch."

"Put a couple of Guinness in the cooler too. It looks like that high-pressure system sitting on the Four Corners is going to continue giving us some great autumn weather. It will be wonderful to sip a cool one up there."

"Yeah, the conditions, unfortunately, are not promising for skiing soon. Still, they're perfect just to be."

"Do you think you should make a flight reservation before we head out, just in case? You can always cancel it."

"No, if I go, I'll drive. It will give me time to ponder—or brood, more likely. I can be there by Wednesday evening even if I leave Monday after dropping off my lesson plans."

"What about getting back to school?"

"I have five days of bereavement coming, so I'm good through the week. Plus, I have personal days and tons of unused sick days. So it won't be a problem."

"Sounds good. I'll top off the gas and clean the windshield while you're packing the lunch."

Thirty minutes later, Daniel and Jonathan are heading west on I-70 with Daniel driving and Jonathan lost in his thoughts. Neither says anything over the next two hours until they crest Poncha Pass. Daniel slows and steers their F-150 onto the gravel. "Pit stop," he says.

Jonathan notices his bladder is now full and appreciates stopping. "Good."

The men step from the truck, which Daniel has parked lengthwise to give them more privacy, despite there being few vehicles on the road. They unzip and relieve themselves on the weeds, both staring at and taking in the deep blue sky and inhaling the refreshing mountain breeze, which is uncharacteristically warm for being at nine thousand feet elevation in late October.

After another stop in Del Norte, where they gas up and grab a snack from the luncheon, they begin the final push on US 160 up Wolf Creek Pass. As Daniel negotiates the curves and switchbacks, Jonathan erupts. "He tasks me, he heaps me."

"Oh, give it up. You're not Melville, and he's certainly no killer whale. You're sounding like a pretentious bastard playing Ahab. Despite what you claim, Jonathan, you're still filled with anger and bitterness. If you hope to grow spiritually, you need to let go and learn forgiveness."

"I want to say that's easy for you to say, but I know it's not. Still, I can't let it go. All I wanted to do was tell a story of an incredible man who did amazing things despite the odds. Did I ever tell you my dad and I share something horribly tragic? We both lost our fathers when we were very little boys. He was only five when my grandfather was killed in a factory accident."

"You never told me about how your grandfather died. Interesting. It makes you wonder how that affected your dad growing up. I imagine even though a boy still has his mother, something powerful happens to him when he loses his father, especially when he's so young. It must be like half of his soul is ripped from him."

"That's the perfect way to describe it."

"I've had my father my entire life, and even though he puts on the front of accepting me for who I am, I know he despises it—and me, of course. To be honest, there were times I wished he was dead. I don't any longer, or at least I believe I don't still harbor that awful thought."

Jonathan mutters while shaking his head. "God, I hate this. I thought I had moved past all this, let go of the anger. But right now the idea of going back there is pushing buttons I long thought were defused."

"That's the way it works. We have to go through the talking stage, which you've done with your therapist, but until we're faced with the issue in real time, we don't know if we have, in fact, moved past it. That's part of what Buddhists call practice. Practice isn't only meditating; it's doing real stuff in real time. That's Zen. That's where the action is, not in some temple or church or mosque or stupa."

Daniel and Jonathan cruise in silence for a few miles with Daniel thoroughly enjoying every hairpin curve. He swerves to dodge a boulder that has rolled onto the road.

"You've had a lot of shit in your life. Your dad was killed by a bullet meant for nothing. It robbed him of his life and each of you the joy and necessity of his presence. It was an accident, no doubt about it, but it still happened. You don't remember it because you were too young, yet you do remember it. Memory doesn't begin at age four or five simply because we can pull incidents from that time forward out of our long-term memory. It begins at the moment of birth. Some argue even beforehand, while we're in the womb.

"You're gay, raised in a parochial, traditional family and culture. They don't get it and probably never will. Because they're afraid—afraid of truth upsetting their myth that is grounded in dogma. As your philosophic hero, Albert Camus, says, we find comfort in familiarity and clarity. It's nostalgia for unity, the essential pulse of human drama.

"But excessive longing leads to extremism, which in religion is fundamentalism. Catholics don't have a monopoly on it. Every dogmatic religion has its fringe, its loonies, its fanatics. Samuel Johnson saw patriotism as the last refuge of the scoundrel. Likewise, absolute truth in the form of fundamentalism and never-bending tradition becomes the last refuge of the weak-minded."

Daniel reaches over and takes Jonathan's hand in his.

"Look at your brothers and see how they've been impacted by it all. James is still at home and devoted to his mother's care, unable to make social connections, and he likely never will. Where does he go now? What's his life purpose? Christopher, the brightest, keeps searching for comfort and answers at the bottom of a bottle. Dutiful Paul never got past his Vietnam nightmare. And Andy, God love him, is so creative but so addicted to the shit he got hooked on in Haight-Ashbury. He was the only one your father never held. Don't you think he knows that?

"Your sisters amble on, trying their best. Elizabeth seeks answers in alternative religion; Ruth in her children; Juliana, like her eldest brother, in fundamentalism, and Mary Agnes in avoidance. That's the reason they hold family reunions. It's the same reason they have unquestioned faith: They crave familiarity, clarity, and unity. Thus, they lock onto something called tradition. And as Melville has taught us, the paths of tradition are deep and rutted.

"They're Catholic for the same reason they enjoy and make *holubky*: Your mother was Catholic and she made *holubky*. It's that simple. Unquestioned faith is learned and gives rise to behaviors, like rituals, that provide unity.

"You can allow your anger and bitterness to consume you, to dictate the remaining course of your life's journey, or you can let it go. It's that simple. As we both know, life is a never-ending exercise in making choices. It's in your power, Jonathan, to give up control, to let go of power."

Daniel squeezes Jonathan's hand more tightly, and the two men sit quietly while Daniel steers competently with his left hand.

"Forgive Theodore," says Daniel.

"Forgive him? That's God's job, not mine!" Jonathan shakes his head. "I wish I could. I truly do. I'm simply unable."

"You're simply unwilling. It's pride. You feel you're the victim, so you relish playing the victim. It's the martyr complex helping to justify your suffering."

"No, Daniel, it's not that, at least I don't believe it is. It's as if the ability to forgive anyone for any offense is no longer part of me. Maybe it's because I've been pounded enough, I can no longer be hurt or wounded. And if I can't be wounded, there's no need to forgive."

Jonathan pauses and reflects shaking his head. "I want to. I want to forgive him and all the others. I truly do, but if I would say, 'I forgive you,' it would be a lie, not because I don't mean it or don't want it to be, but because it isn't a fact."

"Okay. Your heart has become numb. But that's a choice as well. Numbness is a choice, like an addiction."

At the top of the pass, Daniel pulls into the roadside parking area. Four other vehicles sit empty, their occupants out walking through the few inches of snow remaining from the last week's snowfall. The sky is absolute blue, and the few pearls adrift overhead mimic in their shapes the mountains they look down on.

Jonathan and Daniel step out, each grabbing his windbreaker from behind his seat and pulling it on. Jonathan walks around the back of the truck toward Daniel. They stand for a moment in silence. Daniel reaches down and takes Jonathan's right hand in his left and they make their way up onto the tundra. Near tree line they spot a boulder to sit on and climb atop it to sit, keeping their faces toward the sun. The warm breeze gently refreshes them. Daniel puts his right arm around Jonathan's shoulders and pulls him close.

"Forgive him," he says.

Jonathan is resolute. "It's not up to me to forgive him. He has to forgive himself."

"The second part is true. He has to forgive himself. Nevertheless, you have the power to let go of him. That's what forgiveness ultimately is—breaking the power two people have over one another. He wounded you badly with what he wrote, and that act gave you power over him. But ironically, by holding on to your anger, he has regained power over you. To break that, you have to let go, to forgive. It is then up to him. It will be up to him if he wants to allow his anger and fear and ignorance to control him so much that he'll go to his grave with it. If so, then he'll have to deal with that in the afterlife."

"There's no such place as hell."

"I'm not saying there is, but there is an accounting once we pass over. That's the reason we're here: to learn lessons and practice outcomes. Call it the Last Judgment or whatever you want, but something happens. Joseph Campbell says life has no meaning, that each person has to give it meaning. For me, the accounting of ourselves in the afterlife is what gives this life meaning."

The two men sit for some time taking in the world of nature around them. Picas cheep while scurrying over the mountain rocks. A marmot scampers nearby, positioning himself for a handout if one were to be had. Against the deep blue sky, a hawk soars, eyeing it all, scoping out and sizing up potential dinner.

"The opportunity is at hand. The funeral is Thursday. What remains of your tribe will be there."

Jonathan sighs. "Yes, they will. You sure you won't come?"

"No, it's your moment. You need to do this. Besides, I have that fundraiser for the homeless to arrange. But know I will be there with you."

Jonathan nods, takes a deep breath, and sighs. "My throat hurts so much. It's throbbing . . . the memories flooding back."

"Yep, that's where you've stored the pain, in your fifth chakra—there and in your fourth, your heart. It's the reason you find giving voice to your stuff and forgiving those who've wounded you so difficult. But the heart center is where courage lies. Remember the root for courage is the Latin word *cors*, which means 'heart.' Just as the Cowardly Lion had to find his courage, so do you. The irony is that the lion, like you, already had courage; he simply needed to have it pointed out."

He pauses and then adds, "But, of course, you know that better than me."

Jonathan looks up directly into his eyes and smiles. "I," he says.

"Don't avoid the issue, mister perfect English."

Daniel jumps down from the boulder, stands in front of Jonathan, and reaches out to grasp his hands. He turns Jonathan's wrists upward and studies his scars as if deciphering a message. "It's your call."

Jonathan follows Daniel's gaze down to the scars, focuses on them, and inhales a deep breath of the thin but revitalizing mountain air. "That I do know. But somehow, Daniel," he says as he looks back up to Daniel's eyes, "I feel as if this is to be my funeral."

"Perhaps it will be. Recall, though, the Buddha's instruction of samsara, the great cycle of existence. If it is to be your funeral, it will also be the final act before your resurrection and rebirth."

Jonathan sits quietly staring at the snow and the vegetation that has found sunlight. With his hands still held by Daniel, he looks up into his life partner's eyes. "Maybe. But maybe, Daniel, it's to be our funeral, my whole family's funeral."

That night, while sitting in bed reviewing the lesson plans he has prepared for the week, Jonathan checks the assigned readings as laid out in the course syllabus. The chapters include the one in which Melville describes the White Whale in depth and how even Ishmael became delirious with the idea of killing Moby Dick. From his copy of *Moby Dick*, he read a portion of that chapter. "I, Ishmael, was one of that crew; my shout had gone up with the rest; my oath had been welded with theirs; and stronger I shouted, and more did I hammer and clinch my oath, because of the dread in my soul. A wild, mythical, sympathetical feeling was in me; Ahab's quenchless feud seemed mine."

Jonathan pauses and takes a sip of his warm herbal tea. He sits and reflects, becoming aware of the significance of the reading. He reads on several more pages, finally getting to the excerpt that seems timely in a ghostly way. ". . . All that most maddens and torments; all that stirs up in the lees of things; all truth with malice in it; all that cracks the sinews and cakes the brain; all the subtle demonisms of life and thought; all evil, to crazy Ahab, were visibly personified, and made practically assailable to Moby Dick. He piled upon the whale's white hump the sum of all the general rage and hate felt by his whole race from Adam down; and then, as if his chest had been a mortar, he burst his hot heart's shell upon it."

A haunting possibility dawns on him. *Oh my God, is that what I've become?*

19

November 2, 1995

WITH BOTH HANDS FIRMLY clutching the altar, the archbishop struggled to stand. For a few moments he stood facing the altar with his back to the congregation. Jonathan looked over to his siblings and noted the looks of concern on several of their faces. Ruth leaned over to Elizabeth and whispered. When he was able to face the congregants, the archbishop took three short halting steps forward and then, one last time, began his descent to the foot of the altar. One of the servers walked to the communion rail, unlatched the gate, and opened both doors wide. He returned to his place at the foot of the altar to await the archbishop.

The acolytes stood, took the candles from the large brass holders, and walked single-file, three from each side, towards the center of the sanctuary to form two rows. They genuflected, turned, and marched out of the sanctuary and past the bier where they stopped and then turned once again towards the altar. Meanwhile, the servers each had retrieved the two instruments the archbishop would need to complete the ritual: a holy water sprinkler and an incense burner that swung from a chain. The archbishop had waited for all to be in order, and once satisfied it was exactly as it needed to be, he followed the retinue out of the sanctuary.

The servers stepped out first, each moving to his side to face the casket. The archbishop stepped from the sanctuary, raised his arms wide, and prayed asking God not to judge their mother harshly nor give her the punishment she deserved. Jonathan clenched his jaw and shook his head, incredulous. He looked up and studied the visage of the stern God that struck fear into him as a boy and shook his head again. He lowered his head and looked across to the statue of the Blessed Mother with her arms outstretched as if beckoning all into her embrace, the words of the Memorare that he faithfully and earnestly prayed each night as a boy flooding back into his consciousness. The conflicting images and messages stunned him.

The archbishop's resolute voice brought his attention back to the ritual.

"From the gate of hell," he said.

The choir responded. "Rescue her soul, O Lord."

Jonathan stood transfixed, bewildered at the words he was hearing. *We should be celebrating her life and deeds, not begging that she not be damned.*

Jonathan tilted his head back one last time to view the heavenly scene as the archbishop's solemn voice intoned the concluding prayer, again beseeching God that she not endure the pains of hell but possess everlasting joy.

At that, the grand, old organ churned and the choir sang the final hymn praying that the angels might welcome his mother into paradise. As they sang, the acolytes turned in unison towards the back of the church, waited for the archbishop, who was preceded by the two servers, and began the procession out of the maw. The four brothers stepped from their pew and each taking a corner, began pushing the bier. The sisters followed two abreast.

Jonathan looked to his right to the aisle where the confessional booth sat. He took a sidestep towards it, paused, and turned to look at his departing sisters.

No, he thought, *you haven't a choice. This has gone beyond your power and our ken.*

As he inhaled and absorbed the mournful strains of the hymn, Jonathan stepped to the center aisle and followed the entourage through the vestibule and into the courtyard. The heavy oak doors that had been propped open fought valiantly against the wind that sought to make all in its path do its will. Flakes of snow swirled and danced at the wind's pleasure. The archbishop's vestments did likewise, as did the garb of his assistants and the outerwear of the mourners.

The brothers pushed the bier through the accumulating wet snow to the hearse where they lifted and slid the coffin into it. Only it was safe from the storm.

The archbishop turned to the family to give his blessing and, with a look that indicated unpleasant surprise, seemed to have finally seen Jonathan, who was standing just outside the church doors. His voice was hoarse but stern. "Why have you come here? You are anathema to us."

"I come, brother, as a witness to the Light and to honor our dear mother."

The archbishop swept his arm towards the gathered. "Vile as you are, you are not welcome among us. You soil our name. Your perversion desecrates the rest of us. You are little more than a cancer, a lesion excreting pus upon our body."

"Thank you for the warm welcome, brother. But I am only

That I Am. I did not create me. I come now as I came into this world, naked and innocent."

"Innocent? By your own admission, you are guilty of engaging in the most despicable of behavior. Sodomy is the vilest of sins."

"Strange. As I recall from my catechism, sodomy isn't even listed. Lust is, but then, every man, including you, I'm sure is guilty of that. Pride is chief of the deadly sins. I believe it's written in Proverbs that pride goeth before destruction; and a spirit is lifted up before a fall."

"Using Holy Scripture to lead the faithful astray is Satan's diabolical trick. My body might be broken, and soon I might be facing God's judgment, but my mind is clear."

"Well, Your Excellency, if there's anything I can do to speed up your meeting with God, please let me know."

"I have no time for your juvenile taunts and insults. I have dedicated my life to truth and exposing and combating error no matter where it lay."

"I've no doubt you're most proud of that, but in that pursuit, most reverend brother, you have littered your wake with detritus of broken minds and crushed spirits and shattered an entity that held incredible potential. You're no different than the religious fanatics in Iran who held our hostages. It's only in the outer expression do you differ from them."

Jonathan's voice rose as he pointed towards his brothers and sisters. "Each of us bears scars for your zealotry. And I bear the physical ones!"

He pulled up his sleeves and thrust his wrists in front of the archbishop's face. His voice trembled with rage. "Look! Look at my scars! Yes, I made the cut, but your hand was on the blade." He seethed as he held his arms aloft for all to see. "Your words and judgment and condemnation went beyond rebuke to shame. Those were the blades that cut me first and most deeply."

Jonathan stepped towards his brother, the archbishop, and as he did, the archbishop took a halting step backwards. Jonathan continued while pointing his finger at his brother, now an old man. "It's one thing to pursue mania within a religion in which only those who believe in it have a stake in the crusade. But to do likewise within your own family shows the mind of a fanatic, an inquisitor who would burn his own mother at the stake," Jonathan said, pointing to the hearse, "if he suspected her."

Jonathan stopped and looked around at the scene that enveloped them: the snow on the ground, the snow on the hearse, and the snow on the shroud of his indefatigable, mighty eldest brother in stark contrast to his black vestment. The wind whipped the ribbons of his brother's miter and the silky hair strands that escaped from beneath.

Jonathan lowered his voice. "Oh, I admit I held tightly to the arms of our mother. Yes, I was a girlie boy, a sissy from your perspective, a fag, a queer. I own that . . . proudly. Now it's time for you to own your crap. We all know what you did, but the ultimate question is why. The military didn't need you. The Church didn't need you."

Jonathan pointed to the hearse and once again raised his voice as he pointed at the hearse. "She did!" Then he pointed to his brothers and sisters. "And they did!" Finally pointing to his own chest, he said, "And I did!"

The archbishop pointed his trembling finger at his

youngest brother and shrilly shouted, "You fool! Heed our Savior's call, or you will not escape Satan's grasp. Ask for forgiveness. I can bestow God's mercy."

"At one time, brother, I bought in to that story, that long, arduous piece of bullshit. I no longer do, and I've forgiven myself for falling for such claptrap. I've forgiven myself for feeling shame, for buying in to the idea that I was less than human because of this very special and very beautiful aspect of my nature. I've forgiven myself for not figuring it out sooner, but that's the power of shame.

"I've forgiven myself, too, for putting others at risk. You, though, will never understand what that means because you refuse to. I've forgiven myself, completely, and if you have hope of redemption, that's what you must do.

"The Sermon on the Mount wasn't all pie-in-the sky. Jesus laid out some pretty heavy stuff. Recall the admonition in Matthew, brother: 'If therefore thou offer thy gifts at the altar, and there thou remember that thy brother hath anything against thee; leave there thy offering before the altar, and go first to be reconciled to thy brother: and then coming thou shalt offer thy gift.'"

Jonathan stopped and closed his eyes, clenching his fists, breathing hard and deeply. When he opened his eyes, he became aware of his brothers' and sisters' bewildered, anxious, and helpless looks fixed on him. They were in the audience rather than being players in this tragedy. This scene was his alone. He had to speak and act his truth. This was his moment, the final step in the firing of his soul's mettle in the crucible.

"Theodore, I know not where my life's journey is taking me hereon, but," he said pointing to the building, "I know the hell from which I have escaped." Jonathan shook his head and bore deep into his brother's eyes. "Why, Theodore? What caused you to be so hardened, so unforgiving, so judgmental? Not one of us holds you responsible for our father's death. It was a hunting accident, pure and simple, a bullet gone astray. Your shot went high. I'm sure Dad understood the risks of hunting. And in my own way, I know Dad does not blame you either.

"But in your manic obsession, you've killed us. This death isn't the result of an unintentional bullet, but of intentional, vindictive malice. It mattered not to you what might befall everyone else as long as you felt justified."

The archbishop's voice weakened and cracked as he spoke. "Don't you understand? I speak God's word. I can save you."

"No, I don't need to be saved from anything, but you ought to be worried since it's you who will be going to hell according to your faith."

Raising his trembling hand, the archbishop made the sign of the cross towards Jonathan. "*Libera nos a malo,*" he said. Then raising his arms as if in supplication, the archbishop tilted his head back, clutched his heart, and, looking up into the falling snow, cried out, "*Dominus!*" He sank to his knees on the shroud of snow and slush, then fell on his back, his miter toppling beside him.

His brothers rushed to him. Paul lifted his head, cradling it while James loosened the fabric around his neck. The archbishop coughed and gasped and pleaded through his hacking. "A priest, please call me a priest."

As the pallbearers lifted their brother from the slush-covered concrete and lay him on the bier, a man stepped from behind, touched Jonathan on his shoulder, and nodded. He moved to the archbishop and leaned over him. "I'm a priest," said Father Daniel. "I'll hear your confession."

Putting his ear atop the archbishop's mouth, Father Daniel listened attentively to the whispering. After a moment, he stood erect and, placing his right hand on the archbishop's forehead, said, "Let us pray for our brother, Theodore." Making the sign of the cross three times he said, "In the name of the Father, and of the Son, and of the Holy Spirit, let there be extinguished in you all power of the devil by the imposition of our hands, and by the invocation of the glorious and holy Mother of God, the Virgin Mary, and of her illustrious spouse, Saint Joseph, and of all the holy angels, archangels, patriarchs, prophets, apostles, martyrs, confessors, virgins, and of all the saints together."

Father Daniel reached into his pocket and removed a small can of oil for the blessing of the sick and dying. After dipping his fingers into the *Oleum Infirmorum*, he anointed the archbishop's eyelids, ears, nostrils, lips, hands, and his soiled and soaked red slippers. With his arms opened over the archbishop, Father Daniel continued praying. Last, he made the sign of the cross and said, "May Almighty God bless you, Father, Son, and Holy Ghost."

Father Daniel turned and stepped in front of Jonathan, peered deep into Jonathan's eyes, and held his gaze. After what seemed eternity, Jonathan lowered and then closed his eyes. He took several deep breaths, opened and raised them, and again looked into his lover's eyes, which were still riveted on him. He nodded, smiled sadly, and noted his throat opening and the mist forming in his own eyes. Jonathan stepped past Daniel over to his brother.

Reaching down and interlacing his fingers through the archbishop's chilled, bony ones, Jonathan peered into the face of the old man who firmly condemned him. Then he looked up and gazed through the prism of the swirling snow at the building in which he had once found protection and safety, warmth and comfort. Its doors were shut tight and its stained glass windows covered in white, enshrouding the scenes they depicted. In the background he heard a siren from an ambulance likely rushing to his stricken brother's aid. The chilly gusting wind cut through him, his siblings, who had formed a circle to help shield their brother, and the entourage standing like the chorus in a Sophocles tragedy.

Still focused on the red brick edifice, he said, "It's a strange world we live in, Master Jack." He shifted his eyes downward and studied Theodore's drawn and pallid face. The old man slowly opened his eyes, so slightly that it was likely only Jonathan could detect it. Jonathan squinted and peered deep into them, feeling his throat constricting slightly. He took a deep breath and then felt the constriction ease. "So, I guess I'd be remiss if I didn't thank you for all you've taught me."

In a gesture unseen by no one but Jonathan, his brother gave him a nearly imperceptible nod. Barely raising the fingers of his right hand, the archbishop made the sign of the cross saying with shallow breath, "*Benedicat te omnipotens Deus, Pater, et Filius, et Spiritus Sancus.*"

Jonathan nodded, and squeezing his brother's hand firmly said through glistening eyes, "*Etiam te absolvo.*"

20

Good Friday, April 3, 2015

"DID HE SUFFER?" JONATHAN asks Mary Agnes.

"No. I don't think he felt much of anything since his stroke at Mum's funeral."

"Perhaps the time since serves as his purgatory."

"That's a good way of looking at it. Will you come back for the funeral?"

"No, there's no point. It's done. He and I made our peace. I'll leave it to you and your sisters to close it up."

Mary Agnes's tone becomes firm. "Our sisters! With Theodore now gone, you're our only brother. I know this is the last place on earth you want to be, but we're still family. If you'd come back, you'd be able to see everyone. It would be wonderful for your nephews and nieces and now your grandnephews and grandnieces to meet and get to know their mysterious uncle."

"A funeral is probably not the best time for reacquainting, but I'll think about it."

"If not the funeral, then maybe for our reunion. We're planning July."

"I'll think about it, but no promises." Jonathan pauses before continuing. "Truth be known, I miss my brothers, Mary Agnes."

"And not your sisters?"

"I don't mean it in a casual way. There's something about relationships between brothers. It can't be described, never addressed, never acted upon, and not realized until they're gone. Maybe it's a guy thing. We are not allowed to say or cannot say 'I love you' like sisters do. And too often, we die without saying those words to each other.

"Think about them: James, the nurturer and provider; Christopher, the intellect; Paul, the protector; and Andy, the lost sheep. Not one of them was able to come to grips with Dad's death."

"Actually, that's something we sisters have talked about among ourselves as we watched you guys go your ways."

"I understand you spread their ashes over our old garden."

"We did. We thought it fitting. James would never leave that house and was so great taking Andy in after Mum's death. He tried to help him, but Andy just couldn't break his heroin addiction. James just wasted away after he found Andy in the garden dead from an overdose. As for Christopher, the bottle finally won, and after all those years, Paul was eaten alive by the Agent Orange sprayed on him in Vietnam, his gift for his service to his country. And now we'll spread Theodore's ashes there too."

"Sounds like their Garden of Gethsemane."

"Now that you say that, I think you're right. Way too much suffering."

"What about the house? If you're going to spread Theodore's ashes there, someone in the family must own it."

"That's true. Elizabeth's boy Gabriel bought it from the estate and lives in it with his wife and children."

"Well, good. I like that. But back to the idea of me coming back for the funeral, as I said, no promises. We didn't get much snow this past winter, so the mud season will end earlier. I really want to finish summiting the rest of the fourteeners.

"How many more do you have?"

"I've bagged fifty, so only four more to go. I'm thinking two in July and two in August though I probably could climb the last one in September. I'll let you know."

"I know it's asking a lot, so I appreciate your thinking about it."

"You're right, Mary Agnes. It's time to let go. Time to let go of the rock I've been pushing up the hill for the past fifty years."

"I think I get what you mean," says Mary Agnes.

21

July 10, 2015

CLIMBING ANY FOURTEENER IS no small feat, but Holy Cross, even though it barely qualifies being a mere five feet over fourteen thousand feet, presents its own challenges. The distance from trailhead to summit is a very long hike, and it is not a straight climb. As a result, many adventurers choose to camp overnight near the East Cross Creek crossing and do the ascent the next day on fresh legs. The more intrepid, or foolhardy from another perspective, opt to complete it in one day.

Pausing to take a draw from his hydration pack a few hundred feet above the 11,600 tree line point, Jonathan surveys what he can see of the climb ahead. What remains hidden is the peak, 2,400 feet above. The trail immediately ahead, though, is solid with no real obstacles. But from his previous attempt, he recalls boulders beyond that will require work, both up and down. He considers them part of the challenge, and they add to the sense of accomplishment.

Given that the mountain was named for its couloir, which the very Catholic Spanish explorers saw as cross-shaped, it is not surprising for a climber with a weighted pack to make a connection between what he or she is doing and carrying a cross, albeit without the ignominious and excruciatingly painful outcome. So while it is true that climbing Holy Cross is not analogous to climbing Golgotha, within a certain context it is.

As he prepares to resume his climb, Jonathan catches the image of a hiker emerging from the trees moving at what seems a strong and steady pace, unlike his. For a stretch of time whenever the trail switches back, he can see the hiker making steady progress towards him and the summit. At about 12,500 feet, Jonathan stops to refresh from his water bladder and realizes the hiker, who is now only about a hundred feet below, is the young man he saw in the parking lot. He takes note of the fact that he is traveling light, hiking in sneakers and wearing shorts and a T-shirt with only a small hip pack strapped on.

What strikes Jonathan as more unusual than being inadequately prepared is the young man stopping to chat when he catches up. Men rarely do that when hiking alone, especially younger, attractive ones. A nod or good morning might be the best one elicits in terms of a greeting and recognition. The young man reveals he is from San Diego, which he pronounces, paradoxically, with a nasal New England accent, and is on his way there from Cambridge, Massachusetts. He has decided to bag a few fourteeners that are adjacent to the I-70 Corridor: Bierstadt, Grays, Torreys, and Holy Cross, which is his last.

Not wishing to alarm or embarrass him but becoming concerned that the young man is inadequately prepared for such a climb as Holy Cross, Jonathan volunteers that while it is likely he need not worry about rain that day, he should still be cognizant of other situations that can add to the challenge of a hike. "The atmosphere is fairly dry and stable, but still, it's always good to summit and start back by noon because you never know with lightning."

After thanking him, the young man moves on, and as he does Jonathan, while being attentive to his own foot placement, keeps a watchful eye on the progress of his new young friend. Periodically, Jonathan catches a glimpse of him picking his way up the trail and over and around boulders that punctuate it. Scree and talus occasionally add to the challenge making it seem like the proverbial two steps forward and one back. Despite that, Jonathan finds himself not wanting to sit and rest or even take the pack off when pausing to take a sip or catch his wind. At one point as he strains to see a trace of movement ahead of him, Jonathan realizes that his focus is no longer on his own progress but on that of the young man he briefly met and spoke to minutes earlier.

Gaining the summit after an interesting final assault that required him to pull himself up and over a few major rock formations, he sees it is not a very large area. Immediately, he spots the young man sitting in a shelter made of boulders. They are the only two who have summited thus far that day.

The young hiker waves to Jonathan. "Remember me?"

"Sure do. You made good time. You must be in great shape."

"Well, it helps to travel light. Weight just slows you down."

"I hear you, and speaking of weight, check this out."

With that, he pulls out the plastic bread bag containing the rock from his pack.

The young man furrows his brow in wonderment. "What the . . .? First I've heard of anyone carrying a rock up a mountain."

"It's a long story, but it suffices to say that this time the judgment of the gods is overturned."

"Sounds like a great story. My name's Benjamin."

"Jonathan."

They shake hands.

After arranging a comfortable spot to settle into, Jonathan pulls the two sandwiches from his pack and noting that Benjamin has only his water bottle, which now looks ominously empty, he offers him one.

"Thanks. I didn't think it would take this long to climb, so I brought only water and trail mix."

Jonathan gently rebukes him. "First rule of climbing is to assume it will take longer, so be prepared. Juice?"

Benjamin smiles sheepishly. "Thanks again. I guess I'm out of water, but it's downhill from here. Well, kinda downhill. Didn't realize that drop into the valley was so much."

Jonathan raises his eyes to him and stares, saying nothing.

"I know, rule number two," says Benjamin.

Jonathan smiles forgivingly. "And three and four." He notices Benjamin shivering. "Cold?"

Benjamin grins weakly as he wraps his arms around his torso. "Yeah."

Jonathan pulls his North Face windbreaker from his day pack and hands it to Benjamin.

"Son, if you are going to climb this high, you need to be prepared. Otherwise, the consequences can be very uncomfortable and potentially deadly. Take it from the valedictorian of the school of hard knocks." Jonathan then grins broadly. "I can imagine, though, that this is thickening up your blood, which goes a long way toward adapting to the cold. I don't imagine you get too much of a chance to do that on the beach, eh?"

Benjamin pulls the windbreaker over his head and laughs lightly. "No, that's a whole different world down there. Very different." He pauses as he seems to notice that Jonathan is still wearing his hiking garb. "I feel guilty about taking your windbreaker."

"Don't feel guilty. I offered and you accepted."

Jonathan reaches deeper into his pack and pulls out a long-sleeved shirt. He pulls it over his head and looks at Benjamin. "Just a bit chilly. It's called layering. Wear a number of pieces and the air between each helps insulate you. In time, if you haven't already figured it out, you'll learn you get colder on the way down even though the temperature rises. Obviously, that's because you're not exerting enough to heat up. So it's good to have extra clothing for the top and the descent.

"I see, wise man."

"Not so wise as much as a lifelong learner in the academy of life. Coming to understand you can't know everything is the first sign of wisdom. Got it, grasshopper?"

"Huh?"

"Let's try, 'Got it, young Skywalker?'"

"Oh, I get it. Thanks, Obi-Wan Kenobi."

The two sit quietly enjoying their lunch, neither seemingly wanting to disrupt the stillness.

"Good idea about the Pringles," Benjamin says after a few minutes.

"Yeah, chips don't get crushed in it."

"Lots of tricks to learn."

Jonathan nods and after a few bites asks point-blank, "So, what's your story?"

"My story? What do you mean?"

"Everyone has one. No exceptions. That's the grand part of being human compared to our four-legged brethren of the animal kingdom."

"Well, I was born, as I told you, in Cambridge, so not too far from Boston. My heritage is mostly Greek. In fact, I'm third generation. My first name is actually Stefanos, but I always liked to be called by my middle name, Benjamin."

Jonathan muses. "Interesting confluence in your name of the two strands of Western Civilization. Stefanos, Greek, so science and rational thought, and Benjamin, Hebrew, thus monotheism—the two of which combined being the cause of our conundrum."

"How's that?"

"How do you account for evil if there is only one source for all, that being God, and he/she/it is all good? Yet, rationalism cannot provide final answers because we humans are limited. We're neither omniscient nor omnipotent."

"Sounds very confusing."

Jonathan tosses Benjamin an orange. "It is if one thinks about it."

"So the answer is not to think about it?"

"Of course not. As Joseph Campbell has explained, we're all searching for answers to three great questions: How did we get here? Why are we here? What happens when we die? So if one is human, he or she is going to think about it. If he or she doesn't, I suggest something's lacking."

"I never thought about it like that. In fact, to be honest, I don't think I ever thought about it at all. Pretty sad, huh?"

"Sad? Not at all. When one is twenty-something, thoughts of mortality are usually far from the mind. Death is for old people, goes the thinking, but even when death comes to the young, the thinking is that it won't happen to me because I'm immortal."

"Hmmm."

"So back to my question: What's your story? You haven't told me anything. What you said are mere details that are incidental, not essential elements."

"I'm not sure what you mean?"

"Okay, I'll get right to it. You're not hiking this mountain alone by chance or on a whim. Something is moving you. You're dealing with something, something huge you cannot get your head around. Also, I don't believe in coincidence other than what Paul Simon sings about the girl walking down the very same street he is on the very same day. Of course, I don't imagine you listen to Paul Simon."

"Actually I do. I think my parents have every record he and Art Garfunkel recorded. I love their music."

"Excellent! Then you should know you can't be a rock or an island listening to the sounds of silence when homeward bound. But you can be a boxer feeling every glove that cuts you open."

"Wow! I never thought about it that way."

Jonathan laughs. "Nor have I, until now. Ben, also known as Stefanos, I'm not going to pry, but I'm assuring you it's okay. It's okay to be vulnerable. In fact, to grow and break the chains that hold one down, vulnerability is a requirement."

Again they sit quietly.

"More juice?" Jonathan asks after several moments.

"Sure, yeah, thanks."

"I said I don't believe in coincidence, but I do believe in synchronicity. Significant events and encounters don't materialize out of the blue. Some call it the hand of God. I call it cosmic intention—the universe acting to bring one to a particular and necessary place and time where and when he or she needs to be in order for something to happen. I don't know, but my gut tells me you're carrying a huge burden and you're taking time, or better yet, you're making time on your trip to figure stuff out. My bet is I'm not the only one who has carried a rock to the top of Holy Cross."

Benjamin reaches back and grabs the hood of Jonathan's windbreaker, pulling it over his head. He clasps his hands in front of his shins, which he has drawn up to his chest, and rests his forehead on his knees. After several more moments, he raises his head, and looks at Jonathan. "There is something," he says. After a moment's hesitation and through a tight throat he continues. "I lied. I'm not on my way back to San Diego. I'm actually heading home from San Diego, where I went to school, back to Cambridge."

Jonathan nods, listening intently and completely.

"I'm engaged to a girl my family adores. She's beautiful, well-educated, and perfect in every way."

He pauses, looking at Jonathan as if anticipating a question, but Jonathan says nothing. He simply sits and listens.

Benjamin continues, his voice breaking. "My Greek family is very traditional. In fact, my uncle is a Greek Orthodox patriarch. It gets pretty heavy."

Using the sleeves of the windbreaker, he wipes the moisture welling up around his eyes. His face reddens, his mouth tightens, and he looks off to the side for a moment. When he turns back to face Jonathan, he takes a deep breath, exhales, and tightens his lips. "I'm gay, Jonathan. Okay? I'm gay."

At first, Jonathan says nothing because he wants to give Benjamin time to regain his composure. Then, in a calm voice, he says, "I know. I knew it from the moment I laid eyes on you in the parking lot."

"How? How can you tell someone is gay or straight just by looking at him?"

"Oh, call it a gut feeling, a sixth sense, or, in this case, 'gaydar.' Regardless, I felt it, and something I've learned big time through my life is to trust my intuition.

"You see, Benjamin my boy, I'm gay too. Maybe it's one of those 'it takes one to know one' things. So I think I can understand your dilemma. I was raised a traditional Roman Catholic in a very homogenous community. Blue collar, salt of the earth, ethnic foods, and cultural traditions. You were raised Greek Orthodox. Okay, different rules and different practices, but same stuff repackaged. All religions are just that. Religion and culture and all that come with them are intermixed."

Benjamin's voice rises. "To be honest, I don't believe in any of that stuff they teach us. I tried to, but I couldn't. It just never made any sense, and still doesn't."

"Good, you're on the path," says Jonathan.

"What do you mean?"

"I'm supposing you're on your way back to share your truth, to tell your family you're gay."

Benjamin nods.

"I'm betting that what you have to say won't be received well and that once you say all you have to say, all hell will break loose."

Benjamin nods again.

"Finally, I'm betting that while it's scaring the hell out of you now, you're convinced that's what you need to do and will do it knowing full well you might not be very welcome around the Thanksgiving dinner table."

Benjamin sighs, dabbing his eyes. "Yeah."

"That's true courage, son, not the bullshit kind the John Waynes of the world brag about. Ever read *To Kill a Mockingbird*?"

"In sixth grade, I think, but yes."

"Remember how Atticus defines courage to Jem? He says courage isn't a man with a gun but knowing you're licked before you begin, yet pushing ahead anyway. Okay, you won't win this battle, but by not ducking it, you'll win your war."

Again, the two men sit quietly for a while.

"Benjamin also known as Stefanos, you're of Greek heritage. How familiar are you with Greek mythology?"

"Funny, you would think I'd be pretty strong in it, but that's not the case. As far as the Orthodox Church is concerned, my ancestors were pagans."

Jonathan shakes his head. "So it goes. Greek mythology is a treasure trove of wisdom. The Greeks were geniuses in many fields, especially in dissecting human behavior, the reasons people do what they do. And they explained it through myth. Their gods reflected the essentialism, if you will, of humans. They didn't put human behavior in cosmic terms, so they did not have a heaven or hell as Christians do. The myth to which

I've related most is that of Sisyphus. I alluded to him earlier. Have you heard his story?"

"No, I can't say I have."

"Well, Sisyphus, the most learned of men, held three essential outlooks: He thought the gods were a joke and, therefore, scorned them. He loved life with a passion. And finally, he despised death so much that he pursued death, managed one way or another to capture her, and finally put her in chains. As you can imagine, Hades wasn't too thrilled with having no new arrivals to welcome to his dark world. So he complained to Zeus who sent Hermes to snatch up Sisyphus and hustle him to the Olympus where he stood trial. It was a farce of a trial, so of course he was found guilty and condemned for eternity to push a boulder up a mountain only to see it roll back to the bottom, where he would have to renew his efforts.

"The twentieth-century philosopher Albert Camus wrote an essay on it called 'The Myth of Sisyphus.' Camus is particularly interested in what Sisyphus thinks as he trudges back down the hill to begin anew a task that he knows in the end is pointless. It's the one time Sisyphus is free to be in his own thoughts, his own world. It's in that context he calls Sisyphus an 'absurd hero.'"

"That seems to be a contradiction. How can a hero be absurd?"

"Absurdity, of course, is ridiculousness. What's the point of doing something if there's no purpose to it, right? Yet, we live lives of pointlessness. We keep going on as if there has to be a reason for our existence. We can't live with the idea that our lives might not in the end have any meaning, that we're simply here. Remember, the question about why are we here is one of Campbell's big three. To answer it for example, Christians concocted the notion that we're here to serve God, which leads to a whole set of other challenging questions."

"I see."

"Camus explores the meaning of the rock itself. He says that in our search for true happiness we become attached to our existence on earth. But we also understand that death is our fate. And since we truly don't know what happens after death, despite what the various religions insist is the case, we cling to life. We long to hold on to this tangible place of experience. Camus calls that longing 'boundless grief,' a grief too heavy to bear. It induces 'melancholy' in us, and when it does, those times become our nights of Gethsemane. That, he says, is the rock's victory."

"Isn't Gethsemane the garden Jesus prayed in the night before he was crucified?"

"It is. Saint John of the Cross called it the dark night of the soul. It symbolizes the times during which we suffer agonizingly and feel there's no hope. Sisyphus has no hope, yet he perseveres. He doesn't despair. Hence, Camus insists Sisyphus is heroic because he keeps performing a pointless task without complaint. Over and over. No cessation. For eternity. The point Camus is making is that in the end, Sisyphus is grander than the gods who cannot suffer or die."

"It makes sense when you describe it, but I think I'm really going to have to sit and think about it all. That's a whole lot to grasp."

"No doubt. I'm in my seventh decade and I still find myself reflecting on it. But what is important is that we do—think about it, that is. Not deny the possibility, but embrace it. As Camus points out, 'crushing truths perish from being acknowledged.' It's the key. By bringing something pernicious into the light, it dies. Like the legend of Dracula. That's even true for you and me in context of our sexuality, what Lord Alfred Douglas called 'the love that dare not speak its name' in his poem 'Two Loves.'"

"Are you calling those who hate or condemn gays and lesbians vampires?"

"In a way, they are. They use fear and shame to hold power over others. But when you bring your truth to the light and say for the world to hear, 'I, Benjamin, am gay,' no one can hold power over you because your truth is revealed."

"I wish it were that simple."

"But it is, Benjamin also known as Stefanos. It is."

"My uncle is a horrid man. He's unrelenting. He has everyone intimidated."

"So? Stand up to him!"

"How?"

"With love and compassion."

"But how do you love meanness and anger and vindictiveness?"

"A little bird, who perchance shares my name, tells us, 'You don't love the hatred and evil.' He says you have to practice to see the good in each person."

Benjamin looks puzzled, but shakes his head as if dismissing his confusion. "I get it, I think. But it's still scary. I've known since I was at least seven that I'm gay, and now I'm twenty-six. You would think in this day of same-sex marriage and increasing acceptance of gays and lesbians, it wouldn't be so hard. But it is. Some days I just feel completely alone, so disconnected from those I love most."

"I get that. I remember Hawkeye on the 1970s TV series *MASH* telling a patient who came out to him, 'Loneliness is everything it's cracked up to be.' Truer words were never spoken, Benjamin, and every one of us who has had or has to endure the terror of coming out has felt it in every molecule of his or her body."

"That gets to another rub of the condemnation we receive. The marginalization we experience forces us into a no-win dichotomy of either suffering alone or putting ourselves at risk by going to dark places in the subterranean world and being in contact with unsavory types who may be out to do us harm. That's not a real choice, so we have had to change the rules by saying, 'Hell, no!' to either alternative."

Jonathan looks at his watch. "And having said that, it's already past noon and good practice dictates we should already be close to or below tree line."

Jonathan and Benjamin gather their belongings and begin the descent talking about traveling, good beer, and other preferences.

As they hike through the tundra, Benjamin stops, bends down, and cups a wild mountain flower. "What are these yellow flowers called? I noticed them on the way up. They all seem to face east, I think."

"They're old-man-of-the-mountains, as opposed to being an old man of the mountain."

Benjamin laughs. "You're too funny."

"What? You think I meant that about me, young Skywalker?"

At the bottom of the mountain, they sit in the cargo area of Jonathan's Explorer and sip the Guinness Jonathan packed in ice and toke a joint Benjamin brought. They say little.

Benjamin embraces Jonathan tightly while standing near his Subaru. "I'm going to miss you. Can I get your number?"

"Oh, for sure. I'll text it to you."

They begin clicking their smartphones.

"Got it," Benjamin says.

"I'd love nothing more than to hear from you, but remember, Benjamin, as Jonathan the bird reminds us, you need to keep finding yourself. That's how you learn to fly."

"It'll be scary."

"Only as long as you hang on to and act out of fear."

Benjamin nods and begins to get into his Subaru when Jonathan says, "One more thing, Benjamin. You said you climbed Bierstadt, Grays, and Torreys. But they're east of here, which means they're in the direction you're heading, not coming from."

A big smile beams across Benjamin's face. "I guess I shouldn't be surprised you'd figure it out."

"So, Mount of the Holy Cross is your first fourteener?"

"It is, indeed, old man of the mountain."

Watching Benjamin drive off, Jonathan senses he will never see him again and wistfully rues that. It then occurs to him that he merely dropped the rock atop Holy Cross and didn't perform the ritual he had planned. He begins to become agitated, but quickly recovers as the profoundness of it manifests in his mind.

"That's okay," he says out loud. "This time Sisyphus wins."

∽о∽

Acknowledgments

When I began writing this book, I did not realize that I was venturing forth into a universe vastly different from any I had previously explored. Thankfully, that universe provided muses, guides, mentors, and friends. I called on the spirit energy of my personal muse, Denise Oaks Moffett, my teaching partner and coconspirator at Summit High School in Frisco, Colorado, who had recently passed after a heroic two-and-a-half-year battle with cancer. As was our wont, Denise and I often spoke in the language of myth, metaphor, allusion, and illusion. In a last conversation, she compared her struggle to Sisyphus's. So, my coyote sister, I offer much gratitude from this plane for sending guiding and inspirational energy from yours.

I found my footing under the mentorship of an earthly muse, my dear friend, Trish Kinkel. "Details!" she drummed into my head. Trish read drafts, offered invaluable, constructive insights, and occasionally threw out a pithy line that I, following the honored belief by writers everywhere that everything is fair game, naturally stole. Thank you, Trish!

Much gratitude, dearest friends—Marcia Holub, Mary Pat Young, Marilyn Buehler, and Owen Youngblood—for your guidance and insights with the piece itself and the thought process behind it. Special thanks to Marilyn who challenged me after a read through. "You're holding back," she admonished. "I don't know what it is, but you do." She was right. I was. And as soon as she said it, I knew what it was. Spoiler alert: It's in chapter 17.

Thank you, Mark Palko, Mardy Wilson, Nanci Hubbard Morse, and Richard Schwent, for wending through manuscript drafts and offering critical thoughts. And thank you, Jason Steinle, for unfailingly prodding and probing about the book. Thanks also, for steering me to the Colorado Independent Publishers Association. Blessings all.

Speaking of CIPA, what a godsend! Because of it, writers need not feel they are at the mercy of agents and publishers whose whims and judgments dictate what hungry readers get. Thanks to all who come together and make CIPA the amazing organization it is, especially my trusted editor and writing magician Melanie Mulhall, who went beyond basic editorial work by diving into my piece to get at its soul. When I turned the manuscript over to Melanie, I was convinced it was well written. It was, but it was not anywhere near great. Melanie has worked her magic, moving it to a plateau that astounds. Thanks as well to Veronica Yager for her brilliant website work and Nick Zelinger for his creative genius capturing the story's essential message in his inviting and intriguing cover and interior design.

A debt of gratitude to my LGBT brothers and sisters, who have led the way by blazing trails, pushing their rocks up the mountain to become the fulfilled aspects of creation they are intended to be. Without their ceaseless efforts to bring the plight of LGBT people into society's awareness and consciousness, works such as this would not be possible.

Finally, in addition to the aforementioned, a note of appreciation to Steven Pressfield for his inspirational *The War of Art: Break Through the Blocks and Win Your Inner Creative Battles,* which provided the final boost during the final stages of the writing and publishing processes.

About the Author

Jerry Fabyanic with great-nephew, John Hrivnak, atop Grays Peak

Standing atop a snowfield at 12,000 feet in July 1975, Jerry Fabyanic scanned the expanse and said, "Holy, shit! This is it." He quit his job, packed his truck, and headed west without looking in the rearview mirror. Deciding that the only thing he ever wanted to be was a teacher, Jerry began his literal journey into the world of public education and his symbolic journey into the world of myth and story. He counts Herman Melville, Mark Twain, John Steinbeck, and Joseph Campbell among the most influential thinkers and greatest heroes in his life.

Over the years, Jerry's love affair with the Colorado Rocky Mountains has only grown deeper. He has learned the importance of paying attention to guideposts, junctures that at first seem coincidental but prove to be path-altering experiences. Whether running at 8,500 feet, skiing moguls at Mary Jane in Winter Park, or reaching for an outcropping at 13,000 feet, Jerry reminds himself of his place and role as a denizen of Mother Earth.

Jerry Fabyanic is a retired teacher of English and social studies living in the historical mining town of Georgetown in Clear Creek County, Colorado. He has been the featured columnist of the *Clear Creek Courant* since 2003 and a radio host on KYGT since 2004. He has run six marathons, has climbed thirty-four of Colorado's 14'ers, and still loves carving the bumps through the powder and timber of Mary Jane's Eagle Wind territory.

You can read more about Jerry and his works at
www.JerryFabyanic.com
and listen to "The Rabbit Hole" at www.kygt.org.